REBORN YESTERDAY

TESSA BAILEY

TABLE OF CONTENTS

For my father, Michael

CHAPTER ONE

H E WAS THE most beautiful man she'd ever seen.

It was a pity he was dead.

Ginny reached into her rubber apron for the television remote control and turned down the volume on *North by Northwest*, muting Cary Grant's velvet baritone and leaving nothing but the buzz of her equipment and tick tock of the wall clock. Watching classic movies was her norm when working, but the man lying on her metal embalming table deserved her undivided attention.

She walked a measured circle around his prone figure, her fingers creeping slowly to her throat, trying to massage the spreading pressure there. Death at such a young age wasn't fair to anyone, but having grown up in a funeral home, Ginny had learned to compartmentalize sadness. *Tuck it away for another day*, her father had always said. Why was she was finding it so difficult to label and store the grief over this young man's life being snuffed out?

What did he die from?

No bullet wounds were visible. No usual signs of

long-term sickness. His body was strong and sliced with muscle. He looked as though he'd lain down on her table and gone to sleep, although for some off reason, he didn't strike her as a man that rested often. Someone had pressed the pause button on an explosive life force. A kingmaker. A dynamo.

A special man.

How she sensed any of this from a corpse was beyond her. She should have been bathing the body by now and yet she hesitated to touch him. Once the embalming process began, that would be it. There would be no more denying that death had stolen this exceptional male from the world.

I need to know his name. Almost clumsily, she lifted a corner of the sheet covering his feet...but her search yielded no toe tag.

"Huh," she murmured, replacing the sheet with a frown. "That's odd."

Despite a warning from her common sense, hope bloomed in her middle over yet another clue that this man couldn't *really* be dead.

Which was another clue in an embarrassingly long line of clues that Ginny needed a social life.

No one wanted to get margaritas with Death Girl, as the (clearly very imaginative) young women in her dressmaking class—Embrace the Lace Dressmaking Endeavors—called her when they thought she wasn't listening. Eavesdropping wasn't even necessary. The fact that they arranged their sewing machines as far away from her as possible, whispered, stared and never invited her for drinks at Dowling's after class was proof enough that they thought death was contagious.

It was a misconception she'd been living with since preschool. She should have been used to it by now, but it was times like these, while pining in eerie silence over a dead man, that Ginny wondered if isolation had taken its toll.

"What do you think, Cary? Have I gone around the bend?" she asked the man immortalized in Technicolor on her television. "Of course I have, you're not even the first dead person I've tried to converse with this week."

Her attention strayed, rather stubbornly, back to the man on her table.

"Might as well make it a hat trick. How do you do?"

No movement on the corpse's end.

"Will there be a million weeping women at your wake?" She tapped a finger to her lips. "There will be, I'm sure of it. The place will overflow with tears. I better make sure our flood insurance is up to date."

As she commenced circling the table once more, her white lab coat scratched against the hem of her green plaid dress, which fell sensibly to her knees. It was cold in the funeral home, especially downstairs where P. Lynn Funeral Home's guests were kept in preparation for their final goodbye, so she'd pulled on thick black stockings with a flower pattern before coming below to work the night shift.

Dressing with care was Ginny's way of showing respect to the people she worked on—a fact her stepmother and reluctant business partner often scoffed over—but a T-shirt and jeans simply didn't cut the mustard when she'd been entrusted with a loved one's care. Ginny had designed and sewn her current ensemble in class and she *definitely* shouldn't be wondering what Dreamboat here would think about the cut and fabric. Or if he'd notice she'd fitted it a touch tighter in the hip zone than usually made her comfortable.

"I need help." She gathered her auburn hair over one shoulder. "You agree, don't you? Finally, you've gotten peace and quiet from your multitude of admirers and here I come, trying to annoy you into reanimation so I can find out the color of your eyes. You must want to die all over again."

Continuing her journey around the table, Ginny's gaze ticked to the clock, reminding her she should have started working half an hour ago. Why was she so reluctant to begin? Where did she get off experiencing the weight of loss when she'd never crossed paths with this individual before?

"Anyway, I know what you're thinking. She's brought up my legion of female fans three times now.

She must be jealous." Ginny stopped beside Dreamboat and looked down at his regal brow, the masculinity of his jaw, and a horrible welling started in her chest. "I think you'd be right," she whispered in a red-cheeked rush. "I think if you'd smiled at me even once on the subway a decade ago, I'd be out avenging your death right now. Isn't that crazy?"

Just to be sure a terrible (wonderful) mistake hadn't been made, Ginny lifted her right hand, letting two fingers hover over Dreamboat's pulse. Her heart rate spiked at the prospect of touching him, which didn't bode well for tonight's task of filling his veins with formaldehyde. How could she give him the proper care he deserved if she couldn't stop shaking?

A bracing breath passed between her lips.

She touched her fingers down to his pulse.

Nothing.

There had been no mistake.

He was thoroughly, devastatingly dead.

"I'm so sorry," Ginny managed, her tears welling at such a rapid pace that one escaped, glopping heavily onto the man's stone cold torso.

His eyes shot open.

His...eyes shot open?

Shock seared Ginny's blood, dizziness rocking her. Around her, the room narrowed and expanded like a funhouse, fireworks popping off in her ears. She stumbled back a step and careened into the cinderblock wall, watching in piercing shock as Dreamboat came back to life. No. No. This had to be her imagination. She'd been lonely so long, her brain was crying out for human interaction and no way, no way, no way was the corpse sitting up—

Only he was.

Unless she'd completely and totally gone bananas, he *was* sitting up, his stunning musculature flexing in the harsh, clinical lighting. She should have screamed, called an ambulance, got him a glass of water. Something. Instead, she clutched at the middle of her chest and whispered, "*Oh, thank God.*"

Slowly, Dreamboat's head turned and eyes of deep emerald green found Ginny's, narrowing almost on a flinch. "N-not a fan of plaid?" she quipped, ridiculously.

His attention ticked down to the fabric in question, burning the skin beneath like an iron, before returning to her eyes. "Where am I?"

How was she supposed to answer simple questions when his voice sounded like a curl of smoke? When he was approximately thirty times more beautiful while alive? Where his shirtless status had been functional before, he was now sitting up, exuding masculinity with a sheet pooled around his hips and therefore, his bare chest had become a sensual attack. Thick hair, black as sin, was brushed away from his face, but a few pieces had escaped to caress his forehead. His jawline flexed over her perusal, but Ginny couldn't stop staring. It was as though she'd been starving for the sight of him.

The cultivated sadness inside of her lifted so quickly, leaving lightness behind, she almost felt hysterical. Like she'd been slingshotted through a tank of helium. "A better question is, where have you been?"

Ginny's hand flew to her mouth trying to trap the question far too late. Where had it come from? Maybe she *was* hysterical. After all, a corpse had just come back to life in front of her very eyes. She'd earned the right to be tongue-tied.

"I'm sorry. What I meant was, you're at the P. Lynn Funeral Home in Coney Island." She sounded winded, yet official, like a weather girl reporting live in front of a tornado. On cue, a rumbling started overhead and she pointed at the ceiling. "See? There's the Q train. Do you want to talk about this?"

"About the Q train?"

His accent was hard to place, but it was spun through with hints of the south. "No. No, I mean..." She separated herself from the wall and stood shifting in her ballet flats. "The fact that you just came back from the dead."

"Yes," he responded slowly, regarding her in way that made her skin feel hot and sensitive. "First, I'd like to talk about why you're not screaming."

Honestly, Ginny didn't have a good answer for his reasonable and very direct question. So she rambled, as she often did in situations where her normalcy was called into question. "If I scream, I could scare you back to death and I think that might make me a murderer." Thus making it obvious that she was quite *abnormal* and making the conversation even worse for herself. "Anyway, it's a happy occasion. You're alive! You'll get right back in the saddle." Her pep talk died on her lips when something terrible occurred. "You didn't happen to hear anything I said *before*. Did you?"

A spark of humor lit his gorgeous eyes. "You were talking to a dead man?"

"Oh good, you didn't hear anything." She swallowed. "But now you think I'm nuts, anyway, so what's the difference?" He watched her curiously as she crossed the room and picked up the receiver of the landline phone. "We should probably call an ambulance. Or at the very least the medical examiner to inform her she needs to keep her day job—"

"Hang it up."

The receiver was back in the cradle before he finished speaking. Ginny stared down at her hand that had moved on its own, goosebumps prickling her arms. "I, um…I can check your vitals, but I can't treat you," she said, just above a whisper. "You should be examined."

He rubbed at the cleft in his chin. "What is your

name?"

"Ginny," she breathed, loving the act of passing that knowledge to him. Even if he forgot her name in five minutes, he knew it right now.

"*Ginny.*" He said her name like a sinner whispering his darkest secrets to a priest in a confessional. "You don't look suited to working in a funeral parlor."

"Oh." A rush of pleasure stole through her, until she realized he could very well follow that statement up with, *you have a future with the circus.* "To what line of work do I seem better suited?"

"Given your ability to keep your sense of humor under stress, either a war general or a comedian."

She laughed. His lips parted at the sound and for some reason, he looked devastated by the sound. Devastated and fascinated.

"And *your* name, sir?"

He didn't raise an eyebrow at the way she spoke, which was nice. Before she learned how to string a sentence together, she was watching black and white movies beside her father on the couch. Combining that with the formal way her father spoke—and her idolization of film star/goddess Lauren Bacall—she'd been accused more times than she could remember of sounding like a blast from the past.

"Jonas," he said, almost too quietly to make out.

Jonas. Jonas.

It was perfect for him. Strong, out of the ordinary, lovely.

She must have sighed out loud, because his head turned sharply.

"Where are my clothes, Ginny? I need to leave."

"I…yes. Yes, of course you do." Her fingers fidgeted with each other. "You must have a family who will be overjoyed at this turn of events."

"No family," he muttered. "Just two idiot roommates with an ass-kicking in their future."

"I'm sorry?"

He glanced away, his humorless laugh hanging in the air. "What the hell. You're not going to remember anything that happened tonight, anyway, are you?"

"Oh. I promise you, I will remember."

"I'm sorry, I can't allow that." Again, his curious gaze swept her, as if trying to take her measure and unable to come up with a straightforward conclusion. "It would seem we're both the victim of a prank. My roommates left me here while I was sleeping." He shook his head. "Every year on my birthday, they insist on doing something dangerous and stupid, although I really thought they'd outgrown it. I'm sorry for any distress this caused you. They'll pay for it, I promise."

Ginny was in disbelief. "How could you sleep through being transported to a funeral home? Did they *drug* you?"

He seemed to choose his words carefully. "I don't sleep often, but when I do, it's rather deep."

"Oh." She pointed at her embalming machine. "Those bozos. What if I'd pumped you full of chemicals?"

"Bozos," he mouthed with a half smile. "My clothes, Ginny. If you please."

"I must talk to my stepmother about our security system. They probably snuck you in during *Survivor*—she doesn't blink while it's on." Still baffled over the fact that a live body had been smuggled into the funeral home without being seen, Ginny nonetheless decided there wasn't much she could do about it now. He had to be freezing on the cold metal table, not to mention traumatized. She couldn't very well make him sit there while she shook her fist over the actions of his reckless friends. "Clothes. You need clothes," she said, centering herself. "Coming right up, Dreamboat."

"What was that?"

Floor, please open up and eat me alive. Sincerely, Ginny. "Nothing. Let me see if they left you anything." She inched toward the table, her intention to open the metal storage drawer beneath where her stepmother normally placed the burial clothing. She had no reason to believe his friends would follow procedure, but she was operating out of habit. The closer she drew to Jonas, the more his fist curled in the sheet. Was it possible she was now repelling the half-dead, as well as the living?

Fabulous.

Trying not to stare at the gorgeous male specimen up close, she stooped down with purpose and slid open the drawer, slightly surprised to find a balled up pair of jeans and a T-shirt. Across the front of the shirt, the words *Birthday Boy* had been written in Sharpie.

Ginny held it up for him to inspect.

He sighed. "Morons."

She rose and handed him the clothes. "Happy birthday. How old?"

Jonas paused in the act of pulling the shirt over his head. "Twenty-five."

"Oh!" Fidget, fidget. She was watching him *get dressed*. "My birthday is coming up, too. We'll be the same age soon."

He went blank. "Right."

Once his shirt was in place—and was trying her hardest not to notice how his biceps barely fit the armholes—she noticed the tag was sticking out. Without thinking, she reached out and tucked it inside the white cotton, her knuckle grazing his skin. Jonas made a rough sound and she snatched her hand back with a sucked in breath. "Jonas, you're still pretty cold. Are you sure I shouldn't call a paramedic?"

"This is my normal temperature, Ginny," he rasped, the sheet sounding as though it was tearing within his grip. "You, however, are very warm." His nostrils flared. "I'm not sure what it is about you, but there's a…difference."

"Between us?"

"Between you and everyone else." He moved suddenly and quickly, so fast that she barely registered him throwing his legs over the opposite side of the table and a flash of firm buttocks, before he'd donned the jeans. "I can't be here."

It was almost alarming how panicked she grew at his imminent departure. Her throat closed to the size of a straw and an engine false started in her belly, chugging and failing, again and again. "Can I drive you somewhere? I'd have to use the hearse, but—"

"You should not be offering me a ride, Ginny. I'm a stranger." He turned to face her over the metal table, looking deeply perturbed. "Do you often give rides to men you don't have the slightest knowledge about?"

"Yes, but they're usually dead. It's kind of a given that they'll accept."

Bemusement stole his irritation. "Who *are* you?"

"You could find out," she whispered, fearing she'd be humiliated about it tomorrow, but unable to stop herself. "You could stay and find out."

Something akin to longing swept his features. "No, I…can't."

What was the cause of these nerves popping in her

fingertips? If she didn't find a way to prolong this association, it would be over before it started and something about that seemed horribly wrong. "We don't have to stay here," she said. "I was just thinking of taking a walk, actually." Before he could respond, Ginny tugged her apron off over her head, tossed it on the closest counter and sped through the embalming room door. "Coming?"

"A walk," he repeated, somehow already right on her heels. "In the middle of the night?"

"It's the best time to go. Everything is so quiet."

"How have you lived this long?" A beat passed. "Please, I can't do this."

"It's okay." Her smile was innocent. "I can go by myself."

With a growl, Jonas reached Ginny's side and she hid a relieved smile.

"One hour," he muttered. "I get one hour."

CHAPTER TWO

LUNA PARK WAS closed for the night, but some of the rides still twinkled where they lined the Coney Island boardwalk. With fall moving in gradually, the wind had a cool bite but summer was still laced throughout, carrying the scent of scorched sand and saltwater. Apart from a handful of people sleeping on benches and the occasional rat scurrying out to retrieve pieces of popcorn and dropped pizza crusts, the boardwalk was empty of life, quiet enough to hear the waves crashing nearby, the sizzle of the whitewash.

Jonas walked beside her with his hands clasped behind has back, staring straight ahead, occasionally mouthing phrases to himself. *I shouldn't be doing this* seemed to be his favorite, with *have you gone insane* coming in at a close second.

I get one hour.

That was her favorite of his mutterings so far.

He hadn't said, "*You* get one hour." He'd said, "*I* get one hour."

And maybe, just maybe, that meant he was enjoying

being with her, even if he looked like he was being boiled alive in a pit of hot oil.

A girl could dream.

"One hour," she murmured now. "And then I won't see you again?"

Grooves formed between his brows. "Correct."

She ignored the pang in her chest. "This is a unique opportunity then."

He seemed reluctantly intrigued. "How so?"

"Since we're never going to see each other after tonight, we can say the weirdest things on our minds without fear of reliving the embarrassment every time we meet. Maybe I can even pass on the secrets of womankind. Aren't you curious why women open their mouth when they apply mascara?"

"Not until now. Why do they?"

"It's reflexive. When a woman is trying not to blink, the oculomotor nerve is activated, triggering the trigeminal nerve that opens the jaw. Mouth open equals no blinking—and our bodies just do it naturally." She beamed at him. "Aren't you glad you came on this walk?"

He laughed, the full, deep sound making her think of underground wine cellars and the dark, less traveled sections of a library. "It's going to be impossible to forget," he said, seeming suddenly at a loss for words.

"What is it?"

"Nothing," he responded, looking over at her curiously. "I just can't remember the last time I laughed…without making myself do it out of politeness."

"Are you always polite?"

"I wouldn't say that, but I always try to do the appropriate thing. The right thing." Under his breath, he said, "Usually, anyway."

Ginny stopped short, something terrible occurring. "Are you married? Is that why you shouldn't be doing this? You said you had roommates and I just *assumed* that meant you were a single man—"

"I am unattached, Ginny." He seemed transfixed by her hair blowing in the breeze. "In a manner of speaking." With a visible effort, he gathered himself. "What about you? Do you always do the right thing?"

"I'm in the funeral business. I like to leave room for a gray area."

Amusement broke across his face. "Care to elaborate?"

Ginny hummed. "We had a client once, back when my father was still alive. The deceased asked to be buried with his gold watches. Jonas, he had *fourteen* of them. Seven on each arm." She shook her head at the memory. "His sons couldn't afford to pay for the funeral or his burial plot, so we snuck them two of the watches inside a Big Mac carton."

He flashed a smile. "I detect no gray area there. What good would fourteen watches do buried six feet underground? You can't take it with you."

"Exactly."

"When you're dead, you can't lift your wrist to check the time, anyway," Jonas said.

Ginny laughed into her palm—and the sound made him misstep and stop walking.

"What is it?"

"I don't know." He opened his mouth and snapped it shut. "It's almost as if I missed your laugh more than mine."

"Oh," she whispered.

When they started on their way again Jonas appeared quite distracted. "All right, my turn for a question. Are you an optimist or a pessimist?"

"Pessimist to the bone. You?"

"Definite optimist."

"An optimist who works in a funeral home?"

"*Owns* a funeral home." She squinted an eye at him. "Jealous?"

He shoved his fingers through his hair, leaving it tousled and directionless. "Christ, Ginny, you are so endearing, it's painful." His jaw set. "Let's head back."

Reluctantly, she turned and they started off in the direction they'd walked. "Why a pessimist?"

"Seen a lot of things go wrong in…my time."

"Name something you've seen go right."

"Is this a technique optimists use to bring one over to the light side?"

"Nope, I just invented it."

His white teeth flashed, but his smile slowly melted away. "Time gets things right, I suppose. The seasons show up without fail, cycle after cycle. People put up their Christmas lights at the same time every year. Nighttime arrives sooner, then later, then sooner again. Children grow up, learn, get married. Time never fails, it keeps going."

Ginny looked out at the ocean, though her attention longed to be on Jonas. "I can't decide if that's beautiful or terrifying. Maybe it's both."

She felt his nod rather than saw it. "Both is right," he said quietly. "Are you enjoying this walk, Ginny?"

"Very much."

"Good. Quit while you're ahead, please." He took her elbow and propelled her along. "Midnight walks aren't safe."

"I never take them anyway." That trickle of honesty broke the dam on the rest of it. "I just didn't want to say goodbye yet and I knew you wouldn't let me go alone."

He frowned. "How could you be sure?"

"I don't know. I just...was." They were off the boardwalk now and onto the regular sidewalk, the El and P. Lynn coming into view in the distance. And if she thought she'd been panicked before when Jonas was preparing to leave, that feeling was sevenfold now, forming a block of ice in her stomach. "It's your turn for a question."

"*Her voice*," he whispered almost inaudibly, closing his eyes. "I can't think of one."

"Try?"

His gaze traveled over her face in an almost desperate fashion. "What do you care about most?"

"Sure, save the whopper for last." Ginny swallowed. "My father's legacy. People thinking of me as reliable. Not having regrets. A perfectly pleated skirt."

When he watched her in static silence for long moments, Ginny realized they were no longer walking, but facing each other beneath a street lamp, right outside the front entrance of P. Lynn Funeral Home.

"There's more, but I can't think of them right now," she murmured.

Jonas reached up and smoothed her flyaway hair. "Oh to be on that list." He seemed to brace himself—and fail. "I'm sorry I have to do this. I'm so sorry."

"I don't understand."

His voice became hoarse. "Look me in the eye, Ginny."

"Why?"

"You can't remember this. We're not supposed to meet."

The ice block in her stomach expanded. "I *want* to remember this."

"Ginny..."

"I don't understand. H-how are you able to make me forget?"

Jonas closed his eyes briefly. When he opened them, the green embers in them glittered, flaring brighter when he took a step farther into her space. And another. Until she had to tip her head back to look up into his magnificent face. He raised a hand, extending it slowly toward the right side of her head, his fingertips ever so slightly brushing her hair—and fangs sliced into view between his lips like daggers.

"Do you understand now?"

The Q train roared past overhead, shaking the atmosphere, in the same manner her insides started to tremble. What...what was wrong with his teeth?

No, not teeth. Not incisors such as her own.

Those were...fangs?

Breath wouldn't come. She was rooted to the spot, hypnotized and drawn closer, despite the voice of caution calling from the back of her mind. Something is wrong here.

Something is wrong.

Comprehension struck and a scream wound its way up her diaphragm, sticking in her throat. Surely he wasn't trying to make her believe something so outlandish.

Something that only existed in fairytales and movies.

Cold skin. A deep sleeper. No pulse. *Fangs.*

"Is this a joke?"

He shook his head. "If only."

Had the whole night been an elaborate setup? Why would he go to such lengths to scare her? Even as her mind posed the questions, she couldn't quite buy into her own suspicions. Intuition wouldn't let her. Did that make her a crazy person or an idiot?

Both. Definitely both.

"You're trying to make me believe you're a vampire?"

"I *am* a vampire, Ginny." His dark brows drew together. "I've never been sorrier about that."

Ginny turned and threw herself at the door, fumbling her keys while trying to insert the right one into the lock. "Why would you do this?" she asked, her voice wavering.

"Don't run from me," he begged thickly.

"Why?" Her vision blurred. "You need to erase my memories?"

"I'm *required* to." She finally got the door open but he easily pushed in after her, bringing them both to a breathless stop in the dark lobby. "But that's not why I'm asking you not to run. I…*God.*" He pinched the bridge of his nose between two fingers. "I've officially lost it. I can't bear to have you scared of me even though you're going to forget I exist in a moment." He stormed in her direction. "Believe in what I am or don't. Just know this. If I could, I would come back tomorrow in the daylight and ring your doorbell. The way it should be done. Flowers and a promise to have you home before curfew."

"I'm twenty-four. I don't have a curfew," she said without thinking. "At least, I don't think so. Besides tonight, I don't go out much after dark."

"*Good.*"

If this man had really been pranking her, hadn't he gotten his payoff? Why was he still standing there? Why did she still want him to stay?

"Can you prove you're a-a...vampire?"

A muscle popped in his cheek and once again, the jewel green in his eyes flared to life, bright and luminous like something from another world.

"The answer is right in front of you," he rasped.

Could be actually be telling the truth?

Ginny's heart raced so fast, she blinked to keep focus and not give in to a dizzy spell. This man had fangs and glowing eyes. No pulse, lest we forget.

Those weren't things that could be faked. Was she simply being human and rejecting what her mind deemed abnormal?

The truth *was* right in front of her.

"You're a vampire."

"Yes."

She blew out a long, shaky breath. "Oh Lord." She pressed her hands to her cheeks. Her body trembled violently, but she didn't run—and couldn't explain why. Maybe it was the way he was looking at her. Like he would keel over out of sheer misery if she took off again. "A dangerous one?"

"Not to you. Never to you." He said those words with his fist crammed to the center of his chest. "Either way, I'm afraid you won't have to worry about any of this for long."

She couldn't recall fictional vampires having the ability to erase memories, but if vampires existed, nothing would be far fetched anymore. "No. Please don't make me forget you."

"I have no choice. I'm sorry."

"We can't even be…friends?"

"God no."

Ginny flinched.

Jonas cursed. He closed the distance between them, slipping his fingers into her hair, cradling her skull, bringing her close until their foreheads almost touched. "You don't understand. I can't be anything to you. And you can't be anything to me. It would put you in danger."

Memories were sacred to Ginny. Memories were her stock and trade. Every day of her life she'd witnessed the value and importance of them. They were all people had during the toughest times of their lives. Stealing memories struck her as the worst kind of violation. And not only that, a sin. She would protect them at all costs.

But how?

How?

The answer came to her in an almost meandering, obvious way. *Tell the truth.*

"You would *put* me in danger, Jonas?" She shook her head. "I'm already in danger."

Her words visibly wounded him. "I said I'm not going to harm you."

"You misunderstand. I'm not in danger from you. It's someone else." She wet her lips. "I'm in serious danger from someone else."

The rotating green in his eyes pulsed and fizzled out, her muscles loosening at the quick loss of invisible support. His hands, however, caught her by the upper arms, holding her steady. "*Who?* Tell me immediately."

"No."

"No?" His confusion was as obvious as his frustration. "Why not?"

Ginny shrugged. "Come back tomorrow night and maybe I'll tell you." She snapped her fingers between them. "Although if you erase my memory, I won't know you from Adam. So I *definitely* won't trust you enough to tell you my life has been threatened. But maybe…over time you'll earn my trust? I'd need my memory for that, though, wouldn't I?"

When had she become the kind of woman who played head games with a vampire?

Tonight, apparently.

But were they really head games if she was merely stating the facts?

Jonas was not happy. "You will tell me right this moment who threatens you and I'll deal with them before sunrise."

"So it's true, you can't go out in the sun?"

"Not without turning to dust."

"I didn't invite you in. I guess that's a myth?"

"Yes. And please stop changing the subject. Who seeks to harm you?"

"Sorry. My lips are zipped."

"One last chance, before I *make* you tell me."

Alarm pinched her spine. "How will you do that?"

This time, when his eyes started to glow, he seemed reluctant about it. "Do you remember earlier tonight when I made you hang up the phone instead of calling an ambulance? I can give you a very strong…suggestion. And you'll be compelled to follow."

"Please don't do that," she said on an exhale. "You'd be taking away my will."

His fingers tightened on her arms. "You're not giving me a choice."

"Yes," she stressed. "I am."

"I can't walk away and leave you in danger. And I can't come back." His gaze fell to her neck and he blinked several times. "You don't know how or what you tempt. I've already stayed around you far too long."

She shook free of his hold, backing toward the hallway that led to the residential section of the funeral home. "I'd rather face the threat alone than have my memories tampered with. Memories are all a person has some days."

He tilted his head curiously at her words, but matched her retreat, step for step. "Tell me now, Ginny," he murmured, smoothly, so smoothly, and her footsteps halted, her thought process trailing off and spinning into a spool of silk. "Tell me who threatens your life."

Instinct ruled her and instinct dictated she make Jonas happy. It was suddenly what mattered most. *Give him what he wants.* She wanted to get on her knees and bow to him, on the off chance he might stroke her hair and grant her some praise—and wait, what? *What is happening to me?*

He's doing this.

Him and his hypnotic green eyes.

The words were right on the tip of her tongue. Words that would reveal the information she'd told exactly nobody. But if she told Jonas about her recent night of peril, this would be the last time she saw him—

and not only was that possibility abhorrent...it also struck her as wrong.

I'm not supposed to let him go.

"Stop," she wheezed, covering her eyes with a hand. "Please stop."

When long minutes passed without him saying anything, she peeked out from between to fingers to find him dumbfounded. "How did you do that? How did you fight me off?" He studied her face. "No one's ever tried, let alone succeeded."

Ginny had worshipped Lauren Bacall her entire life, but she'd never felt more like her than when she laid a hand on the hallway doorknob, flipped her hair and looked back at Jonas. "Better luck next time, Dreamboat," she breezed. "See you tomorrow. You know where to find me."

CHAPTER THREE

THE FOLLOWING AFTERNOON, things got weird.

Weird*er*, more like, although the insanity took a while to gain momentum.

Ginny woke up at approximately two o'clock, when the sun was highest in the sky, par for the course for someone who worked night shifts. Whenever her late starts felt unnatural or she woke feeling as if she'd missed the important half the day, she reminded herself of all the bartenders, subway technicians and bodega staff waking up across Brooklyn at the same time—and went about her usual routine.

She watered the herb garden on her fire escape, waving her green, metal can at Mr. Jung as he watered the sidewalk outside his fish market across the street. She pinched some basil off between her thumb and pointer finger, carrying it to the kitchen to sprinkle over her eggs. If there was a knife missing from the chopping block, she didn't consider it odd. Her stepmother liked a midnight grilled cheese on occasion and routinely left cutlery in odd places.

Like the freezer. Or outside beneath the welcome mat.

Her stepmother Larissa hadn't been an excessive drinker when Ginny's father was alive, but she'd really put the pedal to the metal of late. Ginny didn't blame her. The former pageant queen had fallen in love with a mortician, but she'd never expected to *become* one. P. Lynn Funeral Home had fallen into quite a bit of debt under her father's supervision, however, and after marrying a woman with supremely expensive taste in jewelry and leisurewear, he'd promptly bitten the dust, leaving them with two choices.

Attempt to sell an outdated funeral home (spoiler: no one wanted it) that was rather unfortunately located beneath the Q train, which on more than one occasion had caused a casket to tip over. And some very unhappy online reviews.

Or, option two. Continue on, business as usual, and attempt to dig out from under mounds of small business loans and credit card debt.

Really, they'd only ever had one option. Knuckle down and keep going, a decision that had relieved Ginny greatly. The home might be a heap, but it was *her* home. One her father had built into a neighborhood landmark and managed to make a happy place, despite the dead bodies downstairs. She didn't want to watch everything he'd worked for crumble when she was more than capable of keeping the doors open. There had to be a reason he'd spent countless hours patiently teaching her the family trade, right?

A loud crash above Ginny's head made her drop the fork she was using to scramble her eggs. She tapped her fingers on the counter for several beats while deciding what to do. Larissa had a *no wake ups, no matter the hour* rule and expected Ginny to adhere to it. Okay, *expected* was a kind way of saying Larissa tended to throw hairbrushes or half-full glasses of water at Ginny if she even crept past her bedroom door to reach the bathroom. Many a full-to-bursting bladder had been endured since she'd been sharing a living space with her stepmother.

However. The silence that followed the loud crash convinced Ginny to leave her uncooked eggs on the counter and tiptoe slowly up the stairs.

P. Lynn Funeral Home consisted of three floors. The underground morgue, the first floor above it, which held the office, lobby and viewing areas. On the same middle floor, inaccessible to the public, was their small kitchen and dining room that could be reached through a locked corridor. Upstairs, on the top floor, lay the bedrooms. Three of them. One for Larissa, one for Ginny and an empty one Larissa used as a secondary closet.

On her way up the stairs, Ginny flexed her fingers at her sides, although no amount of warming up her digits would help catch any flying objects. Ginny was hopelessly unathletic. In middle school gym class, she'd earned the moniker No Win Gin on account of her being the kiss of death to whichever team had the misfortune of picking her last. It was just another way she'd become synonymous with bad luck around the neighborhood.

There was no sense in being *tragic* over it.

She had a legion of old movies to keep her company—*To Catch a Thief* was on the agenda for tonight—a place to live and herbs for her eggs. She could sew a mean dress. And while her profession might make people uncomfortable with their own mortality, she felt the opposite about it. People came to her on their worst day and she guided them through a process they often knew nothing about. In a way, she felt a little like a soft landing safety net for mourners who walked through the front door of P. Lynn Funeral Home. In that spirit, she often opened her meetings with a bright and cheerful, "How would you like to celebrate their life?"

An image of Jonas projected itself onto the back of her eyelids and she gave a prolonged blink to absorb it greedily. Had Jonas been given a funeral? Technically, he *was* dead, even if she'd never met anyone who'd crackled with more…existence.

Vitality.

Sexy sexiness.

Would he come back today? She couldn't imagine a world where he didn't. Where their one magical encounter was their first and last one. She'd dreamed of his eyes and the touch of his fingers in her hair. Replayed their conversations over and over in her mind so she'd never forget them. His voice was stuck in her head like a favorite song.

Was it pathetic that she'd deemed their encounter monumental? That's how it felt. She was like one of those people who claimed they'd seen God while in a coma. No one would believe her, but she'd been forever changed nonetheless.

Come back, Jonas, she said in a mental whisper, somehow positive he'd hear.

Would he listen?

Ginny deftly avoided the creaky hallway floorboard and approached Larissa's room. The hair on the back of her neck rose the closer she got. Her stepmother never failed to sleep with the television on at medium volume, usually tuned to the shopping network, but silence reigned from the other side of the door. There wasn't so much as a snore or a rustle of sheets.

"Curious," Ginny whispered, her big toes climbing over one another on the carpet. "Mmmm." She crept closer. "Larissa?"

She ducked on instinct, in preparation for a shrill screech or perhaps her father's brass urn crashing through the closed door and rendering her unconscious. Throwing an urn would definitely be a first for Larissa, but totally in keeping with her escalating behavior. Best to be on guard.

After several more moments of quiet ticked past, Ginny straightened and closed the remaining distance to the door, curling her palm around the knob and turning. At this stage, she was definitely starting to worry.

Dead silence in a funeral home was only a good sign if it was coming from one of their downstairs guests.

"Larissa?" Ginny called, pushing open the door.

She stopped short as soon as her eyes adjusted to the dimness.

There was her stepmother, her prize-winning figure outlined beneath the sheets. One arm dangled off the bed, an empty bottle of Stolichniya within reaching distance. Ginny squinted into the darkness, trying to discern Larissa's back moving up and down in a typical breathing pattern, but couldn't tell for sure. Abandoning the hallway, she moved into the room slowly, her fingers laced together beneath her chin. "Larissa?"

"She'll be fine."

Ginny spun around with a bloodcurdling scream trapped in her throat. She'd never be able to say for sure why she didn't release it, but suspected it had something to do with the smirking moon-haired young woman looking back at her. Quite possibly, she was too fascinated to scream. Who was this person and what was she doing in Coney Island, let alone Larissa's room? In her leather pants, blood red boots and studded bustier, she appeared to have stepped out of a futuristic eighties movie. And she was holding the missing kitchen knife in her hand.

Am I still sleeping?

Perhaps Ginny was having one continuously long dream about vampires and...whatever this woman was. It *had* been an extremely bizarre twelve hours.

Maybe none of it was real.

Maybe the person who'd tried to kill her had partially succeeded and this was one big insane dream brought on by a terrible fever. She might be surrounded by nurses in the Intensive Care Unit right this very second.

"You are saying all of this out loud," said the woman, her voice faintly accented with Russian. "I swear you are awake. But I could pinch you, if you'd like to confirm this?"

"No, thanks." Oh God, was this the person who'd been causing her to look over her shoulder? Had this intruder killed Larissa first so there would be no witnesses? Was Ginny going to die without even finding out why someone wanted her six feet under in the first place? "Is my stepmother dead?"

Two bright blonde eyebrows pulled together. "Were you listening? I just said she would be fine."

"Then...why are you holding a knife?"

"I'm sharpening it for you. Mine is made of the finest silver." She lifted the knife, regarding the blade with disgust. "You think I could even break the skin with a blade this dull?" With that, Moonhair slipped another, larger knife from the small of her back and began striking and dragging the two blades together, setting off sparks in the dark room. "You're welcome."

Ginny gaped. "You're making the knife sharper so my death will be swifter? And you want me to thank you for it?"

Moonhair didn't bother looking up from her task. "I am not here to kill, even though it would much more interesting. Unfortunately, I am here to protect you."

"Protect me from what?" Ginny twisted around briefly to find Larissa's upper half now sagging off the bed. "What did you do to her?"

"A little conk." She used the flat of the blade to tap herself in the middle of the forehead. "Right here. Lights out."

The woman handed Ginny back her sharpened kitchen knife and she had no choice but to take it, bolstered by the fact that, if nothing else, she'd have an easier time chopping carrots now. "Does you being here have anything to do with Jonas?"

"Yes." Moonhair leaned back against the wall, regarding Ginny with smug speculation. "So you are the one, hmm?"

"The one…?"

"The one making the prince tear out his perfect hair."

"The prince?"

"I refer to Jonas, obviously."

"Oh." Ginny scoffed to hide her smile. "Was he…talking about me or something?"

Moonhair let out a throaty laugh. "It goes both ways, I see. This can only end in disaster." She shrugged. "At least it will be entertaining."

"Why did you call him a prince?"

"Among his kind, he is something of a…reluctant leader, one could say." She studied the tip of her blade with a sniff. "He has morals and principles and things of that nature. I can't stand him, really."

This conversation was completely insane and Ginny had no choice but to keep having it. This woman knew Jonas. Having the barest connection to him, even in the form of this potentially murderous woman, replenished her lungs with oxygen. It meant he was real. "What's your name?"

"Roksana." She gave a sarcastic curtsey. "At your service."

An abrupt snore from Larissa almost sent Ginny skyrocketing through the roof. Under Roksana's sharp regard, she pressed a hand over her racing heart and waited for it to slow back down to a normal tempo. "Can we go somewhere else and talk?" She shifted on her feet.

"I'm feeling a little guilty discussing anything other than my stepmother's possible concussion when she's right behind me."

"That's fair." Roksana pushed off the wall and stomped out into the hallway. "Let's talk in the morgue so you can show me the bodies."

"Oh...I was thinking we could use my room."

"Whatever."

Ginny jogged to keep up with the long-legged Roksana down the hallway, around the bend and into the second door on the right. "I'm trying not to be worried that you know exactly where my room is," Ginny said, shutting the door behind her. "How did you know, by the way?"

Roksana frowned as if she'd asked a ridiculous question. "I've been here all night. You think I didn't map the layout?"

"I'm so confused right now."

"Not my concern. I'm only here to make sure no one murders you." Roksana used her index finger to pull down the blinds, the morning sun leaving a stripe of light across her eyes. "That should be the only explanation necessary."

"You can stand the sunlight, so you must not be a vampire..." Ginny murmured, mostly to herself.

Roksana released the blinds with a snap and spat on the floor. "Hell no, I am not one of those pale parasites.

They are a plague. A *disease*."

"I-I thought you were friends with Jonas," Ginny sputtered.

"I'm friend to no one." She lifted her chin. "I have sworn an oath to slaughter the prince and his two shit-for-brains roommates someday soon. Three stakes in the chest—boom, boom, boom. Probably tomorrow. I haven't decided yet."

"Oh." Ginny massaged the throb in her forehead, trying to forestall the urge to push Roksana out the window. She was the furthest thing from a violent person, but something fierce and protective welled inside her at having Jonas threatened. "Please…don't do that."

"If you want to shout, why don't you just shout?" Roksana mused, now standing inches away.

Ginny jerked back and slammed into the door. "Wow, you move fast."

"Yes, I know." Roksana wiggled a finger at her, then the door. "Please try not to give *yourself* a concussion. I'm not positive I could win a battle against Jonas if he's riled over you being hurt. Any other time, I'd take him no problem."

"Right." Ginny swallowed, her brain trying to make sense of the conversation. Of, well…everything. "So you hate Jonas, but he asked you to protect me and you said yes? Why help him if you think he's part of a plague?"

"I slay their kind." Roksana's finger poked the air.

"It's my job."

"Okay. You slay vampires. That's a real thing."

"Yes, of course. I'm just…" A touch of uncertainty passed across her features. "I'm lulling them into a false sense of security. And maybe I'm taking a little bit of a vacation while I'm at it. Tomorrow, though…" She stomped away with a dark laugh. "Tomorrow I slaughter them all."

Lord, this was a heavy conversation to have when her coffee light was on empty. "And in the meantime, you're going to protect me."

Roksana settled a fist over her heart and turned briefly serious. "To the death." She flipped her knife end over end and caught it. "Can we see the bodies now?"

Ginny did not show Roksana the bodies.

She made the vampire slayer breakfast. How often did someone get to say that? Roksana wasn't talkative during the meal and ate with her ankles crossed on the table, but Ginny was thrilled for the company, nonetheless. She wasn't sure how their arrangement was going to work exactly, but quickly found out the slayer would be shadowing her every move.

Roksana trailed Ginny to the grocery store and back. Then to the fabric shop to buy two yards of persimmon chiffon for the new, fall-inspired dress she was planning. Everyone who passed was given a suspicious once-over from Roksana. To be fair, she got quite a few once-overs in return. Coney Island was full of eccentricities and yet Roksana stood out among the crowd. It might have had a lot to do with the knife tucked into the back of her leather pants, but Ginny was only speculating.

Ginny was in her room preparing for the night shift downstairs when Larissa stumbled into her doorway. The former queen of the Coney Island Mermaid Parade was one of the most beautiful women Ginny had ever seen, even in a dressing gown and a head of curlers.

Every year, Ginny and her father had gone to watch the floats and revelers go past, always standing in their same spot outside the Famiglia snackbar. That afternoon in 2015, he'd gone silent as Larissa passed by in the sunshine, completing her pageant wave and dazzling crowds with a movie star smile, which she'd seemed to aim directly at him.

When the parade ended, Ginny's father had found Larissa and asked to take her out for pierogis, an event that had shocked Ginny, considering her father spent his days trying to blend in with the wood paneling that lined their viewing rooms. Still, Larissa had said yes and a week later, she'd moved into the P. Lynn Funeral Home and never left.

"What time is it?" Larissa cried now, wiping at her smeared mascara.

Ginny checked the clock on here bedside table, noticing Roksana was nowhere to be seen. Where had she hidden herself? "It's 6:49."

"I've slept through my entire shift!" She pressed the back of her hand to her forehead. "And I had the strangest dream. A woman was in my room and…" She cupped the air over her breasts. "She had on a leather bustier with studs."

Ginny had checked on Larissa several times through-out the day and she hadn't stirred once, even when Ginny laid a cold compress on the unfortunate lump at her temple. The smell of alcohol on her breath hinted at the possibility Larissa would have slept through her shift even if Roksana *hadn't* conked her on the head. "That *was* a crazy dream," Ginny said. "After all, it's much too brisk outside for a bustier."

"There was a time when I'd have worn one in a snowstorm—and did," Larissa said wistfully. "Did I miss anything while I was sleeping? Any new arrivals?"

"Not today."

Her stepmother stared off into the distance. "Here I am, hoping people die so we can keep the lights on. It's ghastly." She pinched the bridge of her nose. "Have you given any more thought to selling the business at a lower price?"

Ginny felt a stab of guilt. There was part of her that wanted to put her father's legacy on the market and take *far* less than he'd paid for it—thank you, Q train. Just so Larissa would be free. But every time the real estate agent called to ask if they'd consider relisting the home at a lower price, Ginny balked. These walls were the only witnesses besides her to the memories she'd made with her father. If she sold the home and moved, she'd be the only one with those memories. With every change in her life, they faded a little more, like continually washed black jeans.

Also. Was it wrong of her to enjoy her job?

She took responsibility and pride in caring for the dearly departed. Any lingering eeriness she'd experienced as a child learning at her father's side had long since passed. Now the deceased were just people who'd lived, loved, cried, laughed, spilled sodas, rode roller coasters, told jokes, got mosquito bites. They were to be handled with love, and she wasn't confident in many of her abilities, but no one could treat them with more respect or do a better job. This was her profession and she wanted to keep it.

Unfortunately, that meant Larissa was good and trapped. Unless Ginny could buy out her half of the business—and that wasn't happening any time soon.

"I'm sorry, I haven't thought more about selling," Ginny finally responded. "This place is really all I know—"

"But you could change that! Maybe get out of Coney Island and start somewhere fresh?"

"I don't know," Ginny hedged, not wanting to give

an outright no to a friendly suggestion. "If the job is wearing you out, Larissa, maybe you'd like to take some time off? Clear your head—"

"No, no. No. It's fine. I'll be on time tomorrow." She clutched the sides of her robe, bunching the material at the hollow of her neck. "Besides, who would I visit? My parents in Florida? Those retirees in their complex scatter when they see me coming now. They think I've brought death along in my suitcase." She was getting worked up. "I don't know how you've *done* this your whole life."

Ginny shrugged and reached for the pearl earrings on her dresser, putting them on without looking in the mirror. "It's all I know," she said simply, a pang catching her in the sternum. "People don't want to need us. No one's ever ready. But deep down, they're comforted knowing we're here."

"You sound like your father."

"Thank you."

Larissa's smile was tight. "Well. Since I already missed my shift, might as well rest up for the next one." Her stepmother yawned loudly and turned, stretching her arms above her head as she padded down the hallway. "Please give some more thought to unloading this place. The greater good and all that. G'night."

A second later, Ginny heard Larissa's door close, followed by the distinct sound of a bottle cap being twisted off and liquor filling a glass. Ginny idled for a while in the dark corridor, considering her stepmother's repeated requests. Was she being selfish keeping P. Lynn up and running? This was her home. The only one she'd ever known. Where would she go without it? What would she do?

The barest scraping sound turned Ginny around with a gasp.

Jonas stood just inside her window.

CHAPTER FOUR

J ONAS LOOKED DIFFERENT tonight.

And night *had* fallen while she'd been speaking to Larissa, but the sun must have only just gone down. Had he been waiting for the moment it sank behind the horizon to come see her?

Don't be ridiculous.

Ginny's palms grew damp at the sight of him and she tried to be inconspicuous about wiping them on the hips of her blush-colored A-line dress. His unreadable eyes tracked the motion, however, so she stopped and dropped her hands, no idea what to do with them.

Last time she'd seen Jonas, he'd been in jeans and a wrinkled T-shirt. While he'd looked handsome in the clothes, they'd seemed out of place on his robust blacksmith body. They'd almost seemed too modern on a man whose energy reminded her of the Golden Era films she watched. Movies that celebrated a time when men kissed women like they meant it and a glance across the room could speak volumes. Or spark a love affair.

If only she was in a silk robe, brushing her hair and

looking glamorous when the vampire climbed in her window. She'd give him a cool glance over her shoulder à la Grace Kelly and tell him to come back when he'd brought flowers.

You are not Grace Kelly.

Right.

Ginny trundled back to reality.

No, jeans and a shirt scrawled with Sharpie didn't do Jonas an ounce of justice, maybe nothing would, but the gray wool pants and black button-down shirt he wore...they were definitely a fantastic start. Here was the prince Roksana had spoken about. A royal decree would roll right off his tongue.

Jonas's hands were in fists at his sides. "Hello, Ginny."

The way he said *Ginny* reminded her of the lowest note on a piano and made her toes curl into the rug. "Hello," she managed.

He gave a slow headshake. "I shouldn't be here."

"And yet, here you are."

"Yes." His jaw flexed. "Roksana, would you please come out from under the bed? I'd like a report before you go."

"Oh, I simply live to do your bidding, bloodsucker," she said with a snort, rolling out from under her apparent hiding place, before hopping to her feet and sending Jonas a mocking salute. "It's the stepmother who threatens her life."

"*What?*" Ginny frowned, still absorbing the fact that Roksana had been hiding under her bed for the last twenty minutes. "What about my stepmother?"

Roksana ignored her, pacing in front of Jonas—who still watched Ginny like a hawk. "Stepmother wants to sell this place, Ginny does not. Perhaps she plans to murder Ginny, sell this heap and take the full profit for herself. It's a tale as old as time. Family, greed, yada yada yada."

"No," she breathed. "No, Larissa wouldn't do that. If she were planning to kill me, why would she bother asking me to sell? Why not just act? And anyway, she doesn't have the body strength to…"

"To what?" Jonas prompted, eyes narrowing.

Knowing she couldn't give away too much or she'd risk having her memory wiped, she zipped her lips. "Never mind."

A good ten seconds ticked by. "Just so I understand, whoever is threatening you has considerable body strength. You are aware of this because they've used it against you? Is that what you're telling me, Ginny?"

"No. I'm *not* telling you. On purpose."

Jonas made a sound in his throat. "You'll have my protection regardless—"

"Regardless of whether or not you fiddle with my head? That's a huge regardless." She crossed her arms over her middle and asked what she really wanted to know. A question had been prodding her all day long. "Jonas. *Why* are you so determined to protect me?"

His cool mask remained in place. "Maybe I'm not telling you. On purpose."

Ginny gasped over having her words thrown back in her face.

Jonas raised an eyebrow, as if to say, *your move*.

Roksana split a look between them and cackled. "Watching you two is better than pretending to be a lost virgin to bait vampires."

"No way that works," Jonas commented, sparing Roksana a brief glance before gluing his attention back on me. "You're free to go, Roks. Please be back before sunrise to relieve me."

"Dasvidaniya." Roksana threw a leg out through the open window and vanished from sight. Gone. Just like that.

Leaving her and Jonas alone.

"I really don't need round-the-clock bodyguard service," she said into the charged stillness. "I must be keeping you from something important."

Without confirming or denying, Jonas took a slow lap around the room, cataloguing her movie poster for *The Big Sleep*, the Singer sewing machine on top of her dresser, thimbles scattered at its base. He leaned toward one of her bottles of perfume, but seemed to catch himself before sniffing it, cutting her a slightly sheepish sideways glance.

Jonas continued in an arc around her bed, the fairy lights dangling from her canopy highlighting his rich, black hair. He was traveling closer to her and with each purposeful step, the fluttering in her middle intensified. She could practically *taste sounds*, his presence made everything around her so much more vibrant, from the hum of silence to the sharpness of colors.

"I don't have any clients tonight," she said, wetting her dry lips. "When I have an empty morgue, I usually go up to the roof for a while before doing paperwork."

For the briefest of seconds when he turned, she swore his attention clung to the pulse at the bottom of her neck. Totally out of keeping with his polite nod. "The roof." His exhale reached her skin and she shivered. "Take me there."

She turned and walked slowly from the room, her back tingling with Jonas following behind her. Ginny's room was located in the center of the upstairs hallway, with Larissa at one end near the bathroom. Near the third bedroom/closet sat a narrow staircase which led to the roof. "So, um..." *Be cool. Be interesting.* "I noticed you breathe."

"Force of habit. Though I'm told the urge eventually goes away."

"Isn't it nice to have something to look forward to?"

She turned just in time to catch his lips twitching. "Um." She faced front in time to hide her delirious smile. "Won't that be a dead giveaway that you're not human?"

"Dead giveaway," he chuckled quietly. "I don't spend a lot of time around the living, so giving myself away isn't really a concern of mine."

Ginny opened the door leading to the staircase and flipped on the overhead light, remembering too late that the light bulb had burned out a year earlier. Right. Just an average, ordinary evening ascending a pitch black staircase with a vampire at her heels. Nothing to see here.

"So…" she began with a swallow, taking the groaning stairs one at a time. "Why don't you spend a lot of time around the living?"

Jonas didn't respond right away, but when he did, his smoky, touch of the south voice was close, so close, in the dark. "There are rules we live by, Ginny," he said, gruffly. "None of them expressly forbid being around humans, but each of them was devised to make sure we're never discovered. By allowing you to have an awareness of me, I might as well be breaking them."

"What happens when you break them?"

"Excommunication. Death. Occasional mercy. It depends on the mood the High Order finds themselves in on a particular day."

"*Oh.*" At the word *death*, Ginny stopped and turned so fast, she lost her footing, her heel sliding on the old, worn out carpeting. Her feet whooshed out from beneath her, but before she could even brace for her back to land hard, followed by the inevitable bumpy ride to the bottom, she found herself up on the roof in the moonlight, cradled to Jonas's chest. "What just happened? How did we get up here so fast?"

"I caught you." Emeralds flickered in his eyes. "It would be wise of you to remember how easily."

Her pulse rattled in her ears. "What does that mean?"

"It means..." He trailed off with a frustrated sound, settling Ginny on her feet, but seeming reluctant to move away completely. "It means there are *reasons* we live by a set of rules. They're written in stone because they keep people like you safe and prevent us from being discovered."

She shook her head. "I'm safe with you, though, aren't I?"

A pause ensued. "What brought you to that conclusion?"

"If you wanted to hurt me, you would have done it last night."

Her response surprised him, but only momentarily. "Maybe I have stronger willpower than most." He stepped farther into her space, giving Ginny a hit of his addictive scent. Cloves and mint. "Have you considered there might be a limit to it?"

No, she hadn't considered that and frankly, she was

beginning to question her conviction when it came to Jonas. Was she really so reckless as to put herself in dark, private places with a man who could clearly overpower and kill her? Or was there something almost…*familiar* about Jonas that made her so trusting of his intentions? "Why do you need so much willpower?" Ginny murmured. "What are you stopping yourself from doing?"

"Oh, Ginny." He took her chin in his hand, studying her mouth with…fascination? Hunger? Before turning her head to the right and exposing her neck to the moonlight. "What am I *not* stopping myself from doing?"

The speed at which her nipples hardened caused Ginny to blink rapidly. She was already *quite* aware of her attraction to Jonas, but had he just implied he wanted her blood? She didn't imagine it, right? And instead of recoiling like she ought to, a flame licked at her veins like a dragon's tongue. Unexpected, that.

Very unexpected.

She'd liked members of the opposite sex before. She'd even let Gordon Collingsworth bring her to the movies once—an event he'd been eager to repeat ever since—but she'd only experienced a mild curiosity when it came to kissing Gordon. As in, would it be as clammy and moist as his palms? How long would it continue? If she let him French kiss her, would he stop begging her to come to Sunday dinner with his mother?

Things like that.

This was no awkward evening with Gordon. She was on a rooftop in the moonlight with Jonas towering above her and the implication that he wanted something from her still hung in the air. She pulsed head to toe, her lips and neck tingling under his rapt attention—and even in her state of hormonal excitement, there was a sense of finally. *Finally,* she was there with him.

Jonas gave a slight head tilt. "What are you thinking about?"

"Mostly that…this is nothing like my date with Gordon," Ginny mumbled.

He was already so still by virtue of his nature, but he went even stiller somehow, his left eye twitching. "Gordon?"

She waved a hand. "He's neither here nor there."

"Oh? Then where is he?"

"Not here. Not there."

"Well he has to be somewhere."

"I was just thinking…well, I've never kissed him. But I've never *wanted* him to kiss me, the way…" Her blurted words lost steam as his expression shuttered. "The way I think you would kiss me."

"I'm *not* going to kiss you," he rasped, leaning down to speak inches from her face. "You won't be finding out."

His rejection embarrassed her. The fact that her

nipples were still in tight buds didn't help. Had she assumed too much? Had she been around so few men her age that she grasped onto the slightest sign of interest?

He's not a man.

He's a vampire.

Her body and heart clearly weren't making that distinction, no matter how hard she tried to make them. However, her heart *was* sputtering like a five-day-old party balloon that someone had finally got around to popping and squeezing out the dull air. Ginny turned and walked to the other side of the roof, hoping for a few precious seconds to gather herself before asking more questions.

Jonas sighed as she walked away. "Ginny..."

"So what are the other rules?" she asked brightly, settling her forearms on the cool stone perimeter wall. Jonas came up beside her, leaning a hip against the barrier with his arms crossed, a healthy distance away. She ached to look at him, to see his gorgeous face surrounded by starlight and the glittering boardwalk amusement park in the distance. Instead, she tracked the silhouette of the buildings across the street and let the autumn wind cool her flushed face.

His answer came after a stretch of time, his voice more subdued than before. "There are three rules, although breaking one usually means you've broken all three." In her periphery, she could see him count the items off on his fingers. "One, no relationships of any kind with humans. Two, no taking of human life. And three…"

Finally, she judged her face had lost enough pinkness to look at him. "Yes?"

"No drinking from humans." He dropped a hand to the perimeter wall, seeming to hold it in a tight grip. "Not directly, at least."

Her mind raced with the unusual knowledge. "What if you used a straw?"

Jonas's tight expression gave way to astonishment. Slowly, he turned and looked out toward the coast. "How could I not want to protect you, Ginny? How could anyone?" His chin fell towards his chest. "You're funny and brave and so fucking *beautiful* and God, I really should not *be* here."

The organ in her chest swelled and danced so unexpectedly, she almost toppled over the wall. "But…I thought you didn't want to kiss me."

He moved faster than a blink, his image blurring until suddenly her back was pressed to the wall, Jonas's nose an inch away from hers. "Did you hear what I said about the three rules? Breaking one leads to all three being broken." Their lips grazed and both of them swayed, fingers twisting in one another's clothing. "*Think* about it, Ginny. I can't look at your trusting face and spell it out."

"Okay…" She reached out with her mind, trying to grab onto the strings of information, but balloons were floating off with them. How could she think when his eyes blazed down at her with a trifecta of fascination and pain and need? "You can't be in a relationship with me because you'll break rule number three. I think, right? D-drinking?"

"*Yes*," he hissed, dropping his mouth to Ginny's neck and inhaling deeply, those strong hands pulling her closer by the waist of her dress. "I meant what I said last night. There's a difference between you and everyone else. It's as if I already know what you'll taste like. I recognize you." His lips brushed across her pulse. "I recognize *this* like it's welcoming me home."

If her thoughts weren't scattered bits of crumb, due to their blistering proximity and his body, *oh Lord* his body, she might have recalled her earlier sensation of déjà vu. Of trusting him without reason or cause because she knew, without a doubt, he'd never hurt her.

Jonas lifted his chin and pressed their foreheads together. "You're forgetting the second rule, Ginny."

"No killing humans," she whispered. "I remember."

Regret laced his tone when he spoke. "Break one, break three."

"No. That sounds like something that was made up to control your behavior. Like, 'an apple a day keeps the doctor away.' Clearly an apple farmer thought of that. No one ever stops to think of the origin of…of…why are you laughing?"

"You." His lips brushed over her hair. "You refuse to stop making me laugh. And—"

"And you shouldn't be here."

"That's already getting old, isn't it? It's the truth." His gaze mapped her face. "My strength would be a wildcard if I gave in to this. I can't predict how I'd react to kissing you—or more, when I barely understand what you're doing to me without throwing…*more* into the mix." He paused. "This is unusual, Ginny."

More.

That huskily spoken word made that made her thighs want to open. He would press against her hard and she'd wrap them—

"Stop," he breathed. "You're tempting disaster."

"Maybe one kiss?"

He laughed without humor. "It wouldn't stop there," he said thickly, bracing his hands on the wall on either side of Ginny. "It would have to be all or nothing with you."

Jonas flicked her a searing look and she saw his meaning there. Oh, she certainly did. A corresponding moving image came to life in her mind. Jonas moving roughly on top of her, her skirt around her waist…his teeth fastened to her neck. Her thoughts must have translated to her face because Jonas blurred away with a curse, leaving her in a near puddle against the wall.

"Only another eleven hours and seventeen minutes to sunrise," he muttered. "Downstairs, please, Ginny."

"Yes, Dreamboat," she quipped, before blushing to the roots of her hair. Avoiding his questioning look, she slipped past him down the stairs.

"I knew I'd heard you call me that last night." His voice was brisk—and directly behind her. "Do you have a nickname for Gordon?"

"I'm not sure that's any of your business."

"You wanted it to be my business or you wouldn't have brought him up."

"I was befuddled when I did that."

Jonas hummed a skeptical sound. "How do you know him?"

"Am I...putting his well-being at risk by telling you?"

"No. Remember the rules."

Ginny stopped and turned at the bottom of the stairs. "The rules are pretty much the only thing I'm thinking about right now."

He touched the tip of his tongue to his upper lip. "Same."

They held a heated mini staring contest. "What happens when you find the person who has been threatening me? Are you going to slap them on the wrist and ask them nicely to stop? Anything else would be against the rules."

"You don't think I've considered this?"

"What did you come up with?"

He took Ginny by the wrist and guided her in the direction of her office. "You've changed the subject from Gordon. How do you know him?"

"His mother is the founder of my dress making club. She favors a polyester blend."

"Itchy."

"Yes," she agreed fervently. "And not breathable at all."

A corner of his mouth jumped. "So you're in a dress making club. I don't suppose you've made many enemies there."

"No…" she hedged, following him into the office and turning on the desk lamp, casting the small room in a dusky glow. "No enemies, per se…"

"Be *less* convincing."

"Well, I wouldn't say I've made any friends, either." She dragged her index finger across her father's old mahogany desk and the initials she'd scrawled there with a protractor when she was eleven. Her father had scolded her for it, then taken her for a Carvel ice-cream cone out of guilt. "They call me Death Girl, so we haven't done a lot of gossiping over coffee."

Jonas's expression had turned stony.

"You're mad on my behalf," she breathed. "Are you sure we can't kiss?"

"If there was a way, I would have done it already. Several hundred times." He closed his eyes briefly. When he opened them, they were scanning the room and Ginny's stomach was still mid-somersault. "What about unhappy customers? Anyone who stands out?"

She sat down behind the desk, flattening her palms on the spread of paperwork. "Everyone who comes here is unhappy. It's hard to pick just one."

A flash of white teeth. "I see your point. This isn't going to be easy." He took a seat in the chair in front of her desk. With an arm draped along the back of the chair and his hair falling over his forehead, he was straight out of one of her movies. All he needed was a cigarette and high-waisted man pants.

On second thought, scratch the latter.

Some things were better in the modern age.

"It would help if you told me *how* you've been threatened, Ginny. It would help if you told me anything at all."

"I don't know anything at all. I only know...what happened."

There was a tick in his temple. "Start there."

She shook her head. "Tell me about your room-mates."

This time, Jonas shook his head. "It's one thing to

risk exposure on my own, but I can't jeopardize them, too."

"You don't trust me."

"I don't trust my desire to trust you. It doesn't make sense when we only met last night."

"Same," she whispered, a little shaken at how perfectly their feelings aligned. "I understand your wanting to protect them. You don't have to tell me anything." She took a key out of the top desk drawer and used it to unlock the bottom one, pulling out her laptop and firing it up. "I'm just going to return a few client emails—"

"I met them through my work," he growled. "My roommates."

"Oh." She closed the laptop. "Why did you decide to talk about them?"

"Maybe if I confide in you, you'll do the same to me."

"Not unless I suddenly gain the ability to abscond with your memories." She swallowed. "Still planning on doing that?"

He said nothing, but a muscle jumped in his cheek.

In other words, yes. As soon as the mystery was solved.

She'd wake up one morning and not even be aware of his existence.

Trying to rid herself of the discomfort in her throat, she cleared it quietly. "Tell me about your roommates anyway?"

He stared at her hard, looking like he wanted to address her comment about memories, but ultimately he let it sit there between them like a nine-hundred-pound gorilla. "One is very serious. The other takes nothing seriously." He changed positions in his chair, leaning forward and clasping his hands together loosely between his knees. "Like I said, I met them at work. A lot goes into maintaining our cover. Most of us have no issue following the rules set out by the High Order, but new vampires...well, they have a hard time adjusting." He paused. "A really hard time. And I help them."

"You helped your roommates when they were..."

"Silenced. That's how we refer to the newly turned...because their hearts have been silenced. And yes, I trained them, helped them adapt when they were unsure how to fend for themselves." Ginny had at least forty-five follow-up questions. Such as, how were humans turned? What did new vampires do that constituted a "hard time adjusting"? How did Jonas find new vampires to help? But her pressing questions were put on hold when Jonas shook his head. "You already know more than you should."

Reluctantly, Ginny nodded.

Jonas waited, watching, obviously hoping there would be some quid pro quo for what he'd told her about an apparent underworld that operated without human knowledge. When she said nothing, he rose and walked to the door. "I'll be right outside the door while you work."

"Okay."

The room felt empty without Jonas's intense presence and it was hard to concentrate on anything knowing he was mere yards away, but she managed to answer all of her client emails and even make some adjustments to the AdWords she was using to court clients through Google. Larissa wouldn't be happy knowing she kept a budget set aside for advertising, but it was impossible these days to run a business without marketing in some form. Her father had been a huge believer in word of mouth, and truthfully, that's why most people darkened their door, but there was no reason Ginny couldn't add a few modern touches.

Would her father be proud of how she'd been running the business?

It was something she wondered every day. Sometimes she'd even look up from her desk and expect to see him fussing with the catalogues or trimming stray strings on the carpet out in the lobby. Sometimes he'd even used a magnifying glass and would get so lost in the activity, clients would have to step over his crawling form while Ginny greeted and ushered them into the back office.

With a sigh, she put her laptop back in the drawer and stood, confident that tomorrow would be a better day for the business. Yes, that meant that people had to die, but as long as they were doing it anyway, her wish wouldn't do any harm, would it?

Opening the office door and finding Jonas leaning against the opposite wall knocked the wind clear out of her sails. He looked like he'd been counting the seconds until she appeared again. Or was she reading way too much into the way his fist clenched while his shoulders relaxed at the same time?

"How old are you, Jonas?"

"Twenty-five."

The grandfather clock ticked out in the lobby. "How old are you really?"

She only caught a glimpse of the haunted quality that spun through his eyes before he transferred his attention to the ground. "I've been twenty-five since nineteen fifty-six."

"*Ohh*," she wheezed, wishing for a calculator.

He looked and up at her. Waiting for an official reaction?

Possibly even nervous about it?

"A lot of good movies came out that year," she said finally, wetting her dry lips. "Do you want to go watch one?"

He seemed surprised by his own jerky nod.

"I shouldn't be here," Jonas muttered, taking Ginny's hand and walking by her side back to her bedroom. "You won't remember this."

This time, his tone held far less conviction.

CHAPTER FIVE

"YOU REALLY HAVEN'T seen this movie?" Ginny counted on her fingers. "You would have been twenty-one when it came out."

Jonas settled onto the opposite side of the couch from Ginny—and it still seemed too close for his comfort. "No, I don't think I have."

"Maybe it's for the best if you haven't." She punched a series of buttons on her remote. "I'd be jealous if you'd gotten to see *The Quiet Man* in a theater."

His eyes ticked to the black and white movie poster hanging on her wall. "Why do you have such a fascination with movies from before your time?"

Ginny shrugged. "I don't know. My father found it odd, too. That I favored the Turner Classic Movies channel over Disney. But I eventually converted him. After that, we watched them together all the time."

A beat passed. "What happened to him, Ginny?"

"Heart attack." She said the words simply, but an invisible bolt twisted in her neck, like it always did. "He was working downstairs at night and I was sleeping, so I didn't know. I always think, if it had just been a different time of day, he'd still be here. I'd have called the paramedic to save him. He'd be on a strict diet now, but totally cheating on it behind my back." She shook her head. "Useless thoughts."

"They're impossible not to have."

"Do you have them about anyone?"

In lieu of answering, he nodded at the television. "What's the movie about?"

"Oh, it's wonderful. It's about a man who travels to Ireland to buy the cottage where his mother grew up. He falls in love with Maureen O'Hara—at first sight. She lives next door. I'm just going to fast forward to the part. I'm too excited." Ginny pressed the proper button, trying not to bounce up and down on the couch cushions. It had been so long since she'd watched a movie with anyone, let alone a gorgeous man. "Here. This is where he sees her in the field…" She clutched a hand to her chest. "Look at his face. He knows he's done for."

When Jonas had nothing to say about the incredible scene, she looked over and found him watching her instead, lips parted slightly.

A shiver flew up her spine. The moment stretched, this timeless male on one side of her, the modern television on the other. "Does romance between two regular people seem pointless when they only live a short time and vampires have eternity?"

"No." He gestured absently at the screen. "Regular is how it should be. The short time humans have is precious. It's living for eternity that's unnatural."

"You didn't choose to be a vampire?"

"I did, actually." His fingers curled into his palms. "Everyone should be given a choice. Though choosing to become a vampire is always the wrong decision."

His desolation made her wish to give him a hug, but suspected it wouldn't be well received. "Surely there are *some* perks. When you have all the time in the world, you're not under the human pressures. Get a job, get married, save for retirement, start a podcast…"

"You say those things like they're terrible. Do you not want to…marry?"

"Sure. Someday." Puzzling over his sudden frown, she sighed over the beautiful greenery on the television. "I'd rather travel, though. Have you been to Ireland?"

"Yes."

Ginny gasped and melted against the arm of the couch. "Say the first five words that comes to mind when you think about it."

"Damp. Friendly. Fireplaces. Beer. Wool."

She laughed. "Where's the best place you've been?"

"We've only been in Coney Island for a few weeks," he said quietly, his regard sweeping her. "But it's definitely a frontrunner."

Because she was there? Surely not. Though his eyes suggested that's exactly what he meant. Still...no. Couldn't be. "Yes, the boardwalk is pretty great, even in the fall," she said in a rush, narrowly resisting the urge to play with her hair. "Are you planning on staying long?"

"I don't know," Jonas murmured, a line forming between his brows.

Wait. Had he come closer?

Ginny looked down to find it was her that had scooted halfway across the couch. Flushing to her hairline, she reversed until her back met the arm of the sofa.

Jonas chuckled.

Desperate to pull the focus off her behavior, Ginny resumed watching the movie, though it was impossible not to feel Jonas's attention locked on her. "My favorite line is coming up."

"Don't tell me. I want to guess."

A smile stretched her mouth. "Okay."

They watched in silence for a minute and just like always, Ginny got lost in the romance of the scene. The rain that lashed the windows of the small cottage, the music that swelled as the hero searched his house for the intruder. How he pulled his future wife up against his chest. "It's a bold one you are," Ginny whispered, in time with Maureen O'Hara. "'Who gave you leave to be kissing me?'"

Several lines followed in the characters' argument.

Then, "'You'll get over it.'" She dropped her voice several octaves. "'Well, some things a man doesn't get over so easy.'"

"That's the one," Jonas said.

Her mouth fell open. "How did you know?"

"I have my ways." He raised a brow. "Why is that line your favorite?"

Ginny took a moment to think. "It's nice, isn't it? People acknowledging someone affects them, right to their face, instead of leaving them to guess." Cursing her ability to make any situation weird, she wet her lips and went back to quoting the movie. "'Like what, sup-posin'?'"

"'Like a girl coming through the fields with the sun on her hair...kneeling in church with a face like a saint...'"

Ginny sputtered a laugh. "You *have* seen this movie!"

He winked at her. "Opening weekend."

Thinking of him in an old-fashioned theater with red velvet curtains, she made a wistful sound. "Why did you pretend you hadn't?"

"So I could listen to you talk about it."

A fluttering weight dropped into her belly—and once again, she was halfway across the couch before realizing she'd moved. Drawn to him in a way that couldn't be denied or explained. Slowly, like a middle schooler might do, she slid her open palm over the couch cushion toward Jonas, afraid to breathe, afraid he'd think it was a bad idea.

When he slowly lowered his hand to Ginny's and knit their fingers together, cool twined with warm, electricity raced up her arm and Jonas's nostrils flared. But he didn't take his hand away—and they stayed that way until sleep snuck in like a bandit and claimed her.

GINNY WOKE WITH a start the following afternoon to find Roksana doing a walking handstand from one end of her room to the other. The previous night came back to her on a roaring current and she sprang into a sitting position, searching the room—futilely—for Jonas. Of course he wouldn't still be there in the broad daylight, but the reminder of his sunlight allergy did nothing to stop a ditch from opening in her stomach and filling with disappointment.

The last thing she remembered before sleep claimed her around two o'clock in the morning was waking in a slump against Jonas's hard yet welcoming shoulder. She recalled trying to sit up, clear the cobwebs of sleep from her brain and refocus on *The Quiet Man* unsuccessfully.

Some time later, she'd woken again while being carried in his arms from her sitting area to the bed. There were moments she recalled from childhood of being carried thusly, but this had been different. Her body had been lighter than air, kind of how she imagined it would be like to float in salt water in a sensory deprivation chamber. She'd kept her breathing even and pretended to be asleep, profoundly aware of Jonas's lack of heartbeat beside her ear. Instead of laying her down in the bed right away, he'd paced for a while at the foot of her bed. Without him saying a word, Ginny could decipher his internal mutterings. They might as well have spoken out loud. *I shouldn't be here. She'll remember none of this.*

Finally, he'd lain her down in the bed—fully clothed. After rattling the knob to make sure her bedroom door was locked, he sat in the window staring out over Coney Island. As she drifted off to sleep, she sensed his gaze burning over her time and time again, until she'd lost the battle with not only exhaustion, but the safety she felt in Jonas's presence. Surrendering herself to unconsciousness had never been easier with him watching over her.

"Hey!" Roksana hopped up on the foot of the bed and clapped her hands twice. "You are not a Victorian princess. Rise and shine."

"I work nights," Ginny complained. "Noon is early for me."

She rubbed her stomach, which was decidedly bare between a studded bra and low rider jeans. "I was told this job included meals."

Biting back a smile, Ginny climbed out of bed. "Do you want me to prepare you something or should we go get bagels and cream cheese?"

"Option two. And coffee." Roksana leapt off the bed, shadowboxing as soon as her feet touched down. "Maybe we'll get some action today, yes?"

Ginny paused in the act of choosing a dress from her closet to smile over her shoulder. "Yes, I can almost guarantee it."

The slayer seemed to be holding her breath. "Really?"

"Oh yes. My dress making club is always action packed. There will be backstitching, hemming, maybe even some ruffled embellishment."

"Very funny." She flexed her fingers. "Dress making club. This is really a thing? You can buy clothes on the internet."

"Is that where you buy yours?"

"Occasionally." She fingered the strap of her bra. "I have to sort through a lot of ball gags and latex suits to find what I'm looking for, but it's there."

Ginny laughed. "I just never imagined a vampire slayer having a credit card."

"I don't have one. I steal Elias's—"

When the slayer abruptly cut herself off, Ginny looked up from the mint green frock she'd chosen for the day. "Who is Elias?"

Roksana rubbed at the back of her neck. "Forget I said that. He's no one."

"Is he one of Jonas's roommates?"

The other woman approached with what might have been a menacing expression, if she didn't have two spots of color on her cheeks. "I told you nothing. You never heard that name."

"What name?"

"Good girl."

"Elias?"

"*Ginny!*"

She giggled at the slayer's outrage. "You can relax. I won't say anything." Her thumb traced the curved top of the hanger. "Maybe Jonas will tell me himself one day."

"Don't get your hopes up. He's the strictest follower of the rules."

"I guess he has to be, right?" Ginny moved past Roksana and laid the dress out on her bed. "Since he teaches the Silenced how to follow them."

Roksana was silent for long moments. "He told you that?"

Ginny nodded, silently brimming with pleasure that he'd confided something important in her and vowing she'd never, ever make him regret it. "I'm going to go take a quick shower. Then we'll go get bagels."

She breezed from the room before the slayer could respond, though she could feel Roksana's interested gaze following her from the room. Within half an hour, Ginny had showered, dried her hair and thrown on the green dress, receiving a grunting approval from Roksana. She called downstairs to the office to make sure Larissa had woken up for her shift, breathing a sigh of relief when her stepmother answered the phone albeit in a weary tone. After a reminder to Larissa that she'd be at her dress making club that afternoon, she snuck Roksana downstairs and out the back entrance of the house.

Roksana had drunk an extra-large coffee, scarfed her bagel and started on the second half of Ginny's breakfast by the time they reached the club.

Embrace the Lace Dressmaking Endeavors met once a week in the basement of the Our Lady of Solace Catholic Church. It smelled like stale coffee, dust and there was a distinct lack of fresh air, but Ginny found the whole operation glorious. If she could pick one sound to hear for the rest of her life, it would be sewing machines chirping away, set against the cutting of fabric. Women with pins in their mouths and sketchpads at the ready? It was heaven. Perhaps the members of the club hadn't welcomed her with open arms, but because that was the norm for Ginny, she was able to look past their discomfort over her presence and enjoy the atmosphere.

Ginny couldn't remember a time when she hadn't been fascinated by dresses. Not so much the act of looking pretty as the sensation of feeling feminine.

Maybe even a touch dramatic. One couldn't sweep from the room after a witty rejoinder in a pair of jeans. Dresses—bright ones, specifically—were a tale to tell. In pleated pink tulle, she could be delicate, like Audrey Hepburn. In sunset orange, she could be bold, like Sophia Loren.

Ginny couldn't remember a lot about her mother, mainly just blurry memories, muted sounds and the few stories she'd been told by her father. Her favorite one was that her mother used to dance around the kitchen to the Foo Fighters with Ginny on her hip. Her least favorite story was the one about her mother going out for diapers and never coming home. More than once, she'd caught her father reading the note Ginny's mother had left behind, folded beneath his shaving cream can, but she'd never asked the contents.

When puberty reared its head at twelve and Ginny had no one to speak with about the changes happening with her body, she'd expressed those wild mood swings with dresses. The act of making the dresses and focusing that confusing energy had the biggest impact initially, but as she grew older, they became her shield. *Sophia Loren* didn't care about whispers behind her back, and neither did Ginny, as long as she was wearing sunset orange with scalloped edges.

Now, as Ginny and Roksana walked into the basement—a few minutes late, thanks to Roksana having trouble choosing between poppy seed and plain—the cacophony of Ginny's favorite sounded ceased. This was the usual reaction when Ginny arrived to the club meetings, however, the whispers typically followed in short order. Not this time. They gaped at Roksana like a row of codfish along the back basement wall.

"Hello," Ginny called, her voice echoing off the walls. "I brought a friend."

"Friends aren't allowed," came a sing-song voice. It belonged to Galina, one half of the Russian, middle-aged twins who held dominion over the club when the founder, Ruth, wasn't present, which appeared to be the case this morning. Among them were Mercedes, a regal black woman and stay-at-home mother who mainly crafted holiday dresses for her children and Tina, a Florida transplant that talked of nothing but how to get bang for your buck at Disneyworld. "They have to sign up in advance and pay the fee," finished Galina.

Ginny smiled. "Can we make an exception just this once?"

Galina squinted in lieu of a smile. "I'm afraid not."

Roksana sauntered over to the closest table, kicked out a metal chair—*squeeeeeal*—and sat in it backwards. "How about my fee is not kicking your a—"

"She can stay," Galina blurted, her smile on the verge of shattering. "But Ruth will be here soon and as founder, *she'll* have no choice but to enforce the rules."

"Yes of course, Galina," Ginny said, taking her usual seat at her favorite sewing machine, laying out the fabric she'd purchased the day before.

"These women take dress club very seriously."

Ginny pursed her lips. "*I* take it seriously."

"You would not be unkind about it."

"No, I wouldn't." Ginny fussed with her chiffon. "Look, I know you probably think I acted like a pushover, but I've found it's easier not to engage them."

Roksana gave an exaggerated hum. "*Is* it easier?"

Ginny hesitated. "Yes."

Though…she wasn't quite as secure in that philosophy as she used to be. Pretending to be Lauren Bacall had been easier when she didn't have a vampire slayer and immortal beings populating her life. Roksana was so brave, so daring, so assertive. For the first time in a long, long time, Ginny acknowledged the secret wish that she was better at standing up for herself.

She swallowed. "I hope you won't be bored while I work."

"Eh, I think everything is boring. I kill—" She lowered her voice to a whisper. "I kill vampires for a living. Very hard to top that."

"I see your point." Ginny chewed her lip as the words *Death Girl* drifted toward her from the small group of women. The slayer heard it, too, frowning, and Ginny rushed to fill the resulting silence so they wouldn't have to talk about the nickname. Or the fact that she never did anything to stop it from being spoken aloud. "Speaking of vampires, would you be willing to tell me more about…you know, Jonas's world?"

"Uh-uh." Roksana made a chopping gesture across her neck. "I've been sworn to secrecy."

"By Jonas."

The slayer's expression turned suspicious. "Yes…"

Ginny loaded a spool of white thread into her Singer, absently noting the whispers had commenced on the other side of the room. "Weren't you scheduled to slaughter him and his roommates today?"

She studied her nails. "You're wondering why I keep their secrets when I'm going to kill them?"

"Wouldn't *you* wonder?"

"Perhaps I'm being paid well for my discretion."

"Oh." Ginny perked up. "Are you? Because *that* might make sense."

Roksana leaned back in her chair with crossed arms. "Perhaps you are not such a pushover after all. Deep down, you are Ginny the Not So Meek."

She gasped. "I'm going to stitch that onto a dress."

"Hooray for you." Roksana twisted slightly in her chair to glance over her shoulder. "Don't they serve alcohol at this club?"

"I'm afraid not," Ginny answered, hiding her smile. "Would you need to be drunk in order to let me use you

79

as a dress model?"

"Nyet. You're crazier than me if you think that will ever happen."

Twenty minutes later, Roksana stood on the round, elevated pedestal in front of the three-way vanity mirror used by the club, wrapped in persimmon chiffon, her combat boots peeking out from beneath the uneven hem.

"I will get even with you for this," Roksana swore.

Ginny smoothed and tucked the material, taking a pin from her mouth to secure the adjustment at Roksana's waist. "It's an honor to be penciled in on your slaughter schedule." She stepped back and clasped her hands tightly beneath her chin. "This persimmon color looks incredible on you."

She scoffed. "You're wasting time making me a dress. I won't wear it."

"No special occasions coming up? Or maybe a special someone…?"

Those telltale twin spots of color appeared on Roksana's cheeks. "No. And no. There is no one. Are you almost finished?"

"Yes." While Ginny helped Roksana out of the garment, guilt prodded her in the side. "Sorry, I think maybe I'm forcing girl talk on you because I never get a chance to have it. There doesn't need to be a special someone to dress up, either. Right? Therefore, I'm making you a dress."

Roksana looked like she wanted to protest, but reached out and rubbed the material between two fingers, instead. "Blood would blend in very nicely with this color, I suppose."

"That's the spirit!"

Ruth, founder of Embrace the Lace Dressmaking Endeavors, blew into the church basement with an arm full of fabric sample books. Her son, Gordon, and Ginny's one and only date, trailed behind her with a red Radio Flyer wagon loaded down with a sewing kit and endless bolts of fabric.

"Ladies, I'm so sorry to be late. Please forgive me." Ruth slipped her fingers up beneath her glasses and rubbed at her eyes. "I got all the way here and realized I'd forgotten *everything*, including Gordon."

The son in question grimaced and waved, his gaze searching out Ginny. When he saw her, his spine snapped straight and he dropped the wagon handle. *Clank.*

"Another besotted male, eh, Ginny?" Roksana said out of the side of her mouth. "When it rains it pours."

Ginny started to tell Roksana that this was *definitely* her first downpour, but she quieted when Galina marched in Ruth's direction. On her way, the twin sent a pointed look at Ginny, clearly intending to make a complaint. "Uh-oh."

Roksana sighed. "I really don't like that bitch."

Ginny sighed. "At least she's consistent."

"Ginny," Gordon called, approaching with his wagon once again in tow. "You brought a friend."

"Hi Gordon. Yes, this is Roksana."

Roksana stuck out a hand for him to shake. "Cool wagon."

"Oh, uh…thanks." He scrubbed at the top of his head, making a mess of his ginger hair. "So, listen. Ginny, I was wondering—"

"Yes, yes, Galina. Yes. *A couple of reminders, ladies!*" Ruth's voice rang out, unknowingly cutting off her son. "The dress expo is nearly upon us. Now, we've been preparing for this night for what seems like *ages*! I'm sure you're all very excited to show off your creations to friends and loved ones. But I've been keeping a teeny tiny little secret." Ruth wiggled her hips, fingers crammed to her mouth. "The dress expo will also be a silent auction! All those in attendance will have a chance to bid on your dresses—isn't that *exciting*?"

The members erupted with gasps and squeals.

For Ginny's part, her stomach clenched. Ruth had been planning this dress expo for the better part of the year. Ginny was apprehensive about showing off her designs at first, but steadily grown used to the idea. Now she'd be jockeying for bids?

"One more thing." Ruth sent Ginny a genuinely apologetic look. "Please remember, if you're going to bring a guest, let me know if advance so I can plan for the extra person. We like guests to pay in advance and of course, we have limited space."

A leak dripped nearby, echoing in the barely filled basement. Roksana made a huge show out of turning in a circle and pointing out all the empty seats, only stopping when Ginny poked her in the ribs.

"Oh, uh. Mom." Gordon cleared his throat. "I forgot to tell you, Ginny mentioned to me last week that she'd be bringing a friend tonight. She already paid the fee, too. I can't believe I forgot to mention it."

"Oh!" Ruth seemed relieved. "Crisis averted."

"I don't think she knows what crisis means," Roksana muttered, turning to Gordon. "Thank you for the kindness, my dude. However, I see your motive is brownie points with my friend. And while Ginny is not *technically* dating someone, you are in grave peril just standing this close to her—"

"*Roksana!*" Ginny cut in, with a high-pitched laugh. "She's joking."

The slayer scoffed. "I assure you, I am not—"

"I think it's time to go." Ginny shuffled Roksana away from Gordon. "See you at the expo, okay, Gordon?"

"Actually, I was thinking I'd come by for a visit."

"Sure, sure," Ginny said, not really registering what he'd said. As quickly as possibly, Ginny packed up her material and tools, tucking them in her burlap tote bag. Gathering her courage, she called a goodbye to the ladies on the opposite end of the basement, not expecting a response and not receiving one, either.

She shrugged at Roksana. "Oh well. Maybe next time."

Roksana started to follow Ginny from the room, but stopped in the doorway and turned to glare at the foursome. "Good luck sewing yourself a personality," she called, waving her middle finger at them.

"*Roksana*," Ginny scolded her half-heartedly, while trying not to laugh—at least until they were out of earshot. "I can't believe you did that."

She waved Ginny off. "I should have thought of something better."

"No, I *loved* it. It was perfect."

Roksana cracked a smile and sent Ginny some prideful side eye. "I guess."

THAT EVENING, THEY ate hot dogs from a cart on the boardwalk for dinner. While Ginny tried her best to find out more about Roksana, she came away with the barest of details. She'd moved from Russia to Boston as a child and made her way around the major cities, where she claimed vampires liked to congregate. Her preferred music of choice was synthetic pop, she'd been a competitive gymnast into her teens and suffered from seasonal allergies. That last one she'd been most reluctant to reveal because it exposed a weakness.

Sunset signaled the shift change between Larissa and Ginny at the funeral home and that time was approaching fast. Not wanting to risk getting caught with the slayer, nimble and adept at hiding though she was, they parted ways at the end of the block. Ginny entered through the front entrance, waving at Larissa on her way to the stairs, before detouring and letting Roksana in the back way.

With an hour to go before sunset—and the start of her shift—Ginny left Roksana sharpening her knife on the fire escape and turned on the end of *The Quiet Man*, since she'd missed it last night. Maybe it was the beautiful, green scenery and musical accents of the movie. Or maybe it was the memory of falling asleep against Jonas during the same scene the night prior. Whatever the reason, Ginny found herself lulled to sleep, her face nuzzling into one of her couch's throw pillows.

The dream that crept in was unfamiliar, as in she'd never had it before, but somehow she knew the exact steps to take. Knew what was coming before it happened. There she was, walking through the county fair, the hem of her dress flapping in the nighttime breeze. Around her, lights flickered, games ding-dinged and people laughed. There was a roasted chestnuts smell wafting past and a sense of wonder in the air. The brassy womble of a lone trombone dipped and lifted, coming from the direction of the bandstand. Happiness bubbled in her belly, anticipation, though she couldn't say for what.

She only knew if she turned the corner at the cotton candy stand and left the loud, main drag, she'd see him. That's where he'd been the night before. Standing under the willow tree in the shadows in his newsboy cap and suspenders, watching her. Making no attempt to lure her closer, but luring her nonetheless with the promise of...what?

The mystery he represented excited her. It had excited her the first night of the fair, but she'd exercised caution like she'd been taught and stuck to the crowd. What would she do tonight? Would she play it safe and spend another sleepless night wondering what if? Or would she go find out why, at such a distance, this unknown man could have such a wild pull on her being?

She took a step off the path and his body went on alert, separating from the tree. He shook his head at her. "Don't," he mouthed. "Please, don't."

His warning only made her more determined. More curious.

Another step was taken...

And then the dream changed. Shifted like sand.

One moment she was on the edge of the lively fair

and the next, she was floating. Floating, kind of like last night when Jonas carried her to bed. White haze passed over her like torn shrouds and she left them twisting in her wake. Was she moving? Bright dots of light hung high above her and below, there was a sound of movement. Large movement. Rushing air and muffled music. And it was getting closer. Or, maybe she was moving closer to the sounds?

Ginny tried to open her eyes and find the source of the noise, but her head was muddled in a way she'd only ever experienced after an abundance of cold medicine. Rousing herself was repugnant when she could just float and sleep...

Suddenly, her feet touched down on something hard, jolting her, and the lethargy cleared like it had never been there to begin with.

When she opened her eyes, she was standing in the center lane of a highway with a semi-truck bearing down on her.

CHAPTER SIX

I T WAS THE kind of fear that couldn't be described.

There was no build to it, just a precise slice straight through Ginny's body—a very horrifying certainty that her life ended there. Now. In the middle of a three-lane highway.

I'm going to be road kill.

Would it be painful?

Please don't let it be painful.

The worst part was she'd never know *how* this happened. How she'd gotten there. Oh, something similar to this had happened once before. She'd been lucky to escape. But she wouldn't escape this. The semi-truck's brakes were squealing and the driver was shouting behind the windshield, but he was going too fast, right?

Right.

Ginny closed her eyes and followed her body's instinct to drop into a crouch.

The burn of hot metal screeched to a halt so close to her face, she could taste exhaust and motor oil in her mouth. She opened her eyes to find her pale, petrified face staring back in the truck's front bumper and a shocked sob broke from her mouth, shivers turning to violent shakes as all hell broke loose around her.

"What the fuck are you doing?" shouted the truck driver, coming around the side of the vehicle. He pounded a fist on the grill. "You could have caused a pileup..."

The man continued to rail at her, but her harsh breathing and racing heartbeat drowned him out. *I have to get out of here.* She didn't know where the intuition came from and she didn't question it. Ginny pushed to her feet, stumbling backwards thanks to her trembling knees, and frantically searched for a way out.

Cars were stopped on the shoulders, people getting out to gape at her. Other motorists stuck their heads out of windows, some of them asking if she was okay, others cursing her for holding up traffic. Oh Lord, the smell of burnt rubber and the kaleidoscope of colors was making her nauseous.

Move.

Get home.

"I'm calling the police," said the truck driver, fully breaking her out of her stupor. Grateful she'd put on her work shoes before falling asleep on the couch, Ginny wove through the stopped vehicles and got to the shoulder, sprinting for the exit up ahead. It was her exit, Ocean Parkway. She was close to home.

Honking and shouting ensued behind her, but she didn't turn around and prayed no one would give chase and hold her until the cops arrived. What would she say? She'd woken up in the middle of the Belt Parkway? They'd either think she was crazy or suicidal. They would lock her up in a padded cell somewhere...and apart from her stepmother, there was no one to vouch for her sanity.

In other words, no one. Larissa had too much to gain from her being gone. She'd never considered her stepmother a malevolent person. They'd even formed an awkward yet comfortable bond since her father passed. But in her stark moment of crisis, suspicion reared its head.

For a brief moment while turning at the end of the off ramp and running down the avenue, she considered the possibility she did need mental help. Maybe she required medication? Therapy? Perhaps being around death so frequently and for so long *had* affected her, the way people assumed it had.

The sound of sirens plowed into her thoughts and she detoured hard to the right, cutting between two high-rise apartment buildings, dodging startled passersby in the barren courtyard.

"Where am I? Where am I?" She'd been born and raised in this neighborhood, but she stuck to her routines and followed the same routes. "Go toward the water..."

She hooked a right and landed on another, less congested avenue, smelling the salt air up ahead. Darkness had fallen and headlights trundled past, televisions flickered in the living rooms of houses. She was out of her skin, existing in some disturbing nightmare, ruled by adrenaline. But she kept going and finally, finally, she recognized the bagel shop a few blocks from P. Lynn. Sirens continued to blare back toward the Belt, urging her legs to pump faster, even though her heart was definitely about to beat out of her chest.

Lord, she'd never been more grateful to see the funeral home. Beautiful, beautiful place. She almost collapsed at the sight of it beneath the El. Knowing she'd never be able to explain herself to Larissa, she snuck in through the backdoor and jogged toward the stairs—

Shouts coming from Ginny's room halted her progress.

Jonas.

Roksana.

They were arguing loud enough to wake the dead...and now that she knowingly lived in a world where the undead had their own government, she really needed to come up with a better phrase to describe something unlikely.

Ginny had only stepped foot on the first, creaky stair when her bedroom door flew open to reveal Jonas in extensive distress. She was only afforded the briefest of glances at his wayward hair and fraught expression before he moved in a whirlwind of color down the stairs, collected her and shut them back inside her bedroom a second later.

"Where..." he rasped, trapping her against the door, "*were* you?"

She couldn't answer. For one, her equilibrium had been compromised by their atom-splitting ascent of the stairs. Two, she had no idea if Jonas would believe her story. And three, if she told him the truth about what took place tonight, she'd have to confess what happened *before* and their acquaintance would be that much closer to being over. Wouldn't it? Once he found out wherein the danger lay, it would be sayonara, Ginny.

"I...I..." Casting about for a lifeline, Ginny spotted Roksana over Jonas's shoulder and noticed for the first time that the wise-cracking slayer had a towel pressed to her temple, trying to stem the flow of blood gushing from an apparent wound. "What happened to Roksana?" Ginny gasped.

"Don't worry about her right now. Look at me," Jonas ordered, and Ginny's chin jerked a precise two inches to the left to obey him.

A fire lit in her belly. "Don't command me like that. And keep your voice down. Larissa will hear you."

"She's sleeping. Soundly." While Ginny processed the fact that her stepmother had either been *conked* again or compelled to sleep by Jonas, he visibly reined himself in. When he spoke again, however, his tone remained brittle, ready to snap. "When I arrived, Roks was unconscious on the floor and you were gone. What happened, Ginny? *Are you hurt?*"

"No."

Jonas tilted her face up, scrutinizing every feature. "You're only half lying."

"How can you tell?"

"Your pulse. It changes when you're not truthful or if you get excited. That's how I knew your favorite line in *The Quiet Man.*" His chest rose and fell rapidly. "An explanation. Now. Or I'll have no choice but to make the command."

"Don't you *dare.* Last night, you talked about about the importance of choices. Well you can't talk out of both sides of your mouth, Jonas. Preaching about choices while stealing my free will."

He flinched. "This is different. Your silence prevents me from protecting you."

"Promise to never compel me again and I'll talk."

A short standoff ensued. "Done."

Heat rushed to the backs of her eyelids, panic springing up in her middle like a geyser. This was it. Once she gave up the information she'd been hiding from Jonas, she gave up the only bargaining chip she had to maintain her memories. But if tonight had proven one thing, it was that she couldn't protect herself against an unseen force that could pick her up in one location and drop her in another. She couldn't defend against something she couldn't see, but Jonas might. Her options had run out.

In short order, so would her time with him.

"Two weeks ago, I woke up in the ocean," she whispered, recalling the chill of the black, bottomless water, the taste of salt on her tongue. "It was pitch dark, but I could see lights in the distance and I swam toward them. It took me…hours, it seemed like. And I have no idea how I got there. Only that I slept so deeply before it happened, almost like I was in a trance. Something or someone lifted me up and took me there."

Jonas had gone still as a marble statue, his hands going from cool to icy where they held her face.

"A-and tonight, the same thing happened, except…"

"Tell me."

"When I woke up, I was in the middle lane of the Belt Parkway."

A choked sound left him.

His hands dropped away from her face.

"This time, I remember…floating. I was floating. I can't remember that happening the night I ended up in the ocean."

"Vampire," he growled.

"A powerful one," Roksana added, sounding fearful for the first time since Ginny had met her. "What the hell, Jonas?"

Ginny came off the door. "A vampire is the one doing this to me?"

"It doesn't make sense," Jonas muttered, fingers plowing through his inky hair. "I could understand if I'd made her a target, but I've only known her two days. The first incident was weeks ago."

Ginny waved her hands. "Can we please start from the beginning? Vampires can make people fly?"

Roksana lowered the towel from her head and Ginny got a look at the gigantic red lump. "You've obviously noticed Jonas can compel your actions. He probably wouldn't be able to levitate you, though." Gingerly, she prodded the knot on her head and winced. "That's a skill reserved by older, more seasoned bloodsuckers."

"But…" Ginny made a grab for the missing pieces. "I thought it was against the rules for a vampire to kill a human."

"They didn't kill you," Jonas said, tone ominous. "They put you in a situation where you're likely to…" He dragged a hand down his face. "It's not a direct violation of the rule, but someone is definitely playing fast and loose. Why, though?" He paced for a moment. "I'm the first vampire you've had contact with," Jonas asked Ginny, even though he didn't exactly phrase it as a question.

"Yes. That I'm aware of."

He nodded, satisfied with her answer.

"I'm not in love with the fact that you're a human lie detector."

"Don't lie to me and you've got nothing to worry about."

"I rarely lie at all."

"I know. Only by omission—and you're loath to do even that. Your honesty is one of the reasons I…"

"What?"

He seemed to be judging the wisdom of continuing. "One of the reasons I can't stand to be away from you," Jonas said, just above a whisper, before stepping closer, face tortured. "You're sure you're not hurt?"

He can't stay away from me. The omission made her want to be truthful. "I think I might have strained my Achilles running from the police."

Jonas's right eye ticked. Twice. "Christ."

The next thing Ginny knew, she was being settled onto the edge of the bed with Jonas kneeling in front of her. He started to roll up her pant leg, but paused, his gaze ticking to hers. "No blood anywhere?"

"No." She rolled her lips inward. "Wouldn't you…smell it?"

Briefly, his grip tightened on her calf. "I smell your blood at all times, but *seeing* it…"

Ginny's mouth went dry at the way Jonas stared up at her, as if it took all his inner strength to keep from pressing her backward onto the bed. *Oh my.*

"Farewell, lovebirds. I hereby resign my post," Roksana announced dramatically from her position at the window. "I apologize for failing you tonight, Ginny. You could have been a pancake and all because some parasite got the drop on me."

"Roksana, no." Ginny reached a hand in her friend's direction. "If this vampire is as powerful as you say, what could you have done to—"

"Let her go," Jonas cut in, never taking his attention off of Ginny. "Roksana is right. She didn't do her job."

"I will take some time to train and once again become unstoppable." Roksana turned and gave them a final, anguished look. "Dasvidaniya."

With that, the slayer's blonde head ducked out of view, leaving Ginny and Jonas alone in the bedroom. Shaken at the sudden loss of her friend after everything she'd already been through that night, Ginny smacked Jonas's hand off her leg. "Why didn't you make her stay?"

"Tonight you could have…" He broke off, nostrils flaring. "Hell, two weeks ago, you could have been gone and I never would have met you."

"That wouldn't have been her fault, either."

His hand landed back on her knee and smoothed down, around to the swell of her calf, massaging there. "I'm quite aware I'm not being rational about anything concerning you, Ginny."

Lord, it was hard to argue when he was touching her. She never had this manner of skin to skin contact with a man and could only liken it to being hugged in a towel fresh from the dryer. Or sinking into a hot bath. The cool temperature of his skin did nothing to stop the goosebumps from rising on her arms or the tiny wrench to twist beneath her belly button.

Fight the distraction. She had to. Jonas knew there was a vampire purposefully putting her in dangerous situations and she had no information left to withhold. This could be the last time she looked into his eyes and knew him.

But then, his thumb found her Achilles, pressing and sweeping along the sore tendon—and Ginny moaned.

Jonas's open mouth dragged up her bare thigh, searing her skin, stopping just short of her dress's hem. "This is madness. How do you pull me under like this?"

"You do the same to me," she managed, breathily, sliding her fingers into his hair. "Don't make this go away. Please."

His hand tightened on her leg. "The longer I let you keep your memories of me, Ginny, the harder it will be once they're gone." He pressed his face to her stomach, using his grip on her calf to tug her closer. Until she could feel the outline of his features against her belly. "You'll lose days, weeks, as opposed to hours."

"And once I've forgotten you exist, you'll stay away, just like that?"

Jonas's shoulders tensed, his fingers on her skin. "We'll have to wait a little longer to find out," he said hoarsely. "Knowing it's a vampire trying to bring you harm, and not some easily overcome human, changes everything. I need you alert and I need you to trust me implicitly. Without Roksana to watch you during the day, I have to bring you somewhere without sunlight. To protect you until this is over."

Oxygen trapped itself in her lungs. "Meaning?"

Jonas leaned away, the green sparks shooting off in his eyes telling Ginny how much their closeness was affecting him.

"Pack," he said, doom lacing his tone. "You're coming with me."

CHAPTER SEVEN

"I'M SORRY, WHAT did you say?"

"You're coming with me." Jonas gave Ginny's legs one last, longing look and stood. "I can't and won't leave you here alone while your safety is in jeopardy—and I can't stay."

"There are no windows in the basement. You could stay there."

"With the other corpses, you mean?" he drawled. "I suppose I could stay down there during the day, but you'll have to remain there with me where I can protect you."

"The daytime is Larissa's shift."

"Can you swap?"

"No, she'll refuse. She thinks the morgue is scarier at night, which doesn't really track, because there are no windows. It could be noon or midnight and you'd never be able to tell."

"Then we have our answer." He strode to the window, clenching and unclenching his hands while scanning the street below. "Please get packing."

Ginny shot to her feet and whirled around, wincing inwardly when her Achilles protested. "Who exactly do you think is going to run this place?"

He turned with a regal eyebrow raised. "Are there any bodies downstairs waiting for you?"

"It's been a slow week," she responded, feeling kind of defensive. "Fall is upon us. People tend to try and stick it out through the holidays."

Jonas's sigh was weary and amused, all at once. "So help me God, Ginny..." His throat worked. "It will forever be one of the universe's greatest mysteries that you've remained here for twenty-four years without turning every male you meet into a lovesick fool who worships at your feet."

"That sounds horrible," she whispered, shaken. "I hate clutter."

His laugh was somehow adoring and sad at the same time.

Ginny looked down at her hands. What was she supposed to be doing again?

Packing. Leaving. To go live with the vampires. Right.

"Um. I can leave a note for Larissa about spending the night with a friend. She won't believe it. It's only slightly more plausible than being targeted for death by a formidable vampire. But it will have to do." She turned in a circle, trying to remember where she kept her overnight bag. Did she even own one? "I will need to come back tomorrow night and work, though. I can't neglect this place."

"I know your father's legacy is important to you, Ginny."

Knowing he'd listened and committed her worries to memory made wings flap beneath her breastbone. "Yes. It is." She unearthed a small, dusty suitcase from the back of her closet and piled essentials inside, including a dress for tomorrow, her hairbrush and a bottle of perfume. Before she opened her underwear drawer, she gave Jonas a pointed look and he turned his back like a gentleman.

Satisfied he wasn't watching her dig through her abundance of sensible, full coverage panties, Ginny began to sift. Instead of taking out a perfectly functional white cotton pair, something rebellious lit inside of her—probably sparked by Roksana—and she opened a pack of midnight blue bikini-cut panties she'd never worn once. Some had glittery stars and moons all over them, others were sunshine and clouds. She'd bought them on sale at Kohl's after too much coffee and was grateful for them now. Jonas might never set eyes on them, but maybe they'd make her feel more in control, the way her dresses did.

Feeling herself flush, she quickly stuffed them in her bag. "I'll just get my toothbrush—"

A rumble of air blew hair across her face and then Jonas was standing in front of her with the toothbrush in his hand. "I'd really like to get you somewhere safe," he said, dropping the item into her bag. "Quickly."

"How do you know that's mine and not Larissa's?"

"The other one was electric. You'd never use one of those."

"Wouldn't I?"

"The girl who loves old movies, talks to corpses and doesn't want me to see her underwear? No, I don't think so."

"Does that mean you think I'm boring?"

His lips twisted. "It means I think you're an original. And that you probably like to daydream while you're brushing your teeth and the buzzing sound would deter you."

Pleasure speared her. "You've given this some thought."

"Yes." He gave her his princely profile while zipping her suitcase and picking it up by the handle. "More than I should have."

Ginny followed him to the door of her bedroom and out into the hallway. "Where do you live?"

He sighed. "I can't tell you that, Ginny."

They stopped side by side on the staircase landing. "How are you going to bring me there without telling me…" She trailed off when he took something out of his pocket. "Is that a blindfold? You can't be serious."

"It's for your own safety. The world I live in is a volatile place. You knowing where three vampires live makes you vulnerable."

"You're planning on erasing that information from my head, remember?"

"Remember? I think about it *constantly*," he enunciated, stepping closer. "Like I said, the longer I allow you to keep your memories, the harder it'll be to erase them accurately. I don't want to take chances."

Ginny threw back her shoulders and sailed down the stairs, leaving Jonas to follow behind her with the suitcase. For one fantastical moment, she pretended to be Grace Kelly in *To Catch a Thief*. A rich debutante with a handsome manservant, preparing to depart for Paris. She wished desperately for a pair of white, silk gloves so she could whip them out and don them while looking annoyed. "Now then," she murmured when Jonas stopped beside her at the bottom of the staircase. "Have the driver bring my car around."

"What was that?" Jonas asked, his tone verging on amusement.

"N-nothing."

He tucked his tongue into his cheek and herded her down the hallway, toward the back door. "As luck would have it, we do have a driver."

"Who is it?"

Jonas hesitated with a hand on the doorknob. "One of my roommates, Tucker. Prepare yourself."

"For what?"

He opened his mouth to answer, closed it and pushed open the door instead. She heard the low pump of bass before the black Impala slid into view at the curb, idling for a moment, before the passenger side window rolled down—and smoke billowed out into the night air. It cleared to reveal a Cheshire smile with a cigar clamped somewhere in its midst. The smile belonged to a man who was more like a mountain, a gold chain draped around his thick neck.

Brightly colored tattoos were the only thing covering him, as he was decidedly shirtless, his coloring reminding Ginny of a slightly sunburned Irishman she'd once worked on in the morgue who'd died while on vacation.

"Jonas," called Tucker, taking the cigar out of his mouth slowly. "That's a human girl."

"I'm well aware of what she is. Put out the cigar."

Tucker didn't look happy about stubbing out the stogie in his ashtray. "Are we having her for dinner?" he drawled. "Or having her for dinner?"

Jonas left her wobbling in the wake of his swift departure. One second he was standing beside her, the next he was speaking to Tucker in a low, unintelligible tone through the driver's side window.

After a moment of listening, Tucker threw back his

head and laughed. "The prince himself is breaking the rules. Holy shit, man, this is going to be interesting."

Ginny was in the backseat of the car before she could catch her breath, Jonas pressed in beside her. "What did you say to him?"

"Only that he'd be having stake for dinner if he comes within five feet of you."

"Steak? I thought you don't eat food."

"S-t-a-k-e."

"Oh." Once she'd absorbed that violent implication, she leaned forward. "It's lovely to meet you, Tucker. You're the prankster, are you?"

"At your service."

"I'm sorry Jonas has already threatened your life on my behalf, but you have to admit it's well deserved after leaving him to be embalmed."

Humor-filled eyes met hers in the rearview mirror. "Threats to my life are all in a day's work."

"The day's work of a vampire?"

"Nope." He pointed to the circular sticker in his front window. "An Uber driver."

Ginny chuckled. "I see."

"Don't judge me too harshly for the prank, sweetheart," Tucker continued. "Playing the occasional trick keeps us human. As much as that's possible, anyway. Think of it as me doing him a favor."

"I'll never understand how you get Elias to agree to

these pranks," Jonas muttered. "It's not exactly his style."

"I caught him with a picture of Roksana. I promised not to tell anyone if he'd help me execute the prank." He gave an exaggerated wince. "Whoops."

"Drive the car," Jonas said mildly. "And don't call Ginny 'sweetheart.'"

Jonas was reaching up with the thin, black swath of material, preparing to tie it around Ginny's eyes, when a thought occurred. "Jonas, how do I know you're not the one dropping me into oceans and highways?"

His hands dropped like stones to the seat. Several seconds ticked by. "How can you ask me that?"

She waited.

"I've explained to you, it would take someone older and more powerful to transport you like that."

"How do I know that's true?" Without breaking the intensity of their stare, she reached down and fingered the material of the blindfold. "You're asking for my absolute trust and giving me none in return, Dream-boat."

"She called him Dreamboat!" More raucous laughter from Tucker. "Yes, indeed. This is going to be goddamn interesting."

Jonas's tortured expression was the last thing she saw before the blindfold turned her world black.

GINNY MENTALLY COUNTED the third right they'd taken since leaving P. Lynn Funeral Home, though she couldn't be sure they hadn't doubled back or taken a meandering route to throw her off. Every time they hit a straightaway, she counted the seconds until the next turn and committed the directions to memory, just in case she ever needed them. As a lifelong Coney Island resident, Ginny knew at least four ways to reach the boardwalk. If she wasn't mistaken, they weren't too far from the world-famous planks when Tucker pulled the parking brake.

"I'll park and meet you inside," Jonas's roommate called. "Don't say or do anything worth gossiping about until I get back."

Jonas hummed distractedly. "She'll need food and water. Can you pick up some groceries? Eggs, bread, milk..."

Tucker made a sound. "Gross."

"Get a blanket for her, too."

"Yes, almighty prince."

The back door on Jonas's side opened and then he was lacing their fingers together, sending stardust blustering up her arm. He helped her step out of the car, though Ginny sensed his hesitation before he put an arm around the small of her back, urging her forward. A door opened and cool air crept out, wrapping around Ginny until she was fully ensconced inside of it. That same door closed behind her, dropping them into a total lack of sound. The sounds of traffic, seagulls and car radios cut off abruptly and all she could hear were her and Jonas's footsteps.

"We're going into an elevator now," he murmured near her ear, steering her to the left. "I'll have the blindfold off soon."

She folded her arms across her chest, feeling the metal box lurch downward, followed by the familiar mechanical whine of a moving elevator.

"Are you giving me the silent treatment?"

Ginny kept her lips pressed into a straight line, because yes, she was rather irritated and if she started talking, all manner of smart comments would probably tumble out of her mouth. Just this evening, she'd almost been run over by a semi truck. Now she was being shuffled around by a highhanded vampire who still had plans to apply white out to her memory bank and didn't want Ginny knowing where he lived. He was hedging his bets about her when she didn't have the option to do the same.

"I'm sorry you don't agree with my methods, Ginny," he said in a low voice. "I only want to keep you safe."

Okay. She definitely wasn't cut out to administer the silent treatment. Words were leapfrogging over one another to exit her throat. "Why do you care what happens to me?"

The vein in his temple ticked. "There's a complicated answer to that question."

She took off the blindfold, ignoring his censorious look. "Try."

Jonas stared straight ahead into the metal doors of the elevator. When Ginny followed his gaze, the only face staring back in the reflective surface was her own. A tingle crawled up her spine. She glanced back to find Jonas studying her reaction closely. "If someone put a single scratch on your skin, I would go utterly mad, Ginny, and yet I burn to sink my teeth into your neck every second of the day. I don't know how to uncomplicate that for you." The elevator doors rolled open. "Welcome home."

Her exhale emerged as shaky as her legs. "What would happen if you did?" she managed. "Drink my blood, that is."

Green cinders whipped up in his eyes, his hand curling around the elevator's handrail. "I may have trouble stopping."

"You think you'll kill me, don't you? Break one rule, break them all." She stepped forward. "But I know you wouldn't."

"You're so sure, are you?" His attention strayed to her neck. "We're finished speaking of this," he bit off, reaching down and taking Ginny by the wrist, leading her out of the elevator, into a cement corridor with a single light bulb buzzing in front of yet another door. "I will keep you safe from me *and* whoever is trying to hurt you. That's a promise."

"Will your roommates…" She gestured to her neck. "Will they feel the way you do about the sinking of the teeth?"

He followed the action of her hand with rapt interest. "Me reacting this way to you is unusual enough. Two of us would be unheard of." Jonas took out a set of keys from inside his jacket pocket. "Still, I'm taking no chances with you, so I considered it. If Tucker felt this level of…" He blew out a breath. "…hunger, we'd already know it, since you rode in the same car. If Elias feels even a tenth of my thirst for you, I'll take you elsewhere. He's younger and doesn't have the same willpower to abstain," he said, cutting her a sideways glance. "If mine is testing its limits, someone without the same strength wouldn't be able to cope."

"Oh." She gulped. "Great."

"Ginny," he said, trailing his knuckles down her cheekbone. "You are safe. I would never have brought you here otherwise."

She nodded.

He unlocked the door and she followed him into…what was this place?

They walked into blue. It felt like the bottom of the ocean.

"Sorry about the darkness. We see as well in the pitch black as we do in the light." He walked to the closest sconce and twisted a knob, casting a faint glow. "I'll make sure we keep them on while you're here."

Ginny nodded. "Thanks."

The wide, low-ceilinged room was painted in an azure glow, courtesy of a backlit fish tank arranged against the far wall. To the right was a dining table surrounded by shelving and a counter that ran the length of the wall, to the left was a living space, complete with plush gray couches and a nine-thousand-inch television. A bachelor pad to the extreme, although it wasn't shaped like a typical apartment. Something about the layout and lack of warmth suggested it had been used commercially.

Textured black wallpaper decorated the walls, dotted with golden sconces and frosted glass. Vintage fixtures were everywhere, right down to the embellished grating on the heating vents and elaborate crown molding. Though they weren't turned on, there were lighting fixtures shaped like picture frames in spots—the kind that called to mind an old-fashioned dressing table. Big, bulbs surrounded where the mirrors used to be. Lauren Bacall would have sat in front of one in a silk dressing gown, reading the note on a dozen roses from Bogart.

"There aren't actually fish in that tank. We move around too much to have pets, but Tucker thinks it gives the place atmosphere," Jonas said dryly. "There's no kitchen," Jonas said at her side, gesturing to the left side of the room where a stainless steel appliance hummed. "We do have a refrigerator, so we'll be able to keep your food from spoiling."

"How will I cook the eggs?"

"Huh." He gave her a boyish half smile. "I didn't think of that. It's been a while since I had to worry about meal preparations."

"It's okay. I won't be here long, right?"

"Right." His smile faded. "As soon as I eliminate the danger you're in...I'll bring you home where you belong."

Ginny advanced into the room, worrying over the emptiness in her chest. If she was already sad about leaving, how would she feel when the time actually came? And far more importantly, Jonas had just admitted to thirsting for her blood every second of the day. Why wasn't she screaming for help?

Why did she want to lean against his solid chest and exist quietly inside the silent, unexplainable bond between them?

"Are you going to give me a tour?"

"Sort of." Jonas came up beside Ginny, taking her warm hand in his cool one, guiding her through the apartment and into a wide hallway. "I'm not sure you want to see more of what Tucker considers design choices. And Elias is extremely private. I'm going to give you my room while you're here, so I'll take you there."

"Where are you going to sleep—" Ginny caught herself. "I mean…how often *do* you sleep?"

"Every couple of weeks." His thumb traced the veins in the back of her hand. "I won't be sleeping until this situation is resolved and you're safe, so my bed is free."

"Is it always free?"

His eyebrow quirked. "What do you mean?"

"What?" She turned her head so Jonas wouldn't see her self-directed eye roll. *What is wrong with you?* "I'm not curious about your love life at all."

"Aren't you?" Jonas moved back into her line of sight. "I definitely wanted to know about yours."

"You don't want to know anymore?"

"You've never kissed…" His upper lip curled with distaste. "…*Gordon* and he's the only date you've been on. You're not the casual affair type. I think I've got it figured out."

He knows I'm a virgin. Great.

Amusement crept across his face, which was half illuminated in the blue glow of the fish tank. "You're speaking out loud again, Ginny."

"Oh." She shifted. "Well, do you *want* to tell me about your…"

"Love life." He tucked his tongue into his cheek. "I'd rather not."

"Why?"

He seemed to be thinking hard about his answer. "I felt something like love once, a long, long time ago. Probably before your parents were born. Between then and now..." He searched for words. "I definitely wouldn't use 'love' to describe any of it."

An unpleasant shock ran through her. "Oh my Lord. Are you a player, Jonas?"

"*What?* No." He shoved impatient fingers through his hair. "No, Ginny. I am not that. Not at all. I'm just finding it difficult to admit I've been with anyone at all. *Ever.* When you're near me, I just want like hell to undo everything."

The shock dulled to a slight pinch. *Honestly, Ginny.* Was she actually jealous? It would be ridiculous to expect a man who looked like Jonas to be celibate, especially considering he'd been alive almost ninety years. "They were...other vampires?"

Jonas's nod was almost non-existent as he crowded her against the hallway wall. "Even though I can't have you, God help me..." His palms molded to her hips. "If I'd known you were out there, I'd have easily abstained—"

A door slammed open just ahead in the hallway and Ginny was swept behind Jonas's back in the blink of an eye. "Do my senses deceive me?" rasped a voice. "Or is that the human?"

The human?

"Elias," Jonas said in a measured tone, as if gauging the other vampire's reaction to her. "This is Ginny. It sounds like you already knew Roksana and I have been protecting her."

"Roksana?" Slowly, footsteps creaked closer. "No, I've been smelling this one on you every time you walk in the door. Whatever and whoever you do in your spare time is none of my business, but I never imagined you'd bring her here." The footsteps stopped. "What the hell does Roksana have to do with her?"

Ginny tried to peek out from behind Jonas, but he sidestepped, thwarting her.

"She's facing a threat—and there's no doubt it's one of our kind. An Elder. I tasked Roksana with keeping her safe." Jonas's paused. "She was unsuccessful, so I brought Ginny here."

"Roksana was *unsuccessful?*" Elias's entire demeanor had been almost bored until now. His energy was instantly alert. "Where is she now?"

"Training apparently," Jonas said. "I don't know where."

Ginny was backed up against the wall as Elias thundered past, his booted feet *whapping* on the floor. She only managed to catch a flash of angry forehead above a flipped overcoat collar, before Elias threw open the front door of the apartment.

Tucker was standing on the threshold with brown

paper bags in his arms, the cigar trapped in the corner of his mouth. "Aw, honey." A puff of smoke went up. "You came to help me carry the groceries?"

"I can smell it rotting," Elias grumbled. "Is this going to be a regular thing?"

"It was kind of nice playing human," Tucker said, striding into the room and setting the bags down on the couch. "Where you headed, El?"

"Roksana," he growled.

The door slammed behind Elias a second later.

"He's even more chipper than usual," commented Tucker, shifting items around inside the bags with his hands. "Hey, prince. Look at this shit." He held up a circular baked good wrapped in plastic. "They make pie crusts out of Nilla Wafers now. Where was this kind of thing when we had a working digestive systems, right?"

Jonas slowly let her out from behind him, but kept her tucked to his side. "Did you get anything practical?"

"Peanut butter and Ritz crackers. That's all I remember eating when I was human." He took out a six pack of Miller Light. "And beer to wash it down."

Ginny perked up. "I've never had beer."

Tucker gyrated his hips, apparently dancing to music only he could hear. "Well hot damn. This calls for a party, sweetheart."

"I've never had a party, either!"

"Call her sweetheart again. I dare you." Jonas tossed

her face down over his shoulder and continued down the hallway. "No one enters my room under any circumstances while she's here."

"Party pooper," Tucker called, then to himself, "Nilla Wafer pie crust. The human race might make it after all."

A smile bloomed on Ginny's face—and only partway because she was eye level with Jonas's flexing backside. "I like Tucker."

He grunted.

Her world turned right side up again when he settled her feet flat on the floor. A light came on—the bedside lamp, she turned to find.

Jonas's room was nothing like she expected. His regal bearing had her picturing expensive bedding, thick oriental rugs and possibly a butler. What she saw instead was sparse, functional. Almost empty.

There was a small bed, devoid of anything but a fitted sheet. An antique dresser with glass knobs. The walls had been painted a melancholy silvery blue and she could almost picture him holding the paintbrush, stroking the wall in lonely silence. A chair sat in the corner by a closed closet door and there was a single shelf hanging in the center of the largest wall, small and out of place, like a single freckle in the center of a pale back.

On it sat a gold picture frame.

She was too far away to make out the photo, so she

ventured closer, feeling rather than seeing Jonas's tension mounting.

Ginny slowed her progress and sent Jonas a questioning look. "May I?"

"Yes, of course."

Inside the frame was a faded sepia photograph of two people who appeared to be in their fifties, sitting at a table with a half-eaten birthday cake in front of them. Jonas stood behind their chairs, smiling. "Is this your family?"

His nod was uneven. "By blood, yes."

"What do you mean, by blood?"

He sat down on the corner of the bed, his fingers loosely hooked together. "Those are my parents." His stare was far off. "Once I became…like this, I couldn't have any contact with them. After hurting them so badly, I'm not sure I deserve to call them my mother and father."

Ginny set down the picture from and sat down beside him on the bed, noting the way his nostrils flared at her closeness. The way his whole body seemed to constrict. "You don't seem the type to hurt them if you could help it."

"At the time, it seemed like it couldn't be helped. You know what they say about hindsight, though." He looked down at his loosely clasped hands. "Another lifetime ago, I was an entrepreneur looking for an investor in this invention of mine."

"What invention?"

His lips jumped. "Super glue."

She bashed him in the shoulder. "Get out of here. You invented super glue?"

Jonas nodded slowly.

"So obviously you found the investor."

"If only I'd known I was going to live forever." He winked. "I would have negotiated a royalty deal."

"This is bananas." She buried her face in her hands, dropping them away. "What does this have to do with you becoming a vampire?"

Based on his facial expression, she could see he was recalling memories and playing them back. "I wasn't getting anywhere. Steel was the big industry. Cars. Manufacturers didn't want to hear about a different version of something that already existed. The name alone sounded like a gimmick. I had to find a way to produce and market it myself. That took money I didn't have." He was quiet for a beat. "My father wasn't able to work after a factory accident. My mother was…entertaining men to make ends meet. I needed to help, Ginny. I thought I *was* helping. But I went looking for capital in the wrong places. One loan shark referred me to another and another until I was face to face with him."

"Him?"

"My sire, Clarence. The man who created what I am. I impressed him with my tenacity, I believe he called it. He…" His laughter lacked any humor. "He took a liking to me. Which is pretty damn ironic when you think about it. Liking someone so much that you barter money for their humanity."

Ginny swallowed the lump in her throat. "You did it for your family."

"Mostly. I also liked someone telling me I was good at something. I'd never…had that. By the time I realized I'd sold my soul to the devil, it was too late to get it back."

"No," she whispered, aching in the center of her belly for what he must have gone through. "You still have it."

His gaze shot to hers. "I've learned some hard lessons about being selfish, Ginny. I won't repeat them."

Even as he said the words she was positive were meant as a reminder to keep a heathy distance, Jonas's body gravitated toward her slightly, pushing a wave of cloves and mint in her direction and muddling her brain. Her lips parted in response, tiny explosions going off at every pulse point. Was he going to kiss her, despite his iron willpower and what he'd revealed about the past?

Lord, she wanted that so bad. When his face was right in front of hers, cloves and mint wafting around them like smoke, she could only think in terms of moments, not forevers or consequences or right and wrong. Only that her senses, and maybe even her soul, told her to move closer and hold on for dear life.

"Ginny?" he breathed.

She could practically hear the jazzy boudoir music simmering in the background, the way it would right before the two onscreen leads had their first dramatic kiss. "Yes, Jonas?" she all but whimpered.

His eyelids drooped and suddenly the bed behind them was a giant, magnetic place, despite it's lack of comforter or decorative throw pillows. What would it be like to have Jonas on top of her when the last of his self-control crumbled?

Divine.

Earth-moving.

Inevitable.

"Yes?" she prompted again, leaning closer.

A curse escaped him. "I'll get you some crackers and peanut butter."

He was off the bed and halfway to the door before she processed her first wave of swamping disappointment. She fell backward on the mattress and threw an elbow across her eyes. "Bring the pie crust, too, please."

Jonas was back within moments, with Ritz box in one hand, peanut butter in the other and pie crust tucked under one arm. He kicked the single chair from the corner of the room into a perfect position in front of the bed and took a seat.

Ginny sat up, ignoring Jonas's amusement when her stomach growled. "Is it against the rules to use your speed to your advantage?"

"It's implied, since it could lead to discovery."

"Has anyone ever gone blurry and gotten caught?"

"Gone blurry." Chuckling, he took a knife out of his pocket and set it on his thigh, going to work on opening the peanut butter. "You should always be suspicious when you hear about a string of nighttime bank robberies or a major natural disaster that only claims one life. Oftentimes, someone has broken the rules and...gone blurry." He spread peanut butter on a cracker and handed it to her, watching closely as she chewed. "The High Order treats the offense the same, whether it's used for good or bad."

"Even if lives were saved and no one saw?"

"We're not meant to be heroes, Ginny. Sometimes, we're the opposite."

Deep in thought, she ate her cracker. "You said you help new vampires—the Silenced. Do some of them turn out to be...the opposite of a hero?"

"Frequently." He paused in the act of making a sandwich out of two crackers with peanut butter layered in between. "That's where I plan to start asking questions about who's hunting you. Among the vampires I've helped. If there's a malignant being nearby, it would be hard for them to completely avoid detection. Someone has to know something."

Her dry mouth had nothing to do with the snack she was eating. "Will you be safe, Dreamboat?"

A crease formed between his brows. "Someone's put you in danger. They should be worried about being safe from me."

"You're the tiniest bit arrogant, aren't you?" She tried to hide her fangirl-esque reaction behind a smile. "That's why they call you the prince."

"That's one of the reasons," he muttered.

Ginny wanted to prod that statement, but he put a Ritz in her mouth and gave her a pointed look. In other words, *don't go there.* She wrinkled her nose at him while she chewed. "How often are people…Silenced? It must be a lot if you're continually having to train new vampires."

"It is. And that's my main objection with the High Order—they enjoy loopholes just as much as your human government." A beat passed. "You see, killing a human outright is not permitted. It's one of the rules. But Silencing them *is* allowed." Every line of his hard body vibrated with irritation. Yes, she'd definitely found a sore spot. "There is no guidance for the freshly Silenced. No resources or education. They're just thrown into the streets and expected to acclimate to an entirely new lifestyle on their own."

"Do you think vampires should be allowed to Silence humans?"

"Never." He held her gaze. "It's tantamount to murder."

Ginny said nothing.

Slowly, he went back to being relaxed. "You want any more?"

"Whatever keeps you sitting next to me." She covered her face with her hands, but not before she watched the emerald kindle in his eyes. "That was supposed to be inside my head."

His laugh made her heart boom so severely, she had to clutch her chest. And he obviously heard it, because he quieted, his expression at once sad and pleased.

"I'll leave everything here," Jonas said, standing and setting the food on the chair he'd vacated. "Sleep now, Ginny. You'll be safe here tonight."

"Okay." She nodded. "I know."

Jonas started to back toward the door, but detoured to his closet instead, taking out an armful of jackets. He returned to Ginny and set them on the mattress, scratching at his jaw with a frown. "Tucker forgot a blanket, a fact which surprises no one. Will you be warm beneath my clothes?"

She forced herself not to dive nose first into the pile. "I suppose."

Lips twitching, he leaned down and spoke beside her

head. "Remember, I can hear your pulse."

"Highly inconvenient."

"Not for me," he said, on his way out the door. "Good night, Ginny."

"Good night, Jonas."

Perhaps it was the utter feeling of safety. Or maybe it was the fact that she ate an entire pie crust without taking a breath. But Ginny dropped into sleep like a boulder into a river. She couldn't say for certain what woke her hours later on high alert. She also couldn't stop herself from getting up to investigate.

CHAPTER EIGHT

"OPEN THE DOOR." Still in shock to find herself locked into Jonas's bedroom, Ginny jiggled the door handle. "I have to use the restroom."

Tucker groaned. "Come on, Ginny. Jonas is going to be back in fifteen minutes. I was told I could only open this door in the event of an apocalypse. Can it wait?"

"I'm afraid not. Where did Jonas go?"

"To buy a hot plate, I think. To cook eggs on."

"I wish you hadn't told me that," Ginny grumbled, pushing the hair out of her eyes. "I'm trying to stay angry about being held prisoner. And suspicious, too. Why does this door lock from the outside?"

"Sorry, what was that?" Tucker made a crackling noise that was clearly just him making Donald Duck sounds into his cupped hands. "You're breaking up on me..."

"Oh, stop that. Open this door. Or aren't you offended that Jonas doesn't trust you to guard me while he's gone?"

"Very clever playing us against each other, sweetheart. I won't fall for it."

Ginny shifted on the balls of her feet. "I can't hold it anymore. *Please.*" There was a click and then the door opened, revealing Tucker with a cloud of smoke obscuring his face. Ginny ducked around him into the hallway. "You fell for that, though, didn't you?"

Tucker blinked. "You don't have to pee?"

She wrinkled her nose at him. "Sorry."

His laugh echoed off the hallway walls. "Women. Dead or alive, you're a tricky breed." He moved past her toward the front of the apartment. "Since I'm already courting the prince's wrath, you want that beer?"

"Yes, please," Ginny called after Tucker. Instead of following him, however, she turned and tiptoed down the dark hallway, stopping in front of the door across the hall from Jonas and opening it. Clearly this was Tucker's room. The pungent smell of cigar smoke hung in the air, dumbbells the size of Ginny were situated in the corner and rap album vinyls were stacked on top of a high-end stereo.

She closed the door quickly behind her and moved on.

The next door was locked. Elias's room, perhaps? He'd come from this general direction earlier, but she couldn't be sure from where.

The snick of a bottle cap being popped off almost made Ginny abandon her Scooby Doo-like investigation.

What was she even looking for? She wasn't totally sure. But there was a driving need to gather knowledge, to remember the tiniest details about her time with Jonas. If she gathered enough information without him knowing, the less likely he would be to make her forget every little thing, if he erased her memory.

She wanted to at least have the option of piecing these moments in time back together if she woke up one morning with gaping holes in her timeline.

There was one final door at the very end of the hallway and she power walked to it now, a shiver climbing her arm as soon as she curled a hand around the knob. A sense of foreboding made her hesitate, but she shooed it to the side and opened the door. She only caught a glimpse of metal shackles attached to a filthy brick wall before a hand shot out above her head, slamming the door closed.

Tucker sighed. "Jonas is never going to let me humansit again."

Ginny whirled on the stocky vampire with wide eyes. "Why are there shackles and chains in there?"

"Would you believe Elias is a kinky bastard?"

She blushed, unable to meet his gaze. "I-I…well, I…"

Tucker barked a laugh and fell silent. "So you're brave enough to go sleuthing through a vampire crash pad, but dirty jokes turn you bright red." He handed her a beer and gestured for her to precede him toward the living room. "It makes more and more sense why my roommate is out trying to find a hot plate at three in the goddamn morning."

Unclear of his meaning, Ginny frowned and took an absent sip of her beer—and promptly choked on the bitterness. "Maybe I'm a fruity drink person," she said, following Tucker into the living room. "This is terrible."

"If I'm remembering my debauched youth correctly, beer tastes better every time you take another sip. Best to keep going."

Ginny took another cautious pull. "Oh! You're right. Not so bad this time."

Tucker executed a bow.

"Now can you tell me about the shackles?"

"Not much for small talk, are you, sweetheart?" He leaned a beefy elbow on the mantle beneath the television. "I'm not sure what I should tell you."

She shrugged and took another long sip of beer. "I'm going to forget all of this, right?"

"Right," he drew out, sighing. "Every once in a while Jonas comes across a freshly Silenced and they require some…time to adjust. Where they can't harm any fragile humans, like yourself. Jonas keeps them put in silver chains. They're impossible for our kind to break free of." His smile reminded her of a jack-o'-lantern. "Having an angry, bloodthirsty rookie chained in silver down the hall makes for some interesting living conditions. You're a much better house guest."

"Thank you."

He plucked the cigar from the corner of his mouth, gesturing at her with it. "You finished your beer."

"I did?" Ginny covered her mouth to prevent a hiccup from escaping. "I did."

"Want another?"

She took stock of the light, fizzy sensation in her head and fingertips. "Yes, I think I do."

Laughing under his breath, Tucker crossed to the refrigerator and opened the door, glancing back over his shoulder at Ginny. Probably to gauge her reaction at the abundance of plastic pouches filled with blood. A finger of disbelief trailed up and down her back and all she could do was stare, trying to imagine Jonas drinking from a plastic pouch.

"Oh, he doesn't," Tucker said, straightening with her beer in his hand. "He pours it into a glass, like a fancy asshole."

"I didn't realize I was thinking out loud. I do that sometimes."

"I noticed. It's probably another reason you drive him crazy."

Ginny rubbed at the funny feeling in her chest and cut a look toward the door, willing Jonas to walk in. His presence was so dense in the apartment, like a heavy cloak wrapped around her, making the need to see him severe and inescapable. "Is he safe wherever he's gone?"

Tucker uncapped the bottle and paused. "Jonas? Hell yeah, he's safe. Dude might be a pretty boy, but he wrangles rookies on a weekly basis without batting an eyelash. Brings them to heel." He handed Ginny the beer. "You're in good hands. Jonas Cantrell is a bad motherfucker."

"Cantrell," she whispered, treasuring the knowledge of his last name.

The vampire did a double take, cursed. "I've got a big mouth."

"It's all going to get erased," she murmured, starting on her second drink.

"Uh-huh." Tucker retreated to the mantle in a blur. "So what do you do for fun, Ginny?" His smile was full of mischief. "Besides tempt the prince to break the rules, that is?"

Her breath stuttered in her lungs at the reality that she could be bad for Jonas. Really bad. She'd been so swept up in the realization that vampires existed and one was possibly trying to kill her for an unknown reason that she hadn't taken the time to think about the implications for Jonas. By protecting her, he was putting himself in jeopardy. "Um," she managed. "I'm in a dress making club. Embrace the Lace Dressmaking Endeavors. We have an expo coming up, actually. With a silent auction and everyth—"

The front door opened and Elias whooshed into the apartment, overcoat spinning around his knees, the collar still guarding his face from view, like earlier.

"Hey, buddy," Tucker called, good-naturedly. "We were just talking about what a kinky bastard you are."

No response, just a tensing of his shoulders.

"We weren't really," Ginny stuck in quickly, shooting Tucker a stern look. "Did you find Roksana?"

"No, I did not," he rasped from behind his collar. "The reckless brat."

Ginny's spine snapped straight at the unfounded name calling of her friend. Her *only* friend, to be accurate. "How do you know she's being reckless?"

Elias turned slightly, without revealing his face. "Have you met her?"

The menace in Elias's voice temporarily muddled her thoughts—along with the beer—and she found herself saying, rather stupidly, "She mentioned you to me."

A very subtle ripple went through him. "Did she."

Ginny nodded, even though he wasn't looking at her. "In a fond way."

Elias went back out the front door with a curse.

Jonas caught the door before it could close, his eyes snapping with green and spearing right into her.

The lights flickered in the apartment, turning the beer in Ginny's stomach to sour sludge. Was he manipulating the electricity? Or was that just a coincidence?

"Honey, it's not what it looks like," Tucker cried. "We thought about you the entire time."

Jonas set down the shopping bag in his hand and flexed his fingers. "You couldn't follow instructions for fifteen minutes?"

"She tricked me."

"It hardly took an effort." She looked down at the bottle, surprised to find it was empty—and why was she holding two of them? Wait, no. One. No...two. "I do have to use the restroom now."

Tucker laughed. "Beer'll do that to you."

"This is very cozy," Jonas drawled, though his expression was tight and intent on Ginny. "Back to my room, please."

She set down her empty beer bottle on the coffee table. "If I'm going to stay here for any length of time, I have to be allowed to roam freely."

"She wants to be a free-range human, prince," Tucker translated.

Jonas's jaw popped. "We'll talk about this when we're alone."

A ding went off somewhere in the apartment. Ginny turned in a circle, searching for the source of the familiar sound. It took her a good fifteen seconds to realize it was coming from the cell phone still stowed in her dress pocket. She used it so rarely, she'd forgotten it was there, but she took it out now and tapped the button to bring up her email. "Oh!" Hot moisture pooled in her eyes. "Great news! We have a body being brought into the morgue tomorrow."

"She's a keeper," Tucker said without missing a beat.

Before Ginny could respond, she found herself being carried down the hallway cradled against Jonas's chest, moving somewhere between a sedate walk and warp speed. "I guess I should thank you for not putting me in shackles."

He slowed outside of a door, measuring her with a look. "Did some exploring, did you?"

"More like memory gathering. You won't get them all. It'll be like playing a whack-a-mole."

With a troubled brow, he shouldered open a door and turned on the light to reveal a small, clean, white-tiled bathroom. With no mirrors, of course. He set her down in the center of the floor, but kept her close. "I didn't mean to make you feel like a prisoner." His one-eyed, sheepish squint made him so handsome she swayed closer out of sheer necessity. "Technically, you weren't supposed to know you'd been locked in. You were supposed to be sleeping."

"I'm sorry I couldn't cooperate."

"No, you went and had a little party, didn't you?" He traced her hairline with his thumb. "I'm being irrational, aren't I? That's the opposite of me. I never have a hard time keeping a lid on my impulses."

"What impulses are you having?"

"Wanting to blind anyone who looks at you," Jonas murmured, his thumb traveling in circles in the hollow of her throat now. "Wanting to deafen anyone who hears you speak, so I'll be the only one who gets to experience the music of your voice. You know, normal, well-adjusted impulses."

Ginny couldn't catch her breath enough to laugh. "I thought we couldn't be together."

Jonas's expression blazed with regret, but it was no less possessive. "I'm going to guard you while you sleep and make you eggs in the morning. That's what I know." His lips brushed her forehead. "When I think too far into the future, I can't focus on your safety. Here and now only."

"Here and now only," she repeated. "I guess that's our only choice." Jonas's body vibrated against hers, those bright green eyes catching on her features, his fingertips moving in her face, neck, chin. Even while held in his thrall, though, something occurred to her. "If you can hear my heartbeat, you can probably hear me…using the ladies room for its intended func-tion…anywhere in this apartment."

Jonas's brow quirked. "That bothers you?"

"I think so, yes."

His laughter was warm as he pushed her gently toward the toilet. "I've got you covered."

As soon as the bathroom door closed behind Jonas, she gathered her skirt in her hands and sat down on the toilet. Seconds later, heavy metal blared from the living room and she laughed into her cupped hands, finally relieving her full bladder.

He was waiting in the hallway when she emerged, looking sinfully attractive with his head tipped slightly forward, pieces of midnight hair brushing his brow, tongue tucked into his cheek. He signaled down the hallway to Tucker and the music cut out, then he tipped his head in the direction of his bedroom. "Ready?"

It might have been the beer, the odd situation—she was living among vampires?—or just The Jonas Effect, but she swore they glided into his bedroom, the way silk might move in water. Effortlessly and sensually, their fingers brushing, every look passed between them heightening a sense attachment, hunger, anticipation of the unknown, even though it might never come to pass.

Jonas's hand slid on to her shoulder, guiding her to the edge of the bed and she went, enjoying the way he watched her nestling into his pile of sweaters and jackets, his clenched jaw making it clear he wanted to join her, yet refraining.

"Sleep as much as you can, Ginny," he rasped. "We have a long night tomorrow."

"Good night." She yawned and watched his eyes soften. "I mean…day. Good day."

The last thing she remembered before falling into a deep sleep was Jonas dragging the room's single chair out into the hallway and taking up his post.

Then he shut the door without touching it at all.

CHAPTER NINE

U PON ARRIVING AT P. Lynn the following night, Ginny opened her digital calendar and her mouth dropped open when a reminder popped up.

Ginny's birthday!

Tomorrow?

Apparently the looming date had been forgotten amongst the dramatic events of the last couple days, but tomorrow she would be twenty-five.

Jonas's age, though, technically he was a great deal older.

Old enough to be her grandfather, really.

Best not to dwell on it too long.

After all, she had work to do. Their guest had arrived during the day and thankfully, Larissa had performed the intake paperwork and consulted with the family about their wishes. Now, while Ginny performed the chemical wash on Kristof, a hardware store owner with a mermaid tattoo in the center of his chest, Jonas sat nearby in the morgue reading a tattered copy of *The Count of Monte Cristo*.

Was he reading, though?

Every time she looked over, he seemed to be watching her above the black and beige book jacket. There hadn't been many page-turning sounds, either. Her cheeks warmed when she caught him again, before his eyes zipped back to the text. The entire back half of her body was alive right now, tingling and sparking under his regard. Her focus was in ninety places at once, when it needed to be on Kristof.

Focus.

Morticians were often viewed as cold, clinical. Creepy. But there was an artfulness to the practice most people didn't know about. Or didn't *want* to know about, rather. She'd been taught by her father to make friends with the deceased. To try and understand who they'd been and where they'd come from. Now that she'd performed the chemical rinse and broken the rigor mortis through a careful massaging of the body, it was time to set her guest's features, since the casket would be open at his wake.

Humming to herself, Ginny leaned over and consulted the family-provided picture sitting on her instrument table. In it, Kristof had one arm propped on the bow of a boat, his other hand stuffed into a rain slicker. A deluge fell around him unacknowledged. Kristof had been a stoic man, it seemed. There weren't many smile or laugh lines around his face and eyes, so it wouldn't do to form his lips into a subtle yet peaceful smile, as she often did. No, they would be sending off a hard-nosed fisherman and furthermore, that would be what Kristof would want those left behind to see. The real him.

Ginny was only beginning to lose herself in the setting of his features when Larissa appeared in the doorway of the morgue, holding a martini glass. "Oh, you're here. Good. I wasn't sure if I'd be running this place alone now."

As inconspicuously as possible, Ginny glanced over her shoulder to see Jonas was nowhere in sight. She hadn't even heard him move. Turning back to Larissa with genuine contriteness, Ginny stripped off her gloves and laid them down beside Kristof's head. "I'm sorry about last night. I hope there wasn't much extra work."

"No. No, I left it all for you." She pressed a thumb to the center of her forehead. "I can just about manage my own shifts without taking on yours, too. Who is this *friend* you were with since last night?"

"Someone from my dress making club," Ginny said, too quickly and too unconvincingly. *Just don't add any unnecessary information. It's a classic tell when someone is lying.* "She's a brunette. Bangs. She has bangs…and she loves an A-line."

Larissa sipped her martini. "Hmm."

Ginny traced a circle on the metal table with her finger. "The thing is, I might be spending more time with her. We're working on a project together...for the silent dress auction that's coming up. Just in case you're wondering where I am."

Her stepmother gestured to Kristof with her martini glass. "I suppose I'm going to handle hosting duties for the wake?"

"Yes. If you could just this once. I'll call the church and book the driver. As soon as I'm finished here, I'm going to send the prayer cards to the printers."

"Flowers?"

"Arriving tomorrow morning, first thing."

"Hmm." She drained her glass. "Then I best get off to bed. I've got another depressing day ahead, don't I?"

"I don't know," Ginny murmured. "There's some happiness to be found in everyone coming together and sharing memories, too, isn't there? Ensuring those moments don't die with their loved ones. Reliving times out loud doesn't have to be encouraged, it's just a human reaction. It's beautiful in a way."

Not a single family member remained on her father's side. Without her mother's side to bolster his funeral guest list, there's been a very sparse turnout. Larissa had family in Florida, but she'd never brought them for a visit, rarely spoke of them and they weren't in attendance.

Oddly enough, it had turned out to be her father's barber who saved the day. Sitting to Ginny's left in the front row, he'd listened to her recount memories of her father, even adding some of his own. Until the day of his funeral, Ginny didn't know her father used to read celebrity epitaphs aloud in the barber shop and buy coffee for whoever guessed their identities correctly.

It was entirely morbid, exactly like him and the story made her feel peaceful when she didn't think anything could.

Ginny realized with a jolt that, while she'd been deep in thought, Larissa had paused at the door. "Did you say something?"

She shook her head. "It was nothing. Sleep well."

"Oh!" Her stepmother jerked her chin toward the lobby. "I forgot to mention that Gordon is here to see you."

The overhead lights flickered.

She swallowed. "Oh. Could you let him know I'll be right out?"

Larissa rolled her eyes and vanished from view, leaving the smell of Dior perfume in her wake. Ginny turned and looked for Jonas, expecting him to return now that Larissa was gone, but his chair remained empty.

After lifting the rubber apron over her head, Ginny washed her hands and meandered out to the lobby, which was empty except for a pacing Gordon.

"Hi, Gordon." Ginny stopped about ten feet away, lacing her fingers together at her lap. "Larissa said you wanted to see me?"

He scratched behind his ear. "Yes, but could we work up to the reason?"

"Sure." She breathed a laugh. "Lovely fall weather we're having, isn't it?"

"It is. I finally broke out the winter sweaters." He gestured to the ribbed, woolen top he wore. "Might have been a mistake, because I'm definitely sweating and perspiration definitely doesn't mix well with wool...odor wise." Finally, he ceased his pacing. "Why am I telling you this?"

"No judgments here. I smell a little like embalming fluid."

A dreamy smile broke across Gordon's face. "You're so kind. Hardly anyone is kind anymore." He tugged on the neck of his sweater. "And I think you smell amazing."

Once again, the lights flickered, dimming the room, before brightening it to the extreme and leaving it like a giant, glowing x-ray machine.

Ginny laughed nervously.

"Is there something wrong with the wiring?" Gordon turned in an observant circle. "I have an uncle that could take a look."

"That won't be necessary, but thank you."

As a matter of fact, she was getting semi-annoyed at the gall it took on Jonas's part to tamper with her electricity in what she was fast beginning to suspect translated to a fit of jealousy.

If he wanted Ginny so badly, he had a funny way of showing it, considering he planned on absconding with her memories of him and moving on, as soon as she was free of danger. Once she no longer knew Jonas, she might choose to date and there was nothing he could do about it. Nothing he *would* do about it. Were these light flickering antics a classic example of not wanting someone, but not wanting *anyone else* to have them, either?

Maybe men were the same, human or vampire.

Ginny crossed her arms and glared at a trembling sconce.

Annoyed or not, maybe it was best to get Gordon out of harm's way.

"Gordon, I'm so glad you stopped by, but I'm in the middle of an embalmment—"

"Your birthday is tomorrow," he blurted, drawing her up short. "I…this is so embarrassing, but you have a Facebook profile and you never post there. Or anything." He let out a rush of breath. "But it does have a blurry picture of you and your date of birth, so that's how I knew. I didn't hire an investigator or…anything like that."

"Of course not."

"I'm just explaining how I knew." He muttered for a

moment under his breath about sounding like a psychopath. "Long story short. I came to see if, um…do you have plans for your birthday?"

The front door of P. Lynn flew open, allowing in a mighty gust of wind carrying leaves, abandoned Metrocards and moisture from God knew where. Ginny lunged out of the line of fire, taking Gordon with her. "*Wow*," she called over the noise. "The weather really took a turn. You should get home before it gets worse."

"Yeah," Gordon hedged. "About your birthday—"

The door slammed hard and one by one, the light sockets started to explode in the lobby, *pop pop pop*.

"Gordon, you need to go," she urged, hustling him toward the door.

"No way, Ginny," he sputtered. "I-I can't leave you here. It's unsafe."

P. Lynn's front door opened a final time and Gordon's body moved backward, seemingly on its own—though, Ginny knew different—and in seconds, he was on the stoop of the funeral home, the door cracking shut on his stunned expression.

"*Jonas Cantrell*," she gasped, searching the dark lobby for his figure and finding nothing in the pitch blackness. "I hope you plan on cleaning up this mess and replacing these lights. Kristof's wake is in the morn—"

Ginny's feet were swept out from beneath her and then she was face down, thrown over Jonas's now-familiar shoulder. "She talks to me of *lights*," he growled.

Uncoordinated as her movements might have been, she tried to wrestle her way off his shoulder and perhaps for the first time, she realized how truly, inhumanly strong Jonas was. Exerting the effort to break his hold winded her in seconds. "Where are you taking me?" she asked, listening carefully to his crisp footsteps to determine if they were on hardwood or carpet. "You might have mentioned up front that you can move objects and explode things."

No answer.

A door closed—forcefully.

Ginny's world turned right side up again, her bottom landing on something hard and she blinked into the darkness. She felt the wood beneath her fingertips and would have recognized the office desk even if lamp light didn't burst into a glow to her left. Jonas stood in front of her with a cool and unreadable countenance, obviously having turned on the light without the use of his hands.

And she wanted answers.

"You just...*did* all of that," was all she could come up with.

Admirable effort, Ginny.

Jonas gripped the edge of the desk, his hands on either side of her thighs. "Are you interested in that child?"

"Oh, I'm not answering that."

"Why not?"

"Several reasons, the first of which is how you phrased it. Gordon is the same age as me, but that's beside the point. You meant it to be condescending." She leaned in close enough to count the individual green sparks in his eyes. Fourteen. "At least he didn't wreak havoc on my lobby."

"It was involuntary," he said through his teeth. "These abilities are usually triggered in a vampire when he or she undergoes something harrowing. More and more every time. And you, love, most definitely fit that description."

"I'm *harrowing*?"

"Your safety being compromised is harrowing. As is another man wanting to take you on a birthday date. Or listening to him compliment your scent. *Harrowing*."

Ginny lifted her chin. "He was only being nice."

"Yes, men typically search for women on Facebook and such because they're planning on being *nice*. I could hear his pulse, remember."

Which reminded Ginny, Jonas could hear hers now, too. Could hear it racing like she'd sprinted home again from the Belt Parkway. Too bad there little she could do about it. "Maybe he does like me. That's a good thing, isn't it? I'll have another fifty to seventy years left on this earth once you wash your hands of me." She ignored his warning look. "Who knows? I might even date once or twice."

A slicing sound rent the air.

Jonas's fangs were out.

Ginny's ears started to ring and she was frozen to the spot, unable to move. She was almost hypnotized by the sight of them. The sharpness, the way the lamplight lent them an almost beautiful glint. Wood creaked beneath her, a telltale sign that Jonas's grip was tight to the point of almost snapping the desk. Her fight or flight instinct revved like an engine, but her common sense told her it would be pointless to run when Jonas could break the sound barrier.

And perhaps stupidly, she still firmly believed he would put a stake through his own heart before harming her.

How could she believe that so insistently?

"I'm sorry," he said hoarsely, self-disgust rolling over his features. "I thought this animal part of me was long dead, but it's not, Ginny. Every time I think I'm getting a handle on my need to…"

"To what?"

"*Possess you*," he growled, dropping his open mouth to her neck, his hands sliding beneath her knees and tugging her closer. "Every time I have it handled, I'm proven painfully wrong. I'd almost fooled myself into believing I was nearly human. Then I meet you, I *smell* you, and I'm reminded I'm a beast. The man knows he can't and shouldn't have you, but the animal refuses to share."

Oh wow. "It's not sharing if you haven't...partaken yet," she whispered, barely able to keep her neck from losing power in the presence of such honest sensuality. *Bite me*, she wanted to say. How bad could it be if it would bring him such pleasure?

Without warning, Jonas yanked her to the barest edge of the desk, settling her inner thighs on his hips. "Partaken," he repeated, inhaling against her neck. "Do you have any idea what that means?"

The thick ridge pressing between her legs gave her some idea. But that's all it was. An idea. She'd never been with a man and knew only the mechanics of what happened in bed. Being with a vampire? She knew *nothing* of that.

Was it even physically safe, considering he was so much stronger?

How much would *drinking* factor in?

Why did she get an almost giddy feeling when she thought of him using his fangs on her? Sustaining himself with the lifeblood than ran in her veins?

"Your excitement is making it very hard to get control of myself."

"Uhm, yes," she breathed. "I'm actually a little worried that what everyone believes about me is true."

Jonas lifted his head and pinned her with concern. "And what does everyone believe about you?"

"That I'm too comfortable with death and blood and ooky things."

He made an amused sound. "Am I an ooky thing?"

"No," she murmured, unable to lie while looking into his eyes. "You're a beautiful thing. When you're not damaging my property."

His fangs sliced back in, followed by a rueful pause. "How can I want to devour you one moment and rock you in my arms the next?" Briefly, he looked down. "I shouldn't ask you this, but I'm starting to sense I'm already up shit's creek without a paddle." A beat passed. "You're worried because the idea of me having you—all of you—body and blood…it excites you?"

"Yes."

Jonas's nostrils flared and it took him long moments to speak again. "Every single thing about you is perfect and natural and right. Don't ever question that."

"You're a flatterer, in addition to being a property destroyer."

Jonas pinched a lock of her hair between his fingers and studied it. "Finish with Kristof while I repair the damage." Unease seemed to settle over him. "We have another stop before the sun comes up."

CHAPTER TEN

TUCKER PICKED THEM up outside the back entrance of P. Lynn, both vampires flanking her and scanning the moonlit rooftops as they hustled her into the back seat. She was already nervous just knowing some otherworldly being wanted her dead, but Tucker and Jonas's overprotective nature really brought it home.

Someone wants me dead.

They could accomplish it and she might never know the reason.

Sure, they couldn't kill her *outright*, but the best case scenario was being dropped into a perilous location and being required to use her wits to survive—and that wasn't a best case anything. It was terrifying.

Jonas must have sensed she'd been spooked, because he pulled her into his side and rocked her gently, his mouth ghosting over her hair. They rode in silence for a moment, before Jonas sighed and took the blindfold out of his pocket, tying it across her eyes.

"For your protection," he murmured near her ear.

Ginny didn't answer.

To be honest, she believed him this time. There was an unusual tension in among Jonas and Tucker, an almost predatory stillness, as if they were preparing for an upcoming battle. A battle on her behalf.

What if something happened to them while protecting her?

The car stopped, interrupting her worry and tensing her muscles. The front passenger side door opened, the vehicle sagging under the weight of a fourth occupant.

"Elias," Jonas greeted the newcomer, before lowering his voice to address her. "I have no choice but to bring you with me tonight, but you'll be protected. You know that, right? There's nothing to fear."

Ginny's pulse sprinted. "Where are we going?"

"I have a meeting with a freshly Silenced."

"Oh." She shifted in her seat. "Sure."

"You'll be alright, Ginny," Tucker called from the front seat. "You've got three bad motherfuckers as bodyguards."

"Could have been four bodyguards if Jonas hadn't run off the slayer."

"Her charge was dropped into the middle of a busy highway," Jonas returned tersely. "I spoke only the truth."

Elias didn't respond for a beat. "If she's gone off half-cocked to get revenge on whoever did it, I'm going to put her over my knee."

"What did I tell you?" Tucker drawled. "Kinky as they come."

"She'll be back," Jonas sighed. "She never stays away long."

Ginny had the distinct feeling that Roksana would return thanks to the obvious connection between her and Elias, but now didn't seem like the time to mention it. There might never be a good time, really, since she found Elias extremely intimidating and she'd never even seen his face. "How do the Freshly Silenced know to come to you, Jonas?"

"He comes highly recommended on vampire Yelp." Tucker said.

"*Really?*" Ginny gasped. "Is that on the dark web or something?"

"He's kidding," Jonas said—and she sensed him smacking the back of Tucker's headrest. "Newbies are easy to spot. Oftentimes one of our acquaintances puts us in contact. This time, Elias happened to…stumble across him while he was looking for Roksana."

"He was feasting on a pigeon under the boardwalk," Elias said. "Noisily."

Ginny's mouth fell open. "Poor little pigeon." She turned in Jonas's protective hold. "You said acquaintances sometimes put you in contact. Exactly how many vampires are there in the area?"

None of them answered.

"Wow. That many, huh?"

Jonas swiped a thumb over the back of her hand. "They can be somewhat...rowdy, so I'll have you stay in the car. It's somewhat confusing for them in the beginning."

"Yeah," Tucker agree. "Suddenly you're catching on fire on your way to get the newspaper and your morning beer tastes like piss."

"Yes, the quintessential experience," Elias said dryly. "I assume we're waiting in the car with the human? After all, it wouldn't be wise for a vampire outside of our immediate circle to know we're fraternizing with her. That information could be used against us with the High Order."

Seconds ticked past. "I'm finding it difficult to have her out of my sight," Jonas said unevenly.

Tucker whistled through his teeth.

Elias said nothing, but Ginny could sense his...dread, perhaps?

She couldn't relate. Maybe she should be experiencing dread, but Jonas's admission only made her feel as light and fluttery as a hummingbird. "I don't like having you out of my sight, either," she whispered.

"Well it's a damn good thing she'll be forgetting you shortly." The front passenger seat creaked. "*Isn't it*, Jonas?"

"We're here," Jonas said abruptly. "If any harm

155

comes to her…"

"On my word, she'll still be as cute as a button when you return," Tucker called over his shoulder.

"It's beyond me why you continue to take these clandestine meetings," Elias groused. "The Freshly Silenced are not your responsibility."

"Someone has to take responsibility for them," Jonas said calmly. "Otherwise the cycle continues. Innocent people are turned. Without any official guidance or somewhere to turn, they kill a human in a blind bloodlust and they're put to death by the High Order."

"Like we've been telling you for years," Tucker started, sounding serious for once. "You're the only one in a position to challenge the King—"

"Enough."

Silence fell like a curtain in the car. After a moment, she felt Jonas's palm slide over her cheek and leaned into it greedily. "I'll be very upset if something happens to you this close to my birthday," she said.

"My only worry is for you, love," he muttered, his lips grazing her mouth. "Leave the blindfold on and stay put, no matter what you hear."

Ginny didn't agree out loud because she didn't want to get caught lying, thanks to a wonky pulse. So she crossed her fingers in the folds of her skirt, instead.

Jonas

WITHOUT THE SOUND of her breath, Jonas was instantly hollow.

The fibers left functioning in his arms and neck twisted like twine around a baseball bat the farther he walked from the Impala holding Ginny. He only made it two steps before turning back around to remind himself she was safe and whole. Although, Christ, look at her through the back window. In her blindfold, she looked like a kidnapping victim.

The side of his mouth tugged. There was no way in hell she'd keep that blindfold on much longer. That reminder of her spirit gave him peace and ravaged it at the same time. He couldn't stop himself from memorizing every facet of her personality, even though they would undoubtedly haunt him forever.

Make her safe before you become a plague on her life.

He would.

That was his mission and he needed to get his mind back on it immediately. Needed to stop pining for something he couldn't have, like some sort of wet behind the ears human. A relationship between them could not be.

It *could not* be.

Of course, that reminder didn't keep him from turning to check on her another three times before reaching the back door of the establishment. She was already growing impatient. Without seeing her hands, he knew her fingers played with the hem of her dress, picking a section of material to rub on her knee. Jonas knew because every time she performed the adorable habit, it drove him wild with the need to push aside the material and kiss the chafed skin.

Or possibly arrange her knees so they were hugging his waist and therefore she wouldn't be able to reach them.

He was staring back at the car again. At her parted lips and windblown auburn hair, the gentle rise and fall of her breasts. It was a crime to cover those guileless hazel eyes for even a second. They were the epicenter of life and spirit and hope.

Beautiful, beautiful girl.

Even from this distance, the scent of her blood loitered in the back of his throat. A thirst like any other that had planted roots so deep, they would remain long after he did what needed to be done—leave her the hell alone.

How will I ever do it?

He could barely make it across the alley to the door, let alone move to a new place where she would be out of his reach. Free to date, free to marry—

Jonas nearly ripped the door off the entrance to Haven. Since meeting Ginny, he'd wondered early and often if a certain amount of blood still ran in his veins, because the narrow passageways crisscrossing through his body had the ability to turn molten, like he'd swallowed liquefied silver. The image of a hand upon her skin that wasn't his own unleashed a swarm of locusts in his ears, chest, stomach, the urge to kill putting the taste of rot in his mouth.

He'd worked so hard to rid himself of the violence inherent in vampires. But it seemed to come part and parcel with the rampant joy Ginny made him feel. He could vacillate between the two in the snap of a finger. Feeling so much, so hugely, was addictive. *She* was addictive.

And endearingly kind. Funny. Gorgeous. Dreamy. Brave, if a little sad.

Smooth. The skin of her neck was so *smooth* and *warm*.

It fluttered with a touch more insistence when she said his name.

Jonas stopped just inside the entrance of Haven and grasped at his throat, ordering his thirst for Ginny back under control.

Who was he kidding? It would never be under control. It stole through him now like a jaguar with a deer in its sights, baring down on Jonas and throttling his throat, burning his eyes and making his hands tremble.

Focus. You need to focus.

Jonas called on his determination, rolling a shoulder

back and striding farther into Haven. The small tavern had been so named by Jonas because that was what this place represented. A place to convene without judgment or fear. A place to discuss resources for their kind and create support systems. The mission Jonas had designated for himself should have been the responsibility of the High Order, but they chose instead to let their population manage alone—until it came time to mete out punishment. They certainly loved that aspect of being in power, but refused to do any of the hard work it would take to avoid executing their own or even helping the Silenced find some semblance of peace.

Jonas hadn't returned to Haven since opening it a decade earlier, as he'd been traveling, finding and helping as many of the Freshly Silenced as he could, but since returning to Coney Island, he'd made many stops there.

Too many.

He stopped inside the small, low-lit dining room and nodded at the manager, who immediately went behind the bar to retrieve blood for Jonas. As if he would be able to enjoy it. Everything tasted like refuse now.

Jonas took a seat along the wall and quelled the urge to return to the alley, have one last look at Ginny. Remind Tucker and Elias that he'd burn them alive if a hair on her head was out of place when he returned.

His hand flexed on the table, craving the silkiness of her skin.

Stay where you are.

Jonas reached deep and centered himself, surveying the bar. Haven consisted of eight tables and they were all full now. Silence had descended like cloth as soon as he walked inside and now, one by one, the vampires in attendance placed hands over their dead hearts. Pledging fealty to Jonas that he didn't ask for, nor did he expect. He was only glad they knew he was there to help, not intimidate or make this life even harder.

The High Order did more than enough of that for everyone.

A chair scraped back and a young man stood, twisting a ball cap in his hands. Several of the vampires patted him on the back as he crossed the tavern toward Jonas. Just before he took a seat on the opposite side of the table, Jonas noticed one of his legs was a prosthesis, though his limp was minimal.

"Hello." He nodded. "I'm Jonas."

"Dobby," said the vampire, hanging his hat on the back of the chair. "They said you could help, but I have to be honest, man, ain't sure nothing is going to help. I've passed this place my whole life and it's always looked like it's under construction. Now I'm in here drinking blood." He choked on a breath. "I guess it beats pigeons."

"I'm sorry this happened to you," Jonas said, briskly. "I'll suggest some next steps and then I'll answer any questions you might have."

There was always the urge to commiserate with the freshly Silenced, to share his own confusing experience, but Jonas never allowed himself to do it. They were in a darker, harsher world now and giving them a shoulder to cry on only gave them false expectations of the life. It was hard, lonely and eternal.

His mind drifted back to Ginny in the car and he could feel the imprint of her body pressed to his side, so trusting. God but she made life far less lonely.

Can't have her.

Jonas shoved an unsteady hand into his coat and took out a leather pouch, placing it on the table and sliding it toward Dobby.

"There are three rules you must obey, if you want to go on living."

Dobby looked down at his dead chest. "This is living?"

The manager set a rocks glass of blood in front of Jonas and while he thanked the vampire, he made no move to pick it up, even though a sip might have helped him swallow the urge to apologize to Dobby for what he was going through. To tell him while it didn't get easier, it could become purposeful.

"Rule one: No relationships with humans. Two: No drinking from humans. Three: No killing humans. Break one of them, you risk breaking all three. Break them and the High Order will be alerted to come dole out your punishment."

Dobby buried his head in his hands.

Jonas closed his eyes briefly, brutally aware of his own hypocrisy, seeing as he had a human waiting for him in the alleyway, not a hundred yards from where he sat. All the more reason to see her safe and remove himself from her perfect orbit. "You need to leave town as soon as possible, I'm afraid. At first, being around your loved ones might seem manageable, but you'll either grow tired of only having your thirst half-quenched and drink from them. Or you'll convince yourself you're doing them a favor by Silencing them, too, the way someone did to you. It's not a favor. Eternal life might sound appealing, but it's—"

"Daunting."

"That's putting it mildly." Especially when he couldn't be with the one he needed beyond measure. "There is a constant sense of backpedaling when you wake up, over and over again, but never age. Never hit milestones or…" Realizing he'd gone off track, Jonas reached across the table and tapped the leather pouch. "There is enough cash here to get you started. I've included contact information for several cities in the US and Mexico."

"Does it have to be a city?" Dobby asked woodenly.

"It's easier to blend in." Jonas gestured to the interior

of Haven. "In each of those cities, I've established a place just like this. You can consult the managers in regards to the local blood sources and ask about job openings. Do *not* take chances with the sun and do *not* accelerate if there's a chance you'll be seen. And we're seen everywhere now at all times, so again, don't take risks."

Dobby stared hard at the table. "Why not just break the rules and let the High Order end it? Why live in this miserable, endless cycle?"

"I don't have an answer for that. Certainly many have gone that route."

He'd considered it himself many times, after the disappearance of his mate, the death of his parents. The only thing that stopped him was the knowledge that no one would remain behind to help the Dobbys of the world. And now? Now Jonas wasn't sure he could court death knowing Ginny was alive and breathing somewhere. Living in a world where she existed made the darkness bearable and unbearable at the same time.

"How can this be allowed?" Dobby croaked, taking Jonas's glass of blood and draining it, surprising a low chuckle out of Jonas. "How can the High Order punish us for drinking from humans, unless we Silence them, too?"

A familiar anger made Jonas's jaw tighten. "To guarantee our continued existence," he growled. "Silencing a human doesn't always work, but the urge...it's always there inside us. Often, a new vampire can't help themselves and they go about Silencing in a reckless way, leading to dead humans and vampires left to face the punishment. Far more humans are Silenced, however, than vampires extinguished, leading to higher numbers of our kind. Numbers that learn through example to fear the High Order. Their contradictory rules have led to nothing but a fucked up cycle—and I'm sorry..." Jonas pushed back from the table, annoyed at himself for going off book. "I'm sorry this happened to you."

"Thank you," Dobby said, laying a hand on the pouch, visibly uncomfortable showing gratitude. "I'm not sure...what I would have done without you."

Jonas nodded. "It's nothing." He hesitated before standing. "Who was it that Silenced you?"

"I don't know," Dobby whispered. "I don't remember anything after walking home from my shift at the diner."

In other words, his memories had been wiped.

Tamping down on a second apology—apparently Ginny's sweet, earnest nature was rubbing off on him—Jonas stood and faced the tavern, waiting for everyone to give him their attention. Most of the faces he recognized, if not from recently, then from the last time he'd been in New York. Some of them seemed to have fared well, others were sullen, their stares empty and trained on nothing. With a heavy gut, he wondered how many locals had been extinguished by the High Order for breaking the rules, their seats now sitting vacant.

"I need to know if anyone has come into contact with someone new in town," he said, in a clear voice, watching for reactions. "An Elder."

Murmurings commenced, along with some nervous shifting.

After all, there was no rule against killing *each other* and no one in Haven was a match for a vampire with the abilities an Elder possessed. Abilities that were earned by living through high stress situations, again and again, year after year. Wars, street battles, deaths of human loved ones, loss of a vampire mate. They each added to the store of energy inside of the being, culminating like a force field ready to be unleashed at a moment's notice.

In his surveillance of the room, Jonas noticed only one vampire in attendance who didn't look surprised by his question.

The vampire waited until Jonas made eye contact, then he slowly and meaningfully looked up at the ceiling.

A loud thud overhead had Jonas retreating as quickly as possible to the alley.

Ginny.

GINNY'S SKIN FELT layered with ice without Jonas in the

car. Moments ago, she'd been secure and content in his embrace, she now sat shivering in the bottom of a well. Desperate for a distraction, she listened carefully for anything beside her own breathing and the drumming of Tucker's fingers on the steering wheel.

At least ten minutes had passed when a door opened and closed outside the car, then nothing, save the sound of water dripping, the distant whir of traffic, a plane flying overhead. Tucker turned on the radio and Elias smacked it off, leading to an argument. Mothers were insulted quite offensively.

Jonas had been gone about twenty minutes when a door groaned opened and closed again. She longed to rip off the blindfold and see if Jonas approached—not to mention where he'd been, but she forced her hands to remain at her side.

In the blink of an eye, the energy in the car shifted.

Ginny felt it and sat forward.

"What the hell is going on?" Elias growled.

She ripped off the blindfold, blinking twice into the glare of a streetlamp, before clawing her way toward the door Jonas had exited, pressing her forehead to the cold glass.

There in a moonlit alleyway stood Jonas.

Another vampire joined him. At least, that was one way of putting it.

Was she dreaming? She had to be. No way one of the

most terrifying beings Ginny had ever seen was *floating down from the rooftop of the building.* As if he were strapped into an invisible harness. The skin of his throat and hands was bluish white and streaked with veins, though most of him was hidden beneath a wide brimmed hat and raincoat. A gray braid of hair ticked side to side on his back, reminding Ginny of a metronome. He moved at a sedate pace, expression smug.

Jonas remained entirely still and watched him land.

"Ever the unfazed prince," Tucker muttered. "We should get out there."

"Wait," Elias said. "We wait. It could be a move to draw us away from her."

A shiver passed down Ginny's spine. "You think that's the powerful vampire who's been moving me in my sleep."

"The question is, why?" Tucker asked. "Just to enforce the rule about vampire-human relationships or is there another reason? Anything is possible."

Tucker could say that again. There were so many more possibilities in this world she lived in now. She was ducked down in the back of a car, good vampires protecting her from other evil vampires. And why? She had no clue. But the life she'd once known seemed like nothing more than an uninformed prologue.

"Get all the way down, Ginny," Tucker instructed.

She complied, but slowly crept back up to watch the

action, Jonas's voice reaching her ears through the window, muffled, yet sharp. Royal.

"I'm assuming this isn't an accidental meeting. What do you want from me?"

The vampire smiled to reveal a row of long, sharp teeth. "Seymour Blithe at your service." He tilted his head to the right. "Have you enjoyed having the loss of a loved one dangled in front of you like a carrot?"

To say Jonas bristled would be an understatement. His muscles seemed to expand and cast larger shadows, and even through the car window, Ginny could hear the slice of his fangs descending. "You tried to kill Ginny," he rasped, his voice nothing more than a rippling ribbon of violence.

"I merely pointed the expendable human in the direction of her demise."

"*Why*?" Jonas shouted.

"We really need to get out there and help," Tucker snapped.

Elias made a sound of disagreement. "He'll have no chance of defeating a being that powerful unless he's protecting her. We stay."

"I'm *motivation*?" Ginny pressed her hands to the glass, aching to fling open the door and scream at Jonas to get back inside. "Fine. Good. I wouldn't leave anyway, just *please* go help—"

Before she could finish, Seymour flicked a wrist and

sent Jonas catapulting to the opposite end of the alley. Ginny swallowed a scream at the sight of his strong body plowing into a row of trashcans. Before she could take her next breath, he was up, a darker shade of green than usual pinwheeling in his eyes. His jaw was tight enough to break—and it almost did when Seymour slashed a hand through the air and Jonas's head went snapping back like he'd been punched, making him stumble.

"*Do something*," Ginny pleaded.

Elias leaned forward in the passenger seat. "Wait for it."

Indeed, there appeared to be a change overcoming Jonas. The malice in his eyes alone transformed him, and Ginny recalled what he'd said to her in the office of the funeral home earlier that night. *These abilities are usually triggered in a vampire when he or she undergoes something harrowing. More and more every time. And you, love, most definitely fit that description.*

In a blur of movement, Jonas whipped off his coat, leaving him in dress pants, suspenders and a dove gray button-down. Déjà vu nipped at her conscious, but she was too focused on praying for Jonas's survival, that she could only disregard it and whisper a rush of words against the glass, fogging it slightly.

"Please, please, please…"

Time seemed to slow as she locked eyes with Jonas through the glass. The slightest downward flicker of his irises sent Ginny into a duck without hesitation—and Seymour's body was thrown up against the car. *Slam.*

"Son of a bitch," Tucker breathed.

Ginny straightened and watched Jonas pull Seymour off the car, using only an outstretched hand, and launch him up against the side of the building. She almost cheered. Started to, in fact, but Seymour chose that moment to rally, blasting Jonas with wavy ribbons of clear energy, throwing him off his feet and onto his back.

Leaving him vulnerable.

"No," Ginny breathed.

A ball of crackling air hovered above the older vampire's palm and he was seconds from hitting Jonas with it. While he was down.

No, she couldn't let it happen.

If she was the catalyst for his abilities taking hold, then she'd do her job. She'd help him, instead of standing by like a spare part.

Seymour reared back, preparing to blast Jonas.

She'd have to dig deep for this amount of courage. None of her usual heroines would boost her this time— sorry, Elizabeth, Lauren and Grace. This time around, she was going full Bond Girl. With a deep breath, Ginny threw open the car door and stepped out.

"*No!*" Jonas roared, rolling and lunging to his feet.

Seymour turned with a beastly smile and changed his aim to Ginny instead. "Alas, she makes my task even easier." Her feet lifted inch by inch off the ground, the floating sensation disconcertingly familiar. "Where shall I perch the little birdie this time? A skyscraper, perhaps?"

Seymour's bottomless eyes went blank as his neck snapped. He collapsed into a heap on the ground, dropping Ginny back down to the concrete.

Vampires couldn't die from a broken neck, though, could they?

Her question was answered when Seymour twitched and started to stand, despite the nausea-inducing injuries to his person.

Jonas straddled the man's chest with what appeared to be a broken chair leg clutched tightly in his hand. A makeshift stake? Jonas was saying something, but she could barely make it out. She started to take a hesitant step forward when an arm wrapped around her waist, yanking her backward until she met the side of the car with Tucker and Elias blocking her view.

"That was one crazy move, sweetheart," Tucker said over his shoulder. "She has a couple of beers, all of a sudden she's living life on the edge."

"I can't believe a human is growing on me," Elias muttered from behind his raised collar.

She couldn't take the time to be flattered. Not when she was too eager to hear the exchange between Jonas and Seymour. Holding on to Tucker's jacket sleeve, she inserted her face between her own private vampire shield and listened.

"*Why did you come for her?*" Jonas shouted at the felled vampire. "*Tell me.*"

"Why else?" The old vampire's laugh chugged like an engine, but it held a tinge of sadness. "Your father."

Seymour's head had been bent at an unnatural angle, but his neck shifted slowly now to the sound of tendons stretching. Tucker and Elias tensed on either side of Ginny, a split second before Seymour sprang up and made a grab for the stake—but it was too late. Jonas arced the weapon down with considerable force and penetrated the right side of Seymour's chest, resulting in a loud whistling sound—and pop.

Ashes floated where the old vampire had once been.

Jonas dropped to his knees in the floating debris and hung his head. "Goddammit." A shudder traveled across his shoulder muscles and then he was on his feet, blurring to the spot right in front of her. Tucker and Elias were pushed apart, leaving her crouched sideways like the world's most obvious eavesdropper. "Ginny," he said, his voice lethally quiet. "You got. Out. Of the car."

She straightened and brushed off her skirt, reluctant to witness the accusation and outrage in his gaze. "I was trying to motivate you."

"You agreed to stay put," he gritted out, gripping her shoulders.

"I had my fingers crossed," she whispered, heat stealing up her neck. "Please try and remember we're very close to my birthday."

He made a choked sound. "Do not make jokes when I've just come close to losing you." Twin sparks launched in his eyes. "You are a threat to my very sanity."

Indignation poked her in the side like a thorn. "Do you think it was easy sit here and watch you fight for your life?"

"Forgive me if I'm not prepared to be reasonable over you trying to get yourself killed," Jonas growled, reaching behind her and opening the door, urging her into the backseat while Tucker and Elias reclaimed their spots up front.

Silence cracked in the dark car like a whip.

"Once again, a vampire's hatred for your sire and his cut-throat policies puts you—and this time, *her*—in the crossfire," Elias said finally. "How long are you going to pretend your connection to him is inconsequential?"

Jonas's jaw popped in response. "There are far more vampires that support me than want me dead over some perceived connection to him that no longer exists." He paused. "The threat has been handled. That's what's important now." He frowned out the car window. "Clarence told me stories of Elders developing foresight. Seymour must have been one of them. How else would he have known about Ginny before I met her?"

The question lingered in the air, until Tucker

smacked Elias in the shoulder. "Are we just going to pretend he doesn't have dope-ass abilities now, or..." When he got no response from the passenger, he turned in his seat. "You just staked a billion-year-old vampire like you were spreading mayo on a slice of Wonder Bread. You don't want to chat about it?"

"She was in danger," Elias said. "His *mat—*"

"That's impossible and you know it," Jonas cut in, securing Ginny's seatbelt like she was a three-year-old child. "Drive us to the funeral home."

With a squeal of tires, Tucker accelerated the car and whipped onto the street, turning the stereo on and drumming the steering wheel along with the thumping bass. Jonas found the blindfold on the seat, but before he could tie it over Ginny's eyes, she closed them and turned her face into his chest instead.

His arms came around her slowly, the pressure increasing until he was squeezing her tight.

"Someone tried to kill you, love. Because of who I am. Who I *was*. And yet you trust me, take risks for me...you *cling* to me anyway." He mapped her forehead with kisses. "I should be shaking sense into you. Instead I want to kneel and thank fate."

Ginny's heart twisted so forcefully, she had to gasp for breath. "It sounds like you want to give me more time with you. And my memories."

He shook his head at her ruefully. "The threat has

been eliminated, love. My protection is no longer required," he said unevenly, before casting a morose look out the window. "Besides, do you think we could ever fool ourselves into thinking any amount of time together is enough?"

No. Of course the answer to that question was a vehement no.

Shivers took her over. They'd reached the end of the road.

Tomorrow morning, when she woke up, she would no longer remember Jonas Cantrell or the last few days. The wildfire of feeling inside of her would be doused and there was an extremely good chance she'd never experience a fraction of it again.

Unless she could be very persuasive tonight.

CHAPTER ELEVEN

G INNY SAT ON the edge of her bed, watching Jonas pace.

If she squinted, she could envision him storming back and forth on a stone floor in front of a roaring castle fireplace, a robe billowing out behind him. Servants would hover in the shadows, awaiting orders.

Everything about him was so undeniably in charge and confident, even if now he appeared to be in mental turmoil, muttering to himself under his breath, as he'd been doing for the last fifteen minutes.

He'd brought her home intending to erase her memories, but so far he'd been unable to do it—and that gave her hope. *I'm in the fight of my life.* That's how it felt. The battle to wake up tomorrow and still know what it was like to live with this depth of feeling for another person. How could she live without it?

Get him talking. Isn't that what the experts suggested hostages do in a hostage situation? Establish a rapport. Personalize oneself for a better chance of survival. And that's what she was fighting for, wasn't it? Survival?

"So." she licked her lips. "You're as powerful now as the vampire who's been leaving me in oceans and on highways. How do you do it? What does it feel like?"

He stopped pacing and looked down at his hands. "Normally, my eyesight can pick out the smallest things. Dust motes, an insect several yards away. But this..." He huffed a sound. "Tonight when you climbed out of the car, it was like my fear crystalized everything. I could see molecules in the air, pick them out and manipulate them. Objects were no longer objects. They were just masses of atoms to be broken apart or moved. It's...hard to describe."

"I'd say you did a pretty good job," she said. *Keep him talking. Cause delays.* "Can you explain why someone would target you...and in turn me, because of Clarence?"

Agitated fingers plowed through his hair. "Ginny, I can't confide in you only to take the knowledge away...that makes me an even worst bastard."

"I won't know you're a bastard. I won't know you at all."

Torture twisted his expression. "*Love.*"

She flattened her palms on he bedspread and tried to keep her voice calm and not at all pleading. "Just talk to me. For a little while. Please?"

After some visible debate, he spoke in a hushed tone. "Clarence, my sire, is the King of the High Order. He holds the highest power among the vampires. Tonight was not the first time someone has figured out my connection to him and tried to eliminate me. Though it's the first time someone has been vulnerable because of their connection to me. I'm so sorry I didn't see it coming."

"Don't apologize. You protected me."

He snorted and began pacing again. "Not soon enough. I could have still been inside meeting with the newbie when he arrived in the alley. He could have…"

"But he didn't."

"No thanks to you." He flicked her a high eyebrow. "Car leaver."

Smiles ghosted over their lips.

"Will you tell your father…your *sire* about the attack?"

"I try not to associate with him, but he contacts me occasionally, when he can pin my location down before I move on." He blurred past Ginny, ending up at the fire escape window. "Our relationship is complicated. When I was freshly Silenced, he intended for me to follow in his footsteps."

"He wanted you to lead the High Order?"

"God no. He'd never relinquish power. Not voluntarily, anyway," Jonas said. "He wants a second in command to do his bidding. I didn't agree with how he governed, allowing humans to be Silenced and then punishing those who can't temper the vampire nature inflicted on them. It's barbaric." He tucked his tongue into his cheek. "After one too many arguments, I left. Clarence has made it clear many times that he wants me to return, and take my seat in the Order. See, I'm his only progeny. Once a vampire reaches a certain age, his venom dries up and he can no longer Silence a human." He laughed without humor. "It's more likely he wants me to return and give him a vow of fealty so I can never challenge his domination, not because he has some perceived kinship with me. But I'll never go back."

"Not even for Thanksgiving dinner?"

Jonas showed only the briefest flicker of amusement but it faded rapidly. "Staying away from the only family I have is easy compared to what it'll be like keeping my distance from you." He dragged his hands down his face. "Christ, love. I don't know if I'll be able to stand it."

"Don't find out," she whispered. "We can be careful—"

"No. *No*, Ginny," he barked forcefully, his eyes squeezed shut. "You've already witnessed first hand the danger I bring into your life. The King has made countless enemies and because of that, I'm a target. I won't make you one, too."

She swallowed, a tremble passing through her knees. "Then do it. Erase yourself from my mind. What are you waiting for?"

In half a heartbeat, he was standing in front of her.

He heaved a miserable sound, green starting to crackle in his eyes. Go time.

"It's midnight," Ginny blurted.

He started, seeming almost grateful for her interruption. "What?"

"It's officially my birthday."

Jonas fell to his knees and walked forward, pressing his face to her stomach, hands fisting in the sides of her dress. "Forgive me. Forgive me."

Ginny didn't hesitate to tangle her fingers in his hair, softly scratching circles in his scalp. "Only if you give me a present before...before you do it."

When he lifted his head, his expression was wary, but eager. "What would you request from me, love?"

"A kiss," she breathed, almost dizzy thanks to their proximity and the intensity he radiated. "Just one."

The atmosphere around them turned heavy, like a hot raincloud. A trickle of something predatory rode across Jonas's features and in turn, her thighs clenched. The low lamplight seized them in a hazy glow and time turned languid. She sat on her bed with this beautiful, eternal being knelt between her shaking knees and their position made desire lick at her senses. Made her so excited, her nipples beaded inside her bra and the dress she wore suddenly felt like plastic wrap she needed off.

"Just one," Jonas repeated hoarsely. She held her breath as he flipped up her skirt, exposing her to mid-thigh. His palms molded to her knees and slid to the lifted hem. His touch alone would have been enough to send her pulse skyrocketing, but then he lifted her left leg, leaning down to open-mouth kiss her inner thigh. "Where do you want your kiss? Here?"

"I-I mean, that's really, *really* nice. But, um…" What were words? "I was kind of hoping for higher."

With his lips still searing her thigh, he tossed her a wicked smirk.

"Oh Lord," she rushed to say, red faced. "No. I meant my mouth."

His tongue snuck out and dragged in a circle. "What I wouldn't give for the ability to say next time we'll be a lot more adventurous."

Her heart stuttered. What if she couldn't convince him to forgo taking her memories? The possibility of failing rammed into her with such impact that she fell back on the bed, caught between despair and arousal. Jonas's weight dipping the mattress guided her once again toward desire, however. Especially when his face appeared above her, his gaze zeroed in on her lips.

"She won't remember any of this," he whispered to himself, his mouth descending. Closer. Closer. Sending her nerve endings into chaos.

"You will, though," she whimpered.

His breath mingled with Ginny's. "Yes. I will. *Always*," he rasped. "With this kiss, I willingly damn myself to a lifetime of suffering. Happy birthday, love."

What followed defied any preconceived notions she may have entertained about kissing. Lips making contact wasn't merely something that looked pretty on a television or movie screen. It was what happened on the inside that counted.

He started by slanting his head, tasting her with groaning suction. It went on and on, him absorbing that first taste—and her *being* absorbed. Greedily. Absolutely. His hard body settled on top of hers, the momentous pressure making her gasp as Jonas's tongue swept into her mouth. *Ohhh.*

Their tongues greeted each other like star-crossed lovers, demanding and bereft over their separation. Ginny's eyes flew open to find the same wonder blazing in Jonas's, before his lids drooped along with hers, the kiss taking over, sensations making demands and hunger sinking in its claws.

At the next slide of their tongues, Ginny's knees drew up involuntarily and Jonas rolled forward with a growl, locking their lower bodies together. Pressing. Straining. The vast difference in their strength was obvious. As it was also obvious that he tried valiantly to hold his in check, his body shaking with the effort.

Unfortunately, Ginny's body couldn't seem to stop tempting that inhuman strength. Her inner thighs rode up and down his hips and thighs, sobs catching in her throat, releasing into his hot, seeking mouth. *Lord, his mouth.* It was at once skilled and frantic, like he knew damn well what he was about, but couldn't keep up with the onslaught of lust.

Yes. God, this was *lust.*

An epic flood of it that required an ark for survival.

Their hands wrestled above her head, only to be pinned by Jonas. His hips rocked, the hard ridge of his sex riding to the start of her feminine flesh—and pressing down. *Right there.* Even through the material of her dress, she caught enough friction to cry out—and the threadbare sound did something to Jonas.

He leaned harder into the kiss, befuddling her senses with long, sensual slants of hard lips over soft, animal groans kindling in his strong chest, his fingers locked so tightly with Ginny's above her head, she knew his willpower waned.

Good.

More.

Good.

Never stop.

Life wouldn't be possible without this. It hadn't been. She'd just been in a state of existence without the sensual plundering of his tongue, the weight of his body. All of it had been missing. Lost to her.

Ginny's crossed her ankles at the waistband of his pants and arched her back, gasping excitedly when he pounced forward, holding her down with even more intention. Even more urgency. Voraciousness.

"Ginny," Jonas said thickly. "I'm lost."

"No. You're found. Stay with me."

Stay with me.

Those words echoed like a shout in a cave.

An image flickered in front of her mind's eye. Jonas was still atop her, but their surroundings were a moving haze. Multicolored lights and pinging sounds whirred in the distance, loud and disjointed, but she disregarded them as inconsequential. Nothing mattered but the man and the way his essence promised not only pleasure, but an endless source of it.

As fast as their surroundings changed, they were back in her bedroom and Jonas was letting go of her pinned wrists to unfasten the buttons that ran down the front of her dress. When she took over the task, he looked her hard in the eye and hitched the hem of the garment up to her waist. "Remind me I could hurt you if I take you. Remind me there are rules and *consequences.*"

Wetness rushed to the juncture of her thighs on the wings of desire so wild, it didn't have a name. She shook her head in a stubborn no to his command and peeled open the bodice of her dress, revealing the sheer peach lace of her bra, the breasts that swelled out of their cups.

Jonas's fangs snapped into view, his gaze darkening to a dangerous dark green. "No, Ginny," he breathed. "No, love. No. Don't turn your beauty into my enemy."

"You don't have to fight the battle alone," she said, threading her fingers through his hair and pulling him down for a soft kiss. "You don't have to be alone at all. Give us a chance. I'm acknowledging the risk. I'm *taking* it."

A shudder traveled through Jonas. A surrender. His lips peeled back from his teeth and he slowly lowered his mouth to her breasts, rubbing his lips over the peak of her hard nipple. He made a guttural sound and thrust his hips, absorbing Ginny's whimper with that emerald intensity. He seemed to be powerless to do anything but kiss her and he did. Hard. Wild. They dove back into the hungry writhe of lips like they'd never stopped for a moment, and the pace accelerated quickly, making their bodies strain closer, her legs wrapping more securely around his hips.

Jonas broke away to let her breathe, eyeing her pulse while moving closer, closer to it as if drawn by hypnosis. He brushed the flutter of life with his lips and his hands gripped her thighs in a bruising hold, sending a thrill through Ginny, all the way to her toes. His willpower was on full display while he kissed her neck reverently, but when his tongue came out and licked the entire length of her flexed tendon, Ginny wasn't expecting the deluge of lust—and she jolted.

His fang caught on her skin, causing Ginny a flash of pain.

Jonas drew back in horror, the flaming green fire transfixed by her neck. Reflected in his gaze, she watched the red trickle run down the paleness of her skin and couldn't move. Couldn't breathe.

What would he do?

So many times, he'd warned about the three rules and how easily they could be broken. A relationship led to drinking her blood leading to potential death. What if he couldn't help himself? Had she pushed him too far?

With a growl of pure hunger, Jonas lowered his head and licked the trickle of blood from her neck, bringing it into his mouth and swallowing the way someone might with a fine wine. Almost immediately, his body fell forward on top of her. He caught himself with shaking arms right before he could crush her.

A throttled rendition of her name left him. What was that sound?

There was a muted throbbing between them and at first she thought it came from her own rollicking heartbeat, but no...no, it came from Jonas.

He balanced on one hand, tearing at the left side of his chest with the other.

Was his heart beating?

"Mate," he gasped, fangs elongating another fraction of an inch. "*Mate*."

Before she could respond, Jonas threw himself off the bed and landed on his feet. His fists clenched at his sides for a heavy moment, as if he was considering lunging at her, pinning her, but in the space of a second, he'd gone out the window instead, leaving her alone and wheezing on the bed.

Mate?

Ginny was so confused by what had happened, it took her almost an hour of staring into space and replaying the scene to realize...she still had her memories.

CHAPTER TWELVE

GINNY HAD THE dream again that night.

She was edging along the outskirts of the luminous fair, drawn by her very bones to the darkness. Drawn to the tree where the man stood in his hat and suspenders, watching her as though he'd been waiting for her. As if he'd been watching her for a while and memorized the way she moved. Which made no sense since she was positive she'd never seen him before. She would have remembered being magnetized, hot and shivery just being in his presence.

Having no choice but to get closer, she stepped out of the light and watched him push off the tree and go rigid. "Don't," he said, though his voice didn't reach her. His lips spelled out the words. "Please, don't."

For some reason, with those words from the stranger, she expected the moment to dissolve. For the night to fade and fade like a pencil sketch submerged in water. It didn't, though. Another presence tugged her attention to the left, away from where it truly wanted to be—on the stranger beneath the tree. Someone else was there with them, though.

Static crawled up her Ginny's arm. Her head turned toward the other presence lethargically, but there was only an outline of a dark figure surrounded by the yonder lights of the fair.

A figure in a crimson hood.

Ginny bolted upright in bed, a sob caught in her throat.

Her fingers tore at the bed sheets, twisting them in her grip to keep her grounded in the present. In wakefulness, too. Last time she'd had the dream, she'd woken up in the middle lane of the parkway. Not this time, thank the Lord. She was in her bedroom, even if she couldn't shake the gravity of the dream. Part of her even wished she was still asleep, so she would know what happened. What was the stranger beneath the tree distressed about?

And how could every second of it feel so vivid, right down to the gravel and grass crunching under her feet to the smell of roasted chestnuts?

The lingering haze of the dream drifted away and last night's events came hurtling back in. Automatically, Ginny's fingers went to her neck, to the spot where Jonas's teeth had accidentally nicked her and drawn blood. There was no cut, no pain, nothing to prove it had ever happened.

A lead weight sank in her stomach.

Mate.

What had he meant by that?

Mate.

"Any fresh bodies for me to see today?"

A delighted shock ran through Ginny and she scrambled to the edge of the bed to find Roksana lying casually on the floor.

"You're back," Ginny breathed, moisture rushing to her eyes. Before she could stop herself, she rolled off the bed and landed beside the slayer, promptly throwing a leg across her body and pulling her into a bear hug. "Where did you go?"

"I don't appreciate this display of emotion," Roksana said, contradictory laughter in her voice. "It makes me feel lumpy."

"Lumpy?"

"That's what I said. Get off, you crazy animal."

"Okay, fine." Ginny let go of Roksana and scooted back, fairly vibrating with excitement over having her friend back. Since the slayer had left, she'd mostly been worried about staying alive, but seeing Roksana in person now made Ginny realize she'd desperately needed her friend. "You didn't answer me. Where did you go?"

"Upstate. Downstate." Roksana studied her finger nails. "Here and there."

"What made you come back?"

"The prince." She snorted. "Who else?"

Ginny's brow knit. "I don't understand. He took care of the threat last night. I'm no longer in danger."

"Hmmm." Was it her imagination or did Roksana's attention slip to her neck. "Perhaps that is true. Perhaps he thought you shouldn't be alone on your birthday."

When she should have experienced warmth or pleasure over Jonas's thoughtfulness, there was only a scalding, syrupy sense of foreboding. "He isn't coming back, is he?"

Roksana evaded her gaze. "This vampire drama does not concern me. I am only here to party."

"Roksana, please," she whispered. "Something happened last night—"

"Hold that thought," the slayer said quickly, rolling under the bed. "We have company."

No sooner was Roksana out of sight than Larissa stumbled into the room with a bottle of NyQuil clutched to her chest and a wadded up tissue protruding from one nostril. "What the hell are you doing on the floor?"

"Oh, um. Looking for an earring."

"Whatever." She waved the bottle of blue liquid. "I've come down with a cold. This is why I hate hosting the viewings. Every granny in the house wants to blubber all over my shoulder or make me shake their snotty hands. *God.*" She shivered and took a swig of the cold medicine. "Kristof's second viewing is today. I have no idea why they wanted two when barely anyone showed up yesterday, but as long as they're paying, I'm not questioning it." She paused to deliver a wince-inducing scream sneeze. "Can you handle the second viewing, as well as your shift tonight? It's four to six."

"Yes, I can do that."

Anything to get Larissa out of the room. Not to mention, if there was a lack of guests at the wake, she would like the chance to show some support to the grieving family. It's what her father would have done.

"Great." Larissa smiled and tilted her head, but with her red nose and puffy eyes, she kind of resembled the clown from every child's nightmare. "Have you thought any more about selling?"

"Not yet, sorry. I've been a little distracted lately."

The smile turned tight. "There's a big world out there, you know. Much bigger than Coney Island, Ginny. You need to get out there and see it."

Ginny didn't know how to respond to that. Coney Island seemed a lot bigger and crazier than it ever had before.

"Well," Larissa said haltingly into the silence. "I'm off to bed."

"Feel better, Larissa."

Her stepmother turned to leave, but stuck her head back in at the last second. "Oh and…" She chewed her lip, seeming conflicted. "Happy birthday."

The door snicked shut.

Ginny sighed and sat up, watching as Roksana rolled back out from beneath the bed. "I could kill her?" Roksana suggested. "She's already rotting on the inside. I'd be doing her a favor."

"Do *not* kill my stepmother."

"Great. Now I have to figure out a different birthday present."

A laugh bubbled up in Ginny's throat, her gaze straying to the clock. "How did I sleep so late?" She jumped to her feet and lunged for the closet. "I have to get dressed and prepare the visitation room. Put out the flowers and prayer cards…"

"Since you asked nicely, I will help you."

Ginny raised an eyebrow at the slayer. "You just want to see a body."

"It's not fair," Roksana whined. "When you kill a vampire, there is nothing but dust left over. Very anticlimactic."

Ginny selected the one black dress in her closet, which she'd bought at Macy's, then brought home and added a wide, satin belt and a flower on the right side of the collar. "Speaking of vampires, Elias went looking for you."

"I don't care," Roksana snapped, tightening her blonde ponytail. "When? What did he say exactly?"

Sensing she'd stumbled upon an opportunity, Ginny tapped her chin. "I'm not sure I can recall exactly…"

"What is this?" The other woman narrowed her eyes. "Are you keeping information from me to be cagey?"

Ginny stripped off her dress from the night before and pulled on the black one, all too aware that she needed a shower as soon as the wake ended. "I'll tell you what Elias did and said—" With some modifications. Probably best not to repeat the term *reckless brat*. "If you explain why you're *really* here."

Roksana inclined her head, visibly impressed. "This technique of yours might have worked if I cared about the bloodsucker looking for me." She untucked a rectangular, gold object from her pocket and fanned her face with it. "He probably just wanted his credit card back. My new boots exceeded his spending limit."

Ginny finished tying the bow on the back of her dress and swallowed hard, giving the slayer a meaningful look. "Please, I need to know Jonas is all right. We...there was a mishap last night and I'm worried about him." Her fingers tremored, longing for the feel of his cool skin. "I'm worried about him never coming back."

The slayer looked down at the ground, but not before Ginny caught her troubled expression. "Ginny, my calling is to protect humans. And I do not accomplish this by giving you what you want. Not this time."

"He said mate. I think he *called* me his mate. What does that mean?"

"I'm sorry, I can't help you there." Roksana skirted around the bed and perched herself on the windowsill, throwing her legs over the side and dancing gracefully onto the fire escape. "I'll meet you downstairs."

She stood and stared at the fading silhouette her friend left behind, the foreboding in her stomach burning hotter. Something was wrong. What took place in her bedroom last night had been significant and she needed to find out what it was. But how? She'd been blindfolded during the trip to Jonas's apartment. There was a chance she could retrace the turns and figure out how to get there, but intuition told her she'd have to shake Roksana in order to do it.

Her palm cupped around the spot on her neck where Jonas had licked the stream of blood, leaving no wound behind. Was he staying away because he'd liked it too much?

An involuntary rush of pleasure made the fine hairs on her body stand on end, her toes curling into the carpet. It would make sense that he'd enjoyed her taste and was being noble by cutting her off. He'd told her from the beginning her scent, her blood, was different, hadn't he? *If someone put a single scratch on your skin, I would go utterly mad, Ginny, and yet I burn to sink my teeth into your neck every second of the day. I don't know how to uncomplicate that for you.*

Ginny walked in a trancelike state to her dresser,

picking up her hairbrush and running it absently through her hair. Until she hit a snarl that prompted a sense of indignation.

Since meeting Jonas, he'd made all the rules. Assigning bodyguards. Blindfolding her. Locking her in rooms. If she continued to let him dictate their relationship— and there was no other descriptor for what they had, for better or worse—she would end up without him. He'd only been gone a matter of hours and she already knew living in his absence was a cold, cold place.

Ginny hadn't escaped a lifetime of living in a funeral home without learning the value of living like every day was her last. Regrets were a long-lasting poison and if she died tomorrow, she refused to leave any behind.

Relieved to have a sense of purpose, she started to leave the room, already creating a mental list of the tasks ahead—

Pain flared in her side, like a knife being inserted beneath her rib cage. A scream of agony caught in her throat and she stumbled, running into the door, hands clutching the place of impact, searching frantically for a wound and coming up empty. Nothing was there. *Nothing was there.* Why did it hurt so bad?

As fast as the pain hit, it disappeared, leaving her limp and gasping.

She spun around to find the room empty, the only sound her rasping inhales.

Tingles ran through her body, from the tip of her head to her toes and although the pain was gone, the sense of impending doom remained.

Something was off. The universe had tilted. No more waiting to be shuffled around and allowing herself to be protected without detailed explanations of what she was up against. She intended to get answers.

Tonight.

CHAPTER THIRTEEN

GINNY SAT SIDE by side with Roksana in the back row of the viewing room.

Kristof lay in his casket, his face organized in peaceful indifference. There was only one mourner in attendance and she was motionless in the front row, hands folded in her lap with a rosary wound around her knuckles. Ginny had made an attempt to comfort the woman, but like her husband, she'd been somewhat standoffish—and that was her right. Everyone mourned in their own way.

With twenty minutes left to go, Ginny craned her neck, hoping someone would walk through the door, but the lobby remained silent.

"I don't understand this ritual," Roksana murmured, speaking to Ginny for the first time since they'd met downstairs, awkward after their exchange in Ginny's bedroom. "That man is not lying in that box. He's somewhere else."

A sad smile curved Ginny's lips. "This isn't for him."

"Meaning?"

"I've never had to put it into a words before." Ginny

thought for a few moments. "Everyone has a deck of cards for each person they love. You've got your regret cards, your good memory cards, bad memory cards. When one of your people dies, the deck of cards gets thrown up into the air and the cards scatter everywhere. Wakes and funerals are about putting them into a new order. You have to. One half of every memory you had with them is gone. You have to figure out how to live with only your half. It's a lot harder than it sounds."

Roksana jostled her leather clad leg. "Sounds complicated, Ginny. Maybe it's better to have no loved ones."

Before Ginny could respond, there was a loud bang out in the lobby. Seconds later, a woman came rushing into the room with a rolling suitcase behind her. She dropped it at the door and slammed to a halt, as if she'd run into a glass wall. Her hands came up to over her mouth and she proceeded forward slowly. The woman in the front row turned and her blank expression crumpled into relief, followed by an overflow of grief. The newcomer stirred the air as she passed Ginny and Roksana, stooping over to embrace the woman in the front now and a sense of finality rolled into place.

"Forget what I said about the cards," Ginny sighed. "That's what the ritual is really about."

Roksana sniffed inelegantly. "I'm getting drunk tonight and so are you."

"My only experience with alcohol is my stepmother.

Oh! And two recent beers. What if I'm a terrible drunk who ruins everybody's night by dancing on tables and tossing my cookies?"

"That sounds like a party to me, but we're not going *out* out. Not this time." She flicked her wrist. "I'll steal a bottle of vodka from the liquor store and we'll do girls night in. I'll even watch one of your old movies."

"It sounds like there's a reason you want me indoors."

"Don't read into my actions," Roksana grumbled. "It's very rude."

Ginny faced forward, taking in the scene at the front of the room. The women stood in front of the casket, locked in an embrace. Did they have regrets? Maybe a phone call they'd ignored from Kristof or an argument over politics that resulted in weeks of silence? She often wondered what people would do with the gift of foresight. How would they change things if they knew ahead of time what the future would bring?

She knew.

She'd sat in that very chair and watched a parade of regrets, day in and day out, for most of her life. She had no excuse for sitting back and watching life happen around her. For far too long, that's what she'd been doing. After the sudden death of her father, she might have created patterns that distracted her from the grief, but those patterns had become a way of hiding. They didn't open her up to new experiences. Ones that would allow her to feel *new* things.

Starting now, Ginny was taking control of her own destiny. She didn't want to act in ways that were expected. No more safe patterns and coping mechanisms.

Ginny cleared her throat delicately. "I'm going *out* out."

"I had a feeling you were going to say that." Roksana drummed her fingers on her knee. "I could tie you to a chair."

"You won't, though. Not on my birthday."

"Are you one of these disgusting people who call it a birthday week, Ginny? I can't get down with that."

"No, I'm not," Ginny said on a quiet laugh. "But I've got no other leverage with which to bargain for one night of fun and freedom. I'm not immortal. I don't have your incredible skill—"

"Say more."

"At the moment, all I have is the date on a calendar."

And the desire to draw a certain someone out of the woodwork, even if it *did* include dancing on a table. Not that she had any plans to say such a thing out loud. Her plan struck her as kind of uninspired, but what was she to do with no power and no way to reach Jonas?

Furthermore, it *was* her twenty-fifth birthday and maybe that was reason enough to go a little wild. Growing up, her birthdays had consisted of an ice-cream cake in the break room of a morgue while her father warbled out a well-intentioned yet extremely off key version of Happy Birthday.

For the first time in…well, ever…she had a friend with whom to party. If Roksana was there because Ginny was still in danger for some reason, Ginny had full confidence that Roksana wouldn't let anything happen to her a second time. They might even have fun.

"You are putting me in a tough position, Ginny," Roksana said, pushing to her feet. "But we will go out. If only because I've become a dumb dumb who neglects alcohol and dancing because a bloodsucker asks it of me." Her lip curled. "They should all have been slaughtered by now."

Ginny nodded firmly. "Tomorrow."

"Yes, tomorrow. Tonight we fuck shit up." The slayer wagged a finger at Ginny's attire, mischief trickling into her expression. "But first, we find you something a little more exciting to wear. You look like a goth Bo Peep."

CLUTCHING HER JACKET closed to hide her cleavage, Ginny jogged to keep pace with Roksana on the sidewalk. Around them, the sky was streaked with purple and orange, a beautiful twilight sky that seemed to cast a glow over the apartment buildings and food shops that lined Mermaid Avenue. The scent of curry and jerk seasoning carried on the night breeze from the corner Caribbean restaurant, reminding Ginny that between wrapping up Kristof's viewing, showering, blow-drying her hair and modeling outfits for Roksana, she'd neglected to eat dinner.

"Where are we going?"

"A place you won't find on Yelp." A man passing by did a double take at Roksana and she bared her teeth at him. "You'd think he's never seen someone in a red latex jumpsuit before."

Ginny wished they were still home so she could adjust the borrowed thong underwear currently trying to climb into a place it was not welcome. "Is that jumpsuit more or less uncomfortable than what I'm wearing?"

Roksana didn't seem to hear her. She was busy scanning the street and rooftops—for what? Ginny didn't know. And her friend wasn't spilling. "Listen to me, Ginny. If I tell you to do something tonight, obey me without question. If you can do that, we'll maybe, possibly, have an enjoyable time. Do we have a deal?"

"I'm hearing you loud and clear."

"Fabulous." She hooked an elbow through Ginny's and took a sharp right, sending them down a narrow street lined with closed garages and a shallow gully of sewer water running down the middle. "I find I'm feeling guilty for calling you goth Bo Peep earlier. Please say something insulting to me, so I can move on."

"Oh no, I don't want to—"

"I insist."

Ginny inflated one of her cheeks and let the air out slowly. "You're alarmingly violent?"

"I asked for an *insult.* Not a commendation." Roksana sucked her tongue. "Never mind, we're almost there. Quick rundown, the owner is an ex-boyfriend and he still thinks there is a shot. There is not. Do not mention Jonas, Elias or Tucker. Say *nothing* of vampires whatsoever or you'll get us both killed."

"Should we just go to a Fridays?"

"This is a slayer bar." Something unsettled traipsed across her face. "We're safest here. Unless—"

"Unless I mention our primary reason for knowing one another. Got it."

"Sassy. I like it." She guided Ginny between two garages and down a set of steep stairs. "Those clothes are already doing their job."

They stopped outside a metal door at the very bottom of the staircase. It was a regular old door no one would look twice at. One might assume it led to a place to which only the electrical company had access. Not one sound could be heard on the other side. In fact, Ginny was getting ready to ask Roksana if they were in the right place when the metal creaked open—and blasting hip hop music nearly rendered her deaf.

On reflex, Ginny covered both of her ears, so she could only partially hear the exchange between Roksana and the bald, tawny-skinned man in a white leather vest who stood in front of them, the top of his head brushing the doorframe.

"Knew you'd be back," he shouted, giving the slayer an appreciative once-over. "I don't see the flamethrower you stole last time we hung out."

"I'm having it dry cleaned."

He cracked a laugh, before sliding his attention to Ginny. "You usually travel solo. Who's the fresh meat?"

"Her meat is off limits, Luther. We're just here to drink. Is that allowed?"

"I suppose that can be arranged." He shifted to the side and jerked his chin toward the apparent mayhem that lay on the other side of the door. "Welcome to Enders. Save me a dance, Roks."

"No."

Luther threw back his head and laughed.

The eye-rolling slayer took Ginny's hand and led her inside. With so many lights flashing in time with the bass, it was impossible to make out everything while being shuffled forward by a protective Roksana, but she saw enough to know the place was packed to the gills with fit-looking people who seemed in competition with each other to keep their backs closest to the wall.

Symbols Ginny didn't recognize had been spray painted in bright neon greens and whites onto brick, single blacklight bulbs hung from the ceiling, men and women danced on elevated platforms in next to nothing.

"I don't feel so underdressed in my skirt and tank top now."

"Oh good. I was so worried," Roksana deadpanned, situating Ginny in the very corner of the bar. "Stay put until I make a mental list of everyone here."

"You said we were safe in this place. What are you worried about?"

"Ginny, you need to learn no one is ever safe. Not anywhere. At any time."

Ginny took the words to heart. Wasn't it true that she'd been living in one dimension of this world that actually had two dimensions? Maybe more? Several times today when she'd closed her eyes, she'd thought of Seymour floating down from the roof into the alleyway. Her body being transported across the night sky. It was possible that safety was nothing more than a laughable notion.

Especially for humans like herself.

"Get you a drink?"

Ginny had been in the process of taking off her jacket when the bartender approached. Now, she swiveled on her stool to face him, whipping off her jacket at the same moment—and immediately slipped into the skin of one of her film stars. Elizabeth Taylor, perhaps, in *A Place in the Sun*. Yes. Ginny could see her now, the way she entered the glitzy party and cocked a hip on the pool table with a glass in her hand. "I'll have champagne."

The bartender stared back blankly.

Roksana coughed. "Two beers." When the bartender was out of sight, she turned to Ginny. "If they have champagne in this place, it tastes like piss."

"Another time, then."

The slayer's lips hopped at one end. "Sure."

Ginny cozied into her stool and scanned the room, averting her gaze when she made eye contact with two patrons mid-lip lock. "So what happened between you and Luther? He seems nice."

"Yes, that was the problem." Roksana slapped money on the bar in exchange for their beers and drained half of her bottle. "He wanted to set us up on double slaying dates and such things. I would rather slay myself."

Ginny sipped her drink and sighed over the ice-cold bitterness in her throat. "I think this is the same beer Tucker gave me. Or maybe they all taste the same."

"Tucker gave you beer? And Jonas allowed him to keep his head?"

"Jonas knows…" She stopped short, trying to find the right words. "It's a little odd now that I think about it, but Jonas knows I couldn't have an interest in anyone else as long as he exists. Or as long as I'm *aware* that he exists, anyway. And I know the same about him. Somehow that goes unsaid."

A vein ticked in Roksana's temple. "Da, that is how it would be," she said, low enough that Ginny wondered if she'd heard correctly. "What about before you met your...Jonas? Were there boyfriends?"

"No. I had one date with Gordon and I think he'd like another, but—"

"Turn him down." She shrugged. "If you'd like him to live, that is."

"I would," Ginny said quickly. "You're not saying Jonas would—"

"I *am* saying that."

"That's a fine thing to do. Killing off my only potential suitor when he's so dead set on taking my memories and hitting the bricks."

"Killing a man for getting too close to you would be an involuntary thing, Ginny—" Roksana broke off, taking a long pull of her beer. "Beer gives me a loose tongue."

Reluctant to badger Roksana on their night out, Ginny turned in her stool to face the room, noticing the dance floor for the first time where it was tucked in the back corner beneath a neon yellow chandelier. Bodies moved fluidly, together and apart, hips rocking, hands seeking. What would it be like to dance with Jonas like that? With his mouth in her hair and his leg pressed between her thighs?

The bartender completed an order with the group to Roksana's right and before he could leave to service another customer, Roksana tapped his elbow. "Two shots, please. Patrón."

"Yeah," he grunted, skulking away.

Ginny took a deep breath, bracing for her first shot of actual alcohol and felt a ramble coming on, due to her nerves. "How do slayers find this place?"

"Enders has been here for a century. I guess word got around. For me, I ran into Luther when we were stalking the same vamp in Gravesend. He's sort of the unofficial manager. No one has ever met the owner, but there are rumors."

"What kind?"

"They say she is savage. That in her office, she displays the heads of slayers who didn't pay their bar tab. Some say she is a mafia princess. No one knows the truth." Their shots were set down in front of them. Roksana slid one in front of Ginny before hoisting her own. "To your health."

The tequila burned going down. Lord, it burned. Ginny didn't find it unpleasant, though. It spread into a lake of warmth in her belly and gave her a relaxed sense of optimism. "Let's go dance."

Roksana winced. "Can I convince you to dance in your seat?"

Ginny gave her a *sorry, Charlie* headshake. "I don't even know how to dance, so this should be fun."

"Copy me, only. Not the ones humping."

"Deal."

They hopped off their stools and started to weave through the high top tables and groups of people. A step away from the dance floor, Ginny's vision doubled. The music expanded, the words stretching out interminably, like her footsteps. Was she even moving? Were the lights getting brighter?

That's when the pain struck.

"Oh," she heaved, her knees landing on the ground, sending pain shooting up her thighs. But it was nothing compared to the stabbing agony in her stomach. A sharp twist she could only liken to a hot fireplace poker ramming into her gut made her fall sideways and curl into the fetal position. She squeezed tightly into a ball but that only made the pain worse. Nothing helped. Nothing helped.

Oh Lord, make it stop.

"Ginny!" Roksana was beside her, running hands all over her body, her touch leaving fire in its wake. "What happened? What's wrong?"

"I don't know," she gasped, a terrible throb beginning in her throat. There was the sense that she needed something. A cure. *Now now now.* What was happening to her? She couldn't withstand the torture much longer—and all she could think of was Jonas. She needed him there. He'd stop the pain.

Distantly, she realized people were gathering around them. Barstools were shuffled aside and the music trailed off. Roksana's voice reached her, along with a tinny, yet familiar, one. As if it was coming over the phone.

"Bitch at me later," Roksana shouted. "There's something wrong with her...I don't know! If I knew, I wouldn't be calling you. She's in pain, but there's no injury. God, she's...it's like she's *dying*. Tell me what to do! No. He made me promise I wouldn't." There was a heavy pause. "N-no, you can't come here. You *can't*—"

Ginny's pain finally subsided, leaving her gasping and weak on the sticky ground, shaking violently. She couldn't even speak to tell Roksana that she was fine. She wouldn't have had time to say a word, anyway, because that's when the door of the bar blasted open and pandemonium ensued.

CHAPTER FOURTEEN

"WHAT A PAIR of goddamn idiots," Roksana muttered.

Ginny struggled into a sitting position and only caught the quickest glimpse of Elias and Tucker in the entrance of the bar when Roksana dragged her into a corner and ordered her not to move. With her jaw in the vicinity of her lap, she watched every slayer in the establishment whip out a stake.

"Oh dear," Ginny whispered. "Those are terrible odds."

Had Elias and Tucker come to Enders because of her? What could they possibly do to alleviate whatever was wrong with her? Surely she needed a human doctor and not two vampires. Even as the thought ran through her mind, she was levering herself up to see the door, hoping Jonas would walk in behind them. *Begging* him to.

He didn't.

She ignored the rush of disappointment and focused on the here and now—and the very real possibility that something horrible was about to happen. Her friends could be hurt because of *her*. Surely they couldn't take on an entire room of professional vampire slayers between the two of them.

The room was divided in two.

Vampires on one side, slayers on the other.

Roksana stopped in between the two sides and hesitated, her gaze swinging from the the pair to her colleagues. So to speak.

"*Go*," Elias rasped, his face partially hidden by a low-brimmed baseball cap. It was clear to Ginny he was speaking to Roksana, but the slayers around her muttered their speculations. "*Go!*"

Roksana remained frozen.

A male slayer with myriad piercings in the front row lunged, his stake raised high above his head and a battle cry pierced the air. He was headed straight for Elias when Roksana blindsided him with a kick, sending him crashing into a row of tables, sending bottles and candles crashing to the ground.

Roksana stared at the stunned slayer with a torn expression, slowly shifting her attention to the crowd of disgusted slayers.

Luther stepped out of the pack, betrayal etched into his features. "Am I reading this correctly? You protect...a *vampire*?"

Going from nonplussed to bored, she shrugged. "Just

trying to even the odds. No one likes a shutout."

"You're not welcome here ever again," Luther spat.

Roksana sighed. "Does this mean the offer to meet your parents is off the table?"

Elias released a low growl and stepped in front of Roksana.

The slayers bristled.

Ginny slowly got to her feet and made eye contact with Tucker. He shook his head at her almost imperceptibly, so she stayed put, even though her instinct was to sprint toward the exit. That way they could follow her and avoid what was sure to be a deadly altercation. If anything happened to her friends because of her, she wouldn't be able to live with the sadness *or* guilt.

What could she do, though? She didn't have superhuman capabilities and probably couldn't beat someone whose professional job title was *vampire slayer* on their worst day, unless maybe they were playing checkers. She had no choice but to wait and watch.

Luther pointed in her direction. "That one arrived with Roksana. Bring her to the back room."

Change of plans.

Ginny had no time to think as two glowering slayers started closing in immediately. She'd never wished for athleticism harder in her life as when she took a running jump, leapt onto her vacated bar stool and ran across the bar. She only made it five feet before her ankle was captured. She was just gearing up to kick her assailant in the face—probably while apologizing—when a blur of color snatched her off the bar and transported her to the exit.

"Hang on, sweetheart."

Tucker.

He set her onto watery legs and pushed her toward the door. "Go. Run home. We'll meet you there."

Without waiting for her response, he rolled up the sleeves of his shirt and swaggered up beside a battle-ready Elias and Roksana. "Been a while since I had a decent bar fight," he drawled. "Who'm I fuckin' up first?"

All hell broke loose.

The explosion of the battle threw Ginny's back up against the wall and for a moment, she could only gape and marvel at Roksana's skill. She took on slayers two at a time, fighting back to back with Elias, her limbs moving in graceful and deadly blurs. Tucker whooped his way through a string of bar patrons, twisting and dodging with the speed of a hurricane. He plucked stakes from their hands and launched them up at the ceiling where they got stuck, enraging the slayers.

I should go.

Tucker had told her to go, but she couldn't seem to move. All three of her friends were there because of her. Roksana had come to celebrate Ginny's birthday and Jonas's friends were there because of her mysterious illness. She couldn't just leave them to their fate. Not without trying to help.

Even now, the circle of slayers around Elias and Roksana was closing in. They had the upper hand for now, but for how long? Every time they felled one of their opponents, another one stepped in to take their place.

Chewing on her bottom lip, Ginny surveyed the room. The odds were *not* in their favor, but maybe she could do something to even them up.

Create a diversion. That always worked in the movies, didn't it?

We see as well in the pitch black as we do in the light.

As soon as Jonas's words came drifting back to Ginny, she was sliding along the wall toward the bar, hoping her movements remained undetected. Thankfully, the bartender had joined the fray, so there was no one to stop her from going behind the bar and searching for the light switches. There. They were right behind the cash register, beside the fire alarm.

Ginny smacked off the lights and immediately, roars of dismay reached her from the barroom floor. Hoping her friends would use the confusion as a chance to leave, she turned to leave, but changed her mind and pulled the fire alarm for good measure. A liquid sputter preceded a deluge of water raining down from the ceiling—and then the blaring siren started, muffling the exclamations and bodies running into one another.

She wasted no more time sprinting down to the open hatch of the bar and hooking a quick right, praying she didn't trip in the darkness on her way to the door—and she didn't. Because someone picked her up and broke land records on their way out of the bar, up the staircase and onto the street. She was assuming that was the chosen route, anyway. Ginny saw nothing but whipping colors until they were beneath a flickering street lamp on the opposite side of the alley.

Trying to recover from the rush of wind in her ears, Ginny braced her hands on her knees and took a breathless head count. All of them were there and despite a scrape on Roksana's cheek, unharmed. Thank the Lord.

"Nice assist, sweetheart," Tucker chuckled, giving Ginny a high five. "You've got some trouble in your blood, don't you?"

"Speaking of blood..." Elias said from the shadow just outside the circle of light cast by the streetlight. "We should get moving now."

Roksana cursed in Russian. "We're not taking her there. I *promised* him."

"If he knew the separation was going to cause *her* pain, too, do you really think he'd want you to keep that promise?"

The slayer's mouth formed a grim line.

"Exactly." Elias paused, before coming back with a terse, "You going to fix that cut on your cheek or just stand there and bleed to death?"

"I don't exactly have a first-aid kit handy."

"Maybe your boyfriend in the bar has one."

Without missing a beat, Roksana marched in the direction they'd come. "Maybe he does."

Elias caught her by the elbow mid-step. "Don't even try it."

Ginny sidestepped in between them. "What did you mean?" she breathed, her pulse spiking. "What did you meant, cause her pain *too*? Is Jonas in pain?"

"Now there's an understatement," Elias rasped, letting go of Roksana's arm.

He started to say more but slayers rushed into the alley fifty yards away, clearly searching for their foursome to continue to battle. "There they are," someone shouted.

"Five more minutes, Mom?" Tucker whined, cracking his knuckles.

"Please," Ginny pleaded. "I need answers."

Elias sighed. "We'll talk when we get there." He gave his back to Roksana and she climbed on with an eye roll. Ginny did the same with Tucker. "Stick to the alleys. The last thing we need is to get caught accelerating."

They skyrocketed into the night, traveling at such a high rate of speed that this time, Ginny definitely didn't even need a blindfold. Her eyes couldn't settle on one landmark before it vanished in their wake. One second they were powering down the street and the next, she was being set down in the elevator of Jonas's building, surrounded protectively by Roksana, Elias and Tucker. All three of them watched the split of the metal doors warily, balancing on the balls of their feet.

Why?

Ginny's breath started to come faster and faster, the hair on the nape of her neck standing on end. A ding let them know they'd arrived at the basement floor when an earsplitting bellow of denial rent the air.

Jonas?

GINNY'S ENTIRE BEING quite simply *demanded* to be taken in the direction of Jonas's howl. *He's suffering, he's suffering, he's suffering.* Her brain was not part of the operation. Her heart and possibly something baser and elemental jolted her toward the apartment door, her fingers wrapping around the door handle. She was only given the opportunity to yank once and find it locked before Roksana wrestled her back. Away from the place she needed to be.

A sob welled up inside her, breaking free as she struggled in her friend's hold. Her throat swelled until she couldn't draw breath, a magnetic current drawing her back to the door and she didn't want to withstand it. She wanted to get in. Get in now. Go to him. Her vision transitioned into an angry red and her fingers turned to claws.

"Let me go," Ginny shouted. "*Please.*"

Was that her voice?

She sounded almost possessed, but caring was beyond her at that moment. Who cared about anything when her heart was being wrenched up to her jugular, over and over again? *He's in there. He needs me.*

"*Jonas!*"

The lights sizzled in the hallway, dimming, brightening, like a pulse. And then came another roar, this time of her name.

Her lungs seized, her skin feeling like shrink wrap on her bones.

With an agonized whimper, Ginny twisted in Roksana's grip, noticing that Tucker and Elias were now holding her back, too—and that made them the enemy.

"*Let me in*," she begged, eyeing the apartment door like it was heaven's gates.

"Not until you listen," Elias snapped, the steel band of his arm wrapped around the breadth of her shoulders from behind. "Believe me, I'm on your side. I know you going in there is inevitable, but we need to prepare you first."

Roksana pressed a cool hand to Ginny's cheek and nodded at her slowly. "He's okay. He's going to be okay."

Apparently that was exactly what she needed to hear, because she dropped like a puppet with severed strings, Elias and Roksana lowering her the rest of the way to the floor. "Why does he sound like that? What's wrong?"

The slayer sat in front of her on the floor, cross legged, and took Ginny's hands. "This might be a little scary. We should have drunk more tequila." She shifted. "Last night, when Jonas tasted your blood, it became obvious to him that you are his mate."

Warm pleasure blew across Ginny's senses at the word and she stared longingly at the door. "What exactly does that mean? His mate?"

And why do I like it so much?

Roksana hesitated. "Well…"

"I had an inkling when I saw the way he behaved around you," Elias said quietly behind her. "But it's not supposed to be possible for our kind to have a mate…twice."

Jonas's words, spoken days earlier, came back to her. *I felt something like love once, a long, long time ago. Probably before your parents were born.*

"He's had a mate before," Ginny pushed through bloodless lips.

"Briefly," Tucker confirmed. "Very briefly. But the

length of time doesn't matter. It's fate. A connection. For Jonas, both times his mate has been human."

"Which is not only very unusual, Ginny," Roksana said slowly, her gaze uncharacteristically sympathetic. "It comes with some...difficulties."

"What are they?" Suddenly none of them would look at her. Not even Elias, who didn't seem the type to hesitate while delivering bad news. "Just *tell* me."

"A vampire senses his mate, but until he tastes her blood, he remains Silenced," Roksana explained. "Last night...you made his heart beat again."

Pure joy caused her lungs to seize. "How is that a bad thing?" Ginny cried. "Is he...human now?"

Tucker squatted down beside her, sympathy etched in his features. "Far from it. Still can't be exposed to the sun, still has his abilities and needs blood to sustain himself. He's actually *more* vampiric than before—and Roksana is right. It comes with a lot of complications." He sighed. "Now that's he's tasted his human mate's blood, he can't drink from anyone or anywhere else." He rubbed at the back of his neck. "Or he can...but it won't make a dent in the thirst. Won't nourish him and he'll..."

"Weaken," Elias said succinctly. "Die."

Ginny's ribs caved inward. "No." She shook her head and tried to gain her feet once more, pushing at Roksana's traitorous hands. "You weren't going to tell me this? You thought I would let him *die*?"

"He made me promise," she said, lunging to her feet in between Ginny and the door, fending her off with outstretched hands. "Put yourself in his position. He doesn't want you to spend your life as a...as a-a—"

"Snack," Elias pronounced. "A permanent one. Every day of your life."

The ground shook under the intensity of Jonas's next bellow. Dust puffed down from the ceiling, distracting her three friends long enough to allow Ginny to lunge for the door, shaking the handle. "Open it. Let me go to him."

"Think first, sweetheart," Tucker said, oh-so-casually laying a hand on the door to keep it closed. "He's our friend. He saved our lives, once upon a time. We don't want to watch him die any more than you do. But he made his wishes clear."

Ginny's mind went back to their conversation in the alley outside the bar. Before she truly knew what they were talking about. "Elias said he wouldn't want to keep me away if he knew the separation was causing me pain."

"Pain that will subside if he..." Elias paced down the hallway and halted, hands on hips. "When he eventually goes."

Every snapping nerve ending in her body *screamed* at her to get inside the apartment, but she bore down hard on the impulse, attempting to break through the hold desperation had on her. Something inside of her was alive, like a current. And it ran directly to Jonas. But she was her own person. She was a single, solitary woman and in that moment, a trail diverged in front of her.

If she went one direction, her life ahead was a complete mystery. What did it mean to be the mate of a vampire? To quench his thirst each and every day.

She ignored the arousal and satisfaction that tried to make her rush. Instead, she imagined the consequences of embracing this life.

"Will I continue to get older?" she whispered.

Tucker looked down at the floor and nodded.

She absorbed that. "What happens to him when I die?"

"We don't know," Elias said, still turned away. "The few times in the past a vampire mated with a human...they were either executed by the King or..."

"Or?"

"Or their attempt to Silence them didn't work."

Ginny's temples beat heavily, making her dizzy. She closed her eyes and felt Jonas's presence inside the apartment, taciturn and heartsick and miserable. "Me too, Dreamboat," she whispered, splaying a palm on the door.

What if she took the *other* path?

The one with the much clearer future?

She continued to work at the funeral home, surrounded by memories of happy times with her father, while never making *more* happy memories. Of her own.

The very idea of waking up in her bed every morning and knowing Jonas no longer walked the earth flooded her with burning acid. She fell against the door and wheezed through an inhale—and she knew. She knew that searing agony would never go away. It wouldn't fade like the remnants of some crush. Twice now she'd *experienced his pain.* Hadn't she? Yes. A connection like that didn't die. *Letting* it die without a fight would be a travesty.

Furthermore, she wasn't sure she *could* live without him.

Call it intuition, but she was no longer simply herself. Not merely Ginny. She bore the invisible mark of this vampire on her soul. This. Being together. It was supposed to be. Being without him wasn't an option at all. It was taking a machete to the eternal ribbon of fate.

In the firmest voice she could muster, Ginny said, "I understand what I'm doing. Open the door."

Without turning around, she could feel Elias, Tucker and Roksana exchanging looks. That didn't concern her. She was focused on the man on the other side of the door. Now that she'd made the decision to live as his mate, come hell or high water, rightness settled on her shoulders and raised her chin. Whatever obstacles were to come, they would be together. And they would make each other whole.

Elias inserted a key into the lock, twisted and pushed open the door.

Jonas was nowhere in sight, but his scent slid down her throat like warm, minty chocolate, sweet and welcome. Instinct told her where he was—and the realization made her eyes flood with moisture.

"He's chained in that room, isn't he? With the silver?"

"On his order," Roksana said. "We need to leave him chained, Ginny. Until he gets himself under control. He's…not himself right now."

"The control he must have exercised…" Tucker whistled under his breath. "To taste his mate and not only deny himself more, but make it home and lock himself up. It must have damn near killed him."

Ginny's heart twisted painfully. "Well his suffering ends now." She squared her shoulders and strode in the direction of the back room—

Only to be felled by a wave of pain so astronomical, it made the first two episodes seem like a sneeze. In the center of the living room, she doubled over and landed hard on her right shoulder, screaming pitifully at the top of her lungs. Razors slashed at her insides and fire climbed her throat, needing, needing, needing…

Distantly, she heard chains rattling and Jonas's broken shouting of her name.

Roksana dropped down beside Ginny, her expression tortured. "*What do we do?*"

Nothing. There was nothing they could do.

She had to do it.

She had to get to Jonas.

Now. Or something told Ginny the pain would overcome her.

Battling the blistering waves traveling through her middle, Ginny positioned herself onto her stomach and crawled on her hands and knees down the hallway. At some point, Elias ran ahead and opened the door—and revealed Jonas.

Or what used to be Jonas, anyway.

CHAPTER FIFTEEN

HER PRINCE WAS no more.

In his place was the embodiment of sunken eyed starvation. His manacled wrists were bloody and ravaged, hair sweaty and matted to his forehead. He was shirtless for the first time since Ginny had met him, but her perusal of him yielded no enjoyment. Lord no. He was gaunt, his muscles straining beneath waxy skin.

The wild look in his eye stopped Ginny mid-crawl, even though it hurt to put any kind of hitch in her momentum. How would she ever get moving again? Because no matter how feral Jonas looked, she would continue. She *would* go to him. If anything, his appearance made the journey more urgent.

Move.

Ginny slid a knee forward on the wooden hallway floor, smacking a palm down and pulling her throbbing body closer. She completed the movement twice more before she realized Jonas had stopped rattling his chains. A glance in his direction showed him down on his knees, watching her in horror.

"*What is wrong with her?*" Jonas boomed, making the floorboards tremble. He pulled on the chains with a desperate sound. "*Ginny!*"

"We think she's feeling your pain."

His breath left him in a shuddering rush. "*No.*" Slowly, his head started to shake in vehement denial. "No, she can't be feeling this. I can't let it go on. Elias, bring me a stake. Put it through my fucking heart."

"Don't ask that of me," Elias seethed.

Jonas's green eyes blazed over Ginny, his wrists restless in their chains. "She will suffer until I go otherwise. *No.* No, God. It could take *weeks*. Don't you understand?"

"You aren't going anywhere," Ginny managed, almost to the threshold of the room where Jonas had imprisoned himself.

"Stop where you are," Jonas ordered, even as his fangs sliced into view. "Elias. Tucker. Stop her *immediately*."

"I've made my decision." The pain started to lessen in degrees and she barely kept herself from slumping to the floor. "You're my decision, Jonas."

"You don't know what you're saying," he croaked, a hint of his usual regal self peeking through. "Take the way out. Now. Otherwise it's fucking forever, Ginny."

Didn't he think she'd considered that? Didn't he think she'd weighed the fear of the unknown against a life without him?

The pain had left her so weak, it was impossible to form words and breathe at the same time, so she just kept going. He wouldn't be able to deny her once they were touching, so that was her goal.

When she reached him, Jonas's princely presence was once again eclipsed by the starving vampire. He jerked toward her with a growl, teeth bared, his naked chest heaving. "Get out."

"No."

The floorboards quaked beneath her knees, lights flickering in the hallway. "*Get out.*"

In lieu of answering—obviously he wasn't going to listen or give her credit for knowing her own mind— Ginny reached up and molded a palm to Jonas's cheek. A shudder passed through him, his lids turning heavy. He leaned his face into her palm, whispering her name. "Ginny. Love, my love, my love…"

"It's going to be okay now," she said softly, pushing aside his chaotic hair. "You can't make decisions like this without me. Do you know what it would have done to me if you'd died? Because of me?"

"You'd have been safer," he muttered thickly. "Happier."

"Not happier. Never that."

His body was still tense but the air of violence hovering around him had thinned. Now he swayed toward her with a clenched jaw, as if chastising himself for needing to get closer. Well Ginny wasn't having that.

She looked back over her shoulder at their three friends. Elias had his back turned, Tucker looked fascinated by the sight of Ginny and Jonas on the floor. Roksana looked afraid for her, so Ginny tried to reassure her with a small smile. "Close the door, please."

"Are you sure?" Roksana asked.

"Completely."

"Hang the key by the door," Jonas rasped. "Where I can't reach it."

Elias grunted his agreement and hooked the key on a nail that had been hammered into the wall by the entrance. Seconds later, they were alone. Jonas was stretched as close to Ginny as he could get while attached to the chains and his body was beginning to shake. "It won't always be like this, love. I won't wither after a single day without your…"

"My blood."

His swallow was audible. "I've been neglecting my appetite. Some part of me knew the minute we met, nothing would ever taste the same again." He strained against his bonds, sending a ripple across the muscles of his abdomen. "Jesus Christ. I'm so afraid of hurting you, Ginny. *Please* God don't let me hurt you."

"You won't. If you'd lock yourself up to keep from hurting me, if you'd willingly *die* for me, how can I not be safe?"

"I haven't recognized myself these past twenty-four hours. I've never drunk directly from a human before and my first human is *my mate*," he said hoarsely. "You can't know what I'll do."

She took a deep breath to calm the fluttering of her pulse. "I guess that's why we have the chains."

His skepticism did nothing to quell the hungry way he looked at her. As if beckoning her closer with his gorgeous face and seductive green eyes, while worrying at the same time she'd actually obey. That worry thinned and vanished, making way for lustful awe, when Ginny placed a hand on his chest and pushed him into a sitting position. Soothing him with gentle strokes of her fingertips, she climbed onto his lap and straddled him.

An animal groan burst out of Jonas, his hips shifting beneath her, the links of the chains clinking together.

"I made your heart beat," she whispered, pressing her ear to the center of his chest, listening in awestruck silence to the hectic thrum. "It's beautiful."

"*No*. No, it *aches*. It burns. It's heavy with longing for you, but it also needs your blood to keeping beating and that makes...that makes the longing *savage*. You have to get away from me."

"No," Ginny breathed. She patiently waited for him to settle, before sliding closer on his lap. Right up until the tight material of her skirt prevented her from opening her legs to accommodate his shifting hips.

Maintaining their intense eye contact, she reached down tugged the skirt higher, higher, his energy turning more and more fraught with every inch. She intended to stop once her thighs were able to hug him tightly, but something rebelled inside of her and before she knew it, the entire skirt was rucked up around her waist and she was settling her panties atop the ridge in his jeans.

Both of them tested the friction and moaned.

Jonas angled his head and licked into her mouth slowly, threatening to erode her composure. "What *is* this little outfit you're wearing, love?" he rasped, letting his tongue rest on her lower lip. Dragging it side to side. "Did you think by looking the part of a sacrifice, you might help persuade me to take it?"

"I'm not a sacrifice." She shook her head. "I can't explain how I know this, but tonight feels...inevitable. Don't you feel that?"

"*Yes*," he hissed, his handsome face contorting with pain. "I hate that you felt an ounce of this pain. It's going to haunt me forever."

There were painful stirrings inside Ginny, telling her another episode was approaching and while she wanted to avoid that, she wanted to alleviate Jonas's agony just as much. She leaned in and kissed him softly, hating the tremors passing through him, knowing first hand they were unbearable.

"Ginny, I can't have you this close much longer without—"

"I know." She stroked his face. "It won't...make me a vampire?"

"There's a venom inside of us that only releases when a victim is close to..." His eyes squeezed shut. "Dying. It's involuntary, a product of our true nature as predators and it's the only thing that can transform a human...God help me, I won't let it get that far. I'd *never* make you like me."

Entranced by the fangs he'd exposed to her in his vehemence, Ginny gathered her long hair in a fist and arranged it to one side. "I trust you."

And then she offered him her neck.

GREEN EMBERS WHIPPED up in Jonas's eyes. He still seemed determined to fight his obvious thirst for her. To Ginny, his lust was intoxicating. It wasn't only for her blood, either. With her neck exposed and vulnerable, she felt his shaft thicken between her legs and her nipples peaked in response. Her inhales and exhales grew sharp, uneven, and she could no more stop herself from rocking in his lap than she could shoot lasers from her fingertips.

"You make me wish desperately for the use of my hands," he rasped.

"What would you do with them?"

"Hold your ass still before it causes too much trouble."

Oh my. He definitely didn't sound like a prince anymore—and she minded it far less than she could have imagined. "What trouble is it causing?"

"I crave my mate in more ways than one, love," Jonas said, elevating his hips along with Ginny, who could only grasp his shoulders and whimper. "And I've craved constantly for days, though I'd swear it was decades."

Their mouths surged together in a kiss that was at once rough and reverent. Being positioned on Jonas's lap put their mouths level and they couldn't get close enough. He transferred low growls into her mouth, licking them away with his tongue, his lips demanding and seductive and intuitive. By the time he broke away and ordered Ginny to breathe, she was dizzy and aroused. So aroused. Her hands stroked up and down his chest in worship, the word *please* falling from her swollen lips over and over and over.

Though she begged for Jonas to give her what they both needed, she still gasped in shock when he fisted her hair tightly, his expression nothing short of predatory. Nothing short of electric and thrilling.

He leaned down and licked the side of her neck, long and slow. "*Mine,*" he breathed, planting a hot, open-mouthed kiss over her pulse. "Inevitably, undeniably mine. May God help us all."

Ginny braced herself for pain—and she got it. The shocking sting made her body jolt and twist, but a flood of numbing warmth ensued so quickly afterward, she stilled. As if on command. Stilled and felt the sharp fangs sinking into her. Heard Jonas's muffled exclamation against her skin, followed by an exultant groan.

She'd been caught.

Possessed.

She belonged right there, in his lap, locked to his body and accepting his bite, incapable of moving. Even if she could have, she wouldn't. That truth sang in her blood as Jonas took it into his mouth greedily, the flesh between his legs rising further to meet her. *Needing* her.

Ginny's thighs started to tremble around his hips and she longed to rub herself shamelessly on his erection. *Need to move. Need to move.* Heat inundated her, making her skin feel flushed, her femininity restless. If she could just twist a little, she could rub her nipples against his chest and maybe get some relief, because it seemed to be so near.

So near.

Her thoughts started to jumble and her view of the wall winked in and out. Too much? Was Jonas taking too much blood? Her power of speech was absent, so she couldn't warn him. On some level, she even loathed to stop him. He was insatiable for the taste of her, still groaning with as much satisfaction as he had in the first few seconds, his mouth suctioned to her neck like it might disappear. And now it had been...how long *had* they been...doing this...?

Jonas tore himself away from Ginny with obvious difficulty, running his glittering, jewel tone gaze over her face, looking like a man who'd sold his soul to the devil and wouldn't take it back for anything in the world. His fangs were still out and he licked them now, a shuddering wracking him. "My God is your sustenance *sweet*." He laid kisses on her hairline, her cheeks, ending with a hard pull of her mouth. "Tell me you're okay, love. Tell me I didn't go too far. *Ginny*."

"I'm fine." She tunneled her fingers into his hair. "I'm fine."

He pressed their foreheads together. "If you knew...if you only knew what your taste *does* to me. You're a feast after a famine." He shook his head slowly and whispered, "Thank you."

His adoring tone did nothing to dispel the hunger he'd coaxed. Not at all. She was finally able to move and her body sprang into action, trying to make up for the time she'd been immobile. Her fingertips rode up his hard body, nails digging into his shoulders, her hips starting a slow buck she didn't seem in control of. This wasn't mere desire, there was something about the bite that made every sensation fuller, made her limbs languid and light.

"Good," he said thickly in her ear. "Take what you need from me now. If my hands weren't chained, I'd lay you down and give it to you so fucking good."

Since when did epithets turn her on? Maybe since they were delivered in a throaty growl and every tweak of her hips seemed to make him…swell. Harden. Was she really doing this? Seeking relief from Jonas came naturally, even though she'd never been there in her life. Not with him or anyone else. And yet, her body knew exactly where she needed to go and urged her to ride, get there, grind, *get there*.

"You came in here so beautiful and brave," he gritted, leaning back to watch the point where their lower bodies were creating the most frantic friction, cotton panties moving on top of strained denim. "Hiked up your little skirt for me and offered me your gorgeous neck, didn't you?"

"Yes," she sobbed.

"My bite made you wet," he enunciated. "Didn't it?"

She nodded jerkily and quickened her pace, sensing the end of her frustration looming. Finally. *Finally.*

In response to her silent confession, Jonas's head fell back on a moan. "Might be time to get some mirrors. I'd give anything to watch your tight backside pumping all over my lap right now."

A volcano of bliss erupted inside of her, trapping a

gasp in her throat. His words stabbed at her composure like little daggers and she bore down, prolonging the rush of relief by grinding up and back on his thickness. "Oh Lord, oh Lord, oh Lord," she whimpered, raking her nails down his back. "It feels so good."

"Remember that feeling," he said, pressing his bared teeth to her cheek. "You only get it from your mate. *Ever.*"

His satisfaction purred in her ear, but she could still feel that hard part of Jonas prodding her panties—and it was pure instinct that made Ginny crawl backward and kneel between his outstretched legs, though her own were still shaking. She reached for the zipper of his jeans and paused, not only at his sharp curse, but because she was overcome by the sight of him.

Jonas Cantrell sprawled out in nothing but jeans and permanently flexed muscles, arms suspended in the air in chains, his midnight hair in a mess from her fingers? He might have been God's gift to women if he wasn't looking at Ginny with total and utter worship. The kind that let her know *on purpose* that it would only ever be her. And she was dead certain she looked back at him in the same manner. Their pure idolization went both ways.

His worshipful attention gave Ginny confidence, made her feel sexy. Maybe for the first time in her entire life. Jonas might have made her feel *wanted like hell* before, but this was different. She'd just worked out an orgasm on his lap after he'd drunk her blood.

Boundaries? What boundaries?

Before the heady freedom could slide away, Ginny reached down and caught the hem of her tank top, drawing it over her head, leaving herself clad in nothing but a hiked up skirt, thong and a lacy bra.

"Sweet Jesus," he whispered. "You're an angel."

Her fingers skated up his denim clad thighs and lowered the zipper of his jeans. The words she wanted to say bounced around in her throat until she overcome her final vestige of shyness. "I'm *your* angel."

Possession whipped in his eyes. "Oh yes, you are. Even when you're thinking of doing something quite the opposite of angelic."

She leaned down and kissed the trail of dark hair on his belly. "Do you want me to stop?" she asked, exploring the outline of him with her fingertips.

In response, a sconce on the wall zapped and went dead.

"I need to be a gentleman," he grated.

Her lips curled against his skin. "With *that* mouth?"

"Does it…offend you?"

"No." She fisted his length in her hand, awed by the texture, smooth over hard. So hard. And long. "I like it," she whispered.

"Are we talking about my mouth or my—" He cut himself off with a groan when Ginny gave him a test stroke, loving the way his hips lifted as if propelled, his abdomen flexing almost violently. "Christ. It's going to kill me to stop you."

"Why do you want to stop me?"

"*Want* to? No." He yanked on his chains once, then visibly calmed himself. His eyes remained closed for several seconds. "I've never...released, Ginny. Not since I was Silenced."

Her brow knit. "You told me you'd been with—"

"Pleasure is one thing, but without my mate...without you, there's nothing to show for it." His expression was a mixture of humor and hunger. "So to speak."

"Oh."

"I'm going to be inside you when it happens for the first time. And before we ever get there, I'm going to need full use of my hands and mouth."

Wicked images danced in her mind. "Oh."

His lips twitched, as if he could read her thoughts. "I'm already worried about tempering my strength with you, Ginny." Those eyes dropped and raked up her thighs. "I won't have you anything less than ready on top of it."

Her nipples tingled. "Oh," she whispered again, like a simpleton. "When we...will you... get me pregnant?"

"No." Regret shone on his face. "No, I can't. If I did have that ability, you know I would—"

She stopped him with a kiss. His answer didn't inspire a sense of loss or make her question the decision she'd made upon walking into the apartment. She would never have children. It was a fact to be absorbed and not a blow to the system. Her life could still be full, just the same, without this part of life she'd never strongly considered to begin with.

"Okay," she said quietly, rubbing their foreheads together. "Okay."

"Okay?" he breathed.

"Yes."

His throat worked. "One more thing, Ginny?"

"Yes?"

"I derive more pleasure from holding your hand than I've had in my entire goddamn life combined. Just so we're clear."

A pressure she hadn't been aware of living in her chest evaporated like it never existed, leaving warmth and yearning behind. "Can I please unlock you now?"

His nostrils flared. "Yes, I think so."

Ginny pinched Jonas's zipper between her fingers and drew it back up slowly, watching the play of muscles shifting on his stomach. Even while so still, the energy Jonas threw off was electric. Urgent. Focused on her. She almost stumbled when she reached her feet and turned to retrieve the keys. Jonas's growl and rattling of the chains reminded her the skirt was still hiked up around his hips—and that she wasn't wearing a top.

Muttering apologies, she yanked down the skirt and pulled the tank top over her head. Beginning to lose her patience over having him in captivity like some animal, she hastily grabbed the keys. She remained standing while freeing his right hand from the first shackle, her breath catching when he immediately slung an arm around her hips and drew her close, open-mouth kissing her stomach, drawing on it greedily as if it were her mouth.

"Sh-should I keep going?"

He pulled his mouth away, rolling his forehead side to side against her stomach, before withdrawing completely. "Yes." Those eyes found her and held. "I'm in as much control as I'll ever be around you."

With a click, she opened the second shackle and immediately found herself across the small room, trapped between her vampire and the door. "As soon as I get a handle on myself where you're concerned, Ginny," he groaned into her neck. "I am going to fuck you *endlessly*."

Everything south of her belly button clenched. "There's that mouth again."

His grin was so promissory, it almost made her cry. Stepping back slightly, he lifted Ginny in his arms and opened the door without laying a finger on the handle. One look at Roksana where she stood at the end of the hallway and Ginny knew she'd heard quite a bit of what took place in the room.

Elias and Tucker appeared on either side of her, their shoulders relaxing when they deduced that all was well. "Looking good, prince," Tucker called, good-naturedly.

"You get a haircut or something?"

"Funny," Jonas drawled.

Staring up at him with her cheek against his shoulder, Ginny had to admit he *did* look incredible. Even better than the first time she'd met him, which is saying something, considering the man was eight steps above handsome. His eyes were clear now, his skin glowing with health. Sure, his hair was still disheveled from the last twenty-four hours, but it was visibly richer in color. Had she really been responsible for the transformation? Such a thing seemed impossible.

What *didn't* seem impossible anymore?

Jonas carried her into his room, leaving the door open behind them. He laid her down in his bed and pressed a soft kiss to her mouth. "Sleep."

Drowsiness caught up with her with the utterance of that single word and her lids turned heavy. "Jonas?" she asked, noting the wounds on his wrists inflicted by the silver already looked less painful. "What happens now that we're breaking two of the rules?"

Silence ticked past. "My sanity, my soul, my existence, depend on you being mine." He ground a fist to his chest, right above his heart. "*This* cannot be governed by rules. I was a fool to think it ever could." With a final lingering kiss of her lips, he stood and left the room.

The door closed, leaving no sound behind, save Ginny's racing pulse.

CHAPTER SIXTEEN

G INNY WOKE UP to the sound of arguing.

In the absence of windows, she had no way to gauge the time of day. Until she started searching for her cell, she didn't realize it was still at Enders. Along with her purse. With a groan, she climbed out of bed, the events from the previous night coming back to her in a river of color and sensation.

She was Jonas's mate now. For life.

A hot shiver danced across the nape of her neck.

Her new reality felt like anything *but* reality, especially since her old responsibilities remained. She still needed to call Larissa and check to see if they'd received any new client inquiries. Then there was the matter of tonight's dress expo and the finishing touches she still needed to put on her collection. Normal things—she was actually grateful for them, though she wondered if performing her usual routines would ever feel remotely the same again when this aching need for Jonas was now a part of her.

How could she miss him to the point of pain when

he was in the next room?

Pressing a hand to her stuttering heart, Ginny stepped out into the hallway.

The arguing ceased abruptly.

She turned the corner into the kitchen, finding three vampires and one slayer in a state of suspended animation.

Her gaze sought out Jonas immediately. He stood with his palms flat on the kitchen table facing Roksana, agitation lingering on his face. It faded when he saw Ginny. "Good morning," he rasped, scanning her head to toe, his fingers curling on the table.

"Morning," she breathed, tingles breaking out along her limbs. *There are other people around.* Mentally shaking herself, she tucked some hair behind her ear, positive she looked like she'd slept in a bush during a windstorm. "Do you have a mirror, Roksana?"

"I do not," she said, holding out her phone to Ginny. "Flip my camera."

"I'll save you time," Jonas said in a gruff tone. "You look amazing."

"Goddamn. Could you two bring it down a notch?" Elias asked, his face buried in the refrigerator. "It's uncomfortable."

"Not for me," Tucker said, leaning back in his chair. "I'll watch any time. Sign me up."

Jonas slid him a sideways glance. "Not in your wildest dreams."

Tucker shrugged. "Worth a shot."

Ginny held up the reverse camera and winced at her tornado victim appearance, quickly lowering the phone. "What was everyone arguing about before?"

Everyone looked at Jonas.

He pushed away from the table. Started to answer and stopped. "We've been discussing how best to proceed safely. Now that you and I are…" He shoved his hands into his pants pockets. "Now that we're together." Intense eyes ticked to hers. "Indefinitely."

Her abdomen squeezed. "You mean, how to proceed safely so we aren't discovered?"

"Take your seat on the Order and change the laws." Elias smacked the refrigerator shut, but kept his back turned. "You refuse a position many covet."

"Clarence will never change the laws," Jonas intoned. "By trying to convince him to do so for my own gain, I'd only be putting her in jeopardy."

"I don't care what you bloodsuckers decide to do," Roksana sighed. "I'm only here to protect the human."

Jonas shook his head. "Yes, you did a fine job of that by bringing *my mate* to a slayer bar. Didn't you realize how valuable she'd be to them? To draw me out?"

"It's not something a human could sense," Roksana seethed. "She was safe."

"Everyone stop," Ginny said, going to Jonas and

laying a hand on his arm. "There's no point in fighting about it now. I'm fine."

Jonas shuddered at her touch. "Ginny…"

"You were chained in a room planning to off yourself," she said unevenly. "And you have the nerve to shout about me going out for one beer?"

"Ahhh." Tucker laughed and slapped the table. "Human women don't lose arguments, man. They have a filing system of shit you did wrong. You better recognize."

"Is that true?" Jonas asked, amusement softening his expression.

"I don't know." Her nose wrinkled. "I've never won an argument, because I've never been in a relationship."

"Thank God for that," he murmured, leaning in to look at her mouth.

She quickly reared back. "I don't have a toothbrush here," she blurted, covering her mouth. "That wasn't me asking for one, either. I know it's only my second time staying over."

"And?"

"And…I don't know." Heat stole up her neck. "I don't want you to think I'm presuming anything."

Jonas glanced over at Roksana. "What am I missing?"

"Don't ask the slayer," Elias drawled. "She doesn't know how normal women think."

"She's worried you'll think she's a clinger." Roksana

flashed Elias her middle finger. "I usually worry more about the *men* I date getting clingy. So annoying when that happens." With a sharp sound of irritation, Elias blurred from the kitchen so fast, it left a smug Roksana's hair floating in the air. "Touchy touchy."

"Why wouldn't I want you to cling to me?" Jonas asked, ignoring the scene. "I expect you to cling, Ginny."

"It's just that we haven't had a conversation about…logistics. When we'll see each other and where. Are you just going to appear in my bedroom at nighttime? Am I still going to be blindfolded everywhere we go? Am I—"

"She's feeling insecure, Jonas," Tucker called. "Fix it."

"Oh I will," he said slowly, studying her with harder than usual intensity. "As soon as I figure out the most effective way. Although I'm not sure anything says 'I'm committed' more than making a woman one's sustaining life force."

"You're thinking like a vampire," Tucker said. "She's a human. She needs human gestures."

"Hey." Ginny crossed her arms. "Stop talking about me like I'm not here."

Jonas's lips tugged. "Sorry, love. Are you hungry?"

"Yes." She set her voice to a whisper. "Are you?"

"Always," he breathed, lids drooping. "I can wait, though."

"Can you?"

"I'm going to exercise restraint from the beginning." Jonas circled his thumb in the hollow of her throat. "I will *not* overwhelm you."

He turned and zipped to the counter before she could reply, remaining poised with his fists on the counter a moment, before reaching for the carton of eggs on the counter. What would have been her reply? That, oddly, she *liked* how it felt when he took his fill? That it felt like relief and homecoming, all rolled into one? Did that make her shameful or weird?

Ginny shook herself. "Roksana, can I use your phone to call Larissa? I left my things at the bar."

Roksana rolled her eyes over Jonas's growl. "Sure thing, lady."

She took the phone into the living room and sat down on the couch, keying in the number to the funeral home by memory. Ginny's stepmother answered on the second ring. "P. Lynn Funeral Home."

"Larissa. Hi, it's Ginny."

"*Ginny.* Where are you? I came down for a box of tissues because I still feel like shit and there were *five messages* from a man wanting to schedule his son's services. I can't meet with him. I'm like a *zombie*."

She held on to her patience. "When does he want to meet?"

"Tonight. Six o'clock. I know your shift doesn't start

until later, but—"

"Oh, Larissa. I would do it, but my dress expo is tonight—"

"Your what?"

Ginny closed her eyes. "Nothing. I'll just set up late. Can you confirm the appointment and let him know I'll be there?"

"Yes. Fine." She sounded like a deflating raft. "Ginny, we have to sell this place, even if we take a loss. This is like the Groundhog Day from hell. I'm not cut out for being surrounded by death and sad people. I swear I think it's making me ill."

"Okay, Larissa," Ginny pushed through numb lips. "I'll really sit down and consider it this week. I mean that. I don't want you to be miserable."

"Aren't you miserable, too? Don't you want to try something new? We could...I don't know. We could try something new together, even? I'm not that bad, am I?" Her stepmother bit off a curse. "Listen to me rambling. I'm just stressed."

"It's fine." Ginny pressed her lips together. "Bye, Larissa."

The line was already dead.

Ginny let the phone drop to her lap, starting when she found Jonas standing at the end of the couch, watching her with concern.

"Did you hear all of that?" she asked.

Equations solving themselves behind his golden eyes. "Yes."

She nodded, grateful when he didn't press. "I have to go home."

"I know." It was clear he didn't like it, too. "Tonight is important to you. Roksana will stay with you until I can…"

"Go outside?"

Jonas remained unmoving. But for the first time, the differences between them were a long-term problem. They weren't just details that would no longer matter once her memory was erased. Jonas couldn't go outside in the sunlight. They could never walk along the boardwalk together, or even lie in bed on a Sunday morning with light streaming in through the window.

When did she do those things anyway?

In a way, she already kept the hours of a vampire, sleeping through most of the day and working the night shift. Staying indoors during the day wouldn't even be that big of an adjustment for her, but Jonas looked concerned nonetheless.

"It's okay," she said. "I'll miss you until tonight, but it's okay."

"I'll miss you, too. Mercilessly." The vein in his temple ticked as he held out a hand. "Come have breakfast."

It was definitely a new experience, eating breakfast while sitting on Jonas's lap, his thumb brushing back and forth against the small of her back. She was thankful Roksana had some of the eggs, too, so she didn't have to be the only one eating. Once they were finished and they all pitched in cleaning the dishes, her stomach started to jangle with nerves. Because she was leaving Jonas?

That's what it felt like. As if they were going to be on opposite sides of the country, instead of opposite ends of Coney Island.

"I can hear your pulse beating fast, love," he whispered in her ear. "It's going to be all right."

Ginny fanned her face. "Why do I feel like this?"

"I hate letting you go, too, but I don't know if our reasons match." He tucked her head beneath his chin. "Maybe you're worried the pain will come back if you leave me. It won't. Not before I see you again."

"I'd be more worried about the pain coming back for you...but I don't think that's it." She tried to find a way to put her anxiety into words. "Everything feels so fragile. Like this...*us*...could get taken away any minute."

He kissed her forehead hard. "We're the opposite of fragile, you and me."

Still walking on pins and needles, Ginny nodded. *Pull it together*. They couldn't be together twenty-four hours a day. They both had responsibilities. They were independent people. She had to work the funeral home and maintain her interests. He had the newbies to train. If she fell victim now to the impulse to never leave

Jonas's side, she'd never overcome it in the future.

"Why are you worried about letting *me* leave?"

"While *we* are not fragile, love…you are. You couldn't withstand an accident or a long fall or—" He broke off with a rough exhale. "Roksana, *please.*"

"I'll guard her with my life," the slayer said where she waited at the door. "To the best of my ability. You know I will."

"I know we have to worry about the High Order finding out about us now, but Seymour is gone. You took care of the immediate threat last night," Ginny reminded him, pushing off his lap to her feet. "I'll see you when the sun goes down."

"I'll be watching the clock," he murmured, catching her hand and dusting his lips across her knuckles. "Bye, Ginny." She was almost to the door when Jonas appeared between her and the door with a determined set to his jaw. "Will my mate not kiss me goodbye?"

Flowers bloomed in the soil of her nerve endings, sprouting like spring daisies. "Are you sure that's a good—"

Jonas mouth was already on hers, depleting her lungs of breath. He took it into himself and gave it back to her in a greedy exchange. The fingers of his right hand molded to the back of her neck, sliding up into her hair and fisting it, his tongue traveling into her mouth to touch their tongues together. Just a hint. And another. Such gentle friction compared to his hold which might as well have been made of steel bars. Ginny's thighs itched to perch on his hips, but he made her too dizzy to follow through, once again pulling the air from her body and breathing it into her once again.

"I carry you in my veins, you carry me in your lungs."

Dazed, she nodded.

With a satisfied smirk, he turned her to face the door where Roksana was still waiting with her eyes averted. "Tonight, Ginny."

She left in such a daze, she didn't realize until they were standing outside on the sidewalk that Jonas didn't blindfold her. Turning to face the building, she realized she'd been sleeping in the basement of the abandoned Shore Theater all along. The men's apartment was a series of dressing rooms, wasn't it? That's where those big-bulbed frames came from.

"Nothing surprises me anymore," she murmured, staring up at the boarded up arches and vintage stone-work.

"No?" Roksana said, tossing her a wink. "In this world, when things stop surprising you, wait five minutes."

In that moment, Ginny didn't know enough to acknowledge the truth of her friend's words. She would soon enough.

CHAPTER SEVENTEEN

GINNY STEPPED ASIDE to avoid being run over by Larissa and her suitcase.

"What do you mean you're outta here?"

"I'll explain it one more time," her stepmother called over her shoulder. "An investor called and asked if the business was for sale. I told him, yes, of course. That he should get in touch with you to make an offer. But he was only interested in *my* share."

Larissa ran back up the stairs, emerging a moment later with another suitcase, this one bursting at the seams with undergarments.

"I don't know why I never thought of that angle before, but your father's will states that the company would be split fifty-fifty in the event of his demise. There's no language precluding me from transferring my portion to someone else. And it's done." She held up her arms in a touchdown signal. "Hallelujah. I'm out."

"But…" Ginny pressed the back of her wrist to her forehead. "You just sold half of the business without speaking to me?"

"I spoke to my lawyer."

Ginny sat down on the stairs out of necessity. Her legs would no longer support her. "But I don't even *know* this person."

"I'm sorry, sweetie, but that's no longer my problem." Larissa slowed on her third trip up the stairs, sighing as she passed Ginny. "Look, you're a good girl. Kind of weird, but nobody's perfect. I gave it the old college try, honey." She lifted a hand and let it drop. "This place just gives me the fucking creeps."

"Did you really love my father?" Ginny blurted the question, unaware that it had been sitting on her tongue for years without being voiced. More than that, it had been eating at her, wondering if this woman who'd soaked up so much of Peter Lynn's legacy had ever known how quietly extraordinary a human being he was. "Did you, Larissa? Because this place you detest so much…is him. It's so him."

"Yes," her stepmother whispered shakily, her eyes turning to two perfect pools of glass. "I did love him. Why do you think I've stayed this long? Why do you think I've been trying so hard to—" She cut herself off with a headshake. "Yes, I loved Peter Lynn, right down to his uneven beard and mismatched socks."

Ginny closed her eyes. "Thank you."

Genuine grief flashed in her stepmother's eyes. "One last chance to come with me." Larissa playfully punched

Ginny in the shoulder. "Make a clean start somewhere."

"I have to stay."

Larissa nodded. "That's that, then, I guess." She looked like she wanted to say more, but she hopped to her feet once more, as if the poignant moment never happened. "The investor offered me double my asking price for fifty percent of P. Lynn. The only condition was I get out today."

"*What?* Are they planning on moving in here?"

Roksana cleared her throat loudly from her hiding spot in Ginny's room.

Larissa whirled around. "Did you hear that?"

"No." Larissa started to creep along the landing in the direction of the noise—and Ginny panicked. "You know how sometimes dead bodies expel air. That must have been it."

"There are no bodies to speak of."

"Oh I didn't mention," Ginny said, scratching her eyebrow. "A new guest arrived just as I did. Had the whole thing arranged. Didn't I tell you?"

"No…" Larissa paused. "Oh, who gives a shit anymore? I'm done. Let the dead bodies do as they will."

Ginny waited until Larissa had disappeared back into her room before speed walking to her own bedroom and closing the door. "What was that?"

Roksana rolled out from beneath the bed. "Ask for the name of the investor."

With that, she trundled back out of view.

A very unladylike curse hovered on Ginny's lips as she stomped back out into the hallway, calling, "Larissa. What did you say this person's name was?"

"Oh, um…what was it…" She poked her head through the doorframe. "J. Cantrell. Sounded kind of cute, too. Maybe you'll get lucky."

Ginny's jaw hung in the vicinity of her knees. From underneath her bed, she could hear Roksana snickering. She didn't know whether to be relieved or livid.

Livid. Definitely livid.

This was the second time in twenty-four hours Jonas had made a huge decision without even dropping her an email. And that was on the heels of a series of decisions he'd made on her behalf since day one. Oh, she'd walked into this relationship with eyes wide open. Less than a day later, however, she was already questioning her sanity.

"How could he do something like that without even asking?" Ginny breathed, walking back to her bedroom in a stupor. "I never would have agreed to let him bail me out. I was figuring out what to do on my own."

"You asked for human gestures."

"No, I didn't. You and Tucker *decided* I needed human gestures."

"Are you really so upset about this?" Roksana asked, still under the bed for some reason. "Jonas is loaded. He won't even feel it and now we don't have to conk old Larissa on the noggin every time we come over. It's good for everyone."

"He can't make decisions this big when they affect us both. How would you feel if Elias—"

"No no no." Roksana's wagging index finger emerged first, followed by the rest of her. "Don't bring him up and kill my chipper mood."

"What happened between you two?" Ginny asked, being more abrasive than usual because this crazy huge thing just happened and Roksana was acting quite cavalier. They'd see how cavalier she'd be when someone prodded *her* sore spot. "He's the reason you can't slaughter them, isn't he?"

Roksana smacked the floor. "I'm doing it tomorrow!"

Ginny snorted.

Larissa appeared in the doorway, staring at Roksana and her leather bustier like they were a personal offense. "Who are *you*?"

"Death. Here to collect," Roksana said, unsheathing a knife from inside her boot. "Go now and I might let you live."

Larissa ran screaming down the stairs as though wild boars were snapping at her heels.

"Well that was unnecessary."

Roksana flipped her knife end over end and caught it. "She had it coming."

A laugh tickled the inside of Ginny's throat, so she smacked a hand over her lips to trap it. Was this going to be her life now? Swinging between the disturbing to the shocking to the absurd with every tick of the clock?

"Clock," she breathed. "What time is it? I have to finish my dresses before tonight and there's the meeting with that man about his son…"

"I'll just be under here," Roksana intoned, vanishing once more beneath Ginny's queen-sized bed. "Wake me up if they bring the snack cart around."

Shaking her head, Ginny got down to business. She wheeled the squeaky garment rack over to her sitting area and fired up her sewing machine. Thankfully there weren't too many things left undone. She polished the hem on her green, wool A-line, for which a Christmas tree had been the inspiration, then sewed on the red holly embellishment over the chest pocket.

The formal, white silk gown required steam cleaning, along with the faux fur being affixed to the collar. And maybe she needed a trail of rhinestones traveling down between the breasts and spreading along the hips?

With a needle and thread permanently stuck between her lips, she'd never worked faster in her life and by the time late afternoon rolled around, she had a full, finished collection, against all odds.

Ginny eyed her napping couch longingly, but there was no time to rest. She sped through a shower, blow drying her hair and applying lip gloss, mascara and some blush. When her usual go-to for anything fancy—that wasn't a funeral—would have been bright and pattered, she found herself reaching for the red, lightweight chiffon number in the back of her closet. A black belt cinched the floaty material in the waist, layers of ruby red cascading to mid-thigh.

And for once, when putting on a dress, she felt exactly like herself. Not Elizabeth Taylor, Lauren Bacall or even Grace Kelly.

Just Ginny.

"I believe they call this a glow up," Roksana murmured, coming up beside her. "Are we over our tiff?"

"It wasn't really a tiff," Ginny sighed.

"Ahhh. You are saving your wrath for Jonas."

Ginny squared her shoulders. "Like I said, he can't make big decisions that affect us both without some kind of communication. It's not fair." She shook her head. "My heart already trusts him, but my mind is another story. I need both on board. Both are important to me."

"He's used to being the prince. He makes a decree, others obey."

"Why?"

Roksana shrugged. "He inspires loyalty. Even from me."

"Does it have something to do with the fact that Jonas helped Elias when he was freshly Silenced?"

"I thought our tiff had ended," sniffed the slayer.

Ginny hid a smile. "I have to get to my meeting. Could you do me a huge favor and put these dresses in garment bags? It'll save me time when we have to leave for the expo."

"Nyet." She slashed a hand across her neck. "I'm not to leave you alone. The Elder might have been eliminated, but now we have the High Order to worry about, since you've deemed it wise to give yourself to a bloodsucker."

"Five minutes. Please?" Ginny was already backing from the room. "I'm going to be running late as it is. And anyway, the sun doesn't go down for another half an hour. It's nature's vampire repellant."

"I'll walk you to the office and make sure there are no intruders. Or spiders. Or sharp edges. I'm not taking any chances with your fragile humanity."

Ginny rolled her eyes, but didn't protest as Roksana followed her down the stairs. "Maybe I'd be better off if…" She watched closely for the slayer's reaction. "If Jonas made me a vampire."

She didn't necessarily mean it. Not yet. Losing her humanity wasn't something she could ever take so lightly. But she wanted to know if it was possible. She wanted to know what it would take. And more importantly, the consequences. Ginny was more interested in satisfying her curious nature than floating the possibility.

Roksana's face remained stoic, but her steps faltered. "You would no longer be able to sustain him."

A pang hit her in the throat, the memory of him pale and out of his mind with hunger rushing to the fore. "Would anything sustain him if I was Silenced?"

"There've been no cases like yours. Vampire mates with girl, girl becomes only source of nourishment for vampire, girl turns to vampire...I don't know what happens after that."

Ginny processed that, the fear of the unknown weighing in her stomach like a boulder. She stood in the middle of the lobby while Roksana checked every shadow and hiding spot, clomping across the burgundy carpet with a sense of purpose, until finally she gave Ginny the all clear.

"Do not leave this office," Roksana said, punching the air with her finger. "I'll be back. Right after I bag these dresses like I'm someone who earns minimum wage and says things like 'I'll try and get a sitter.'"

"You're the best," Ginny called back, already pulling out her sample books and paperwork in preparation for the meeting. She took out the laptop and opened their trusty—and often malfunctioning—database to read through the information Larissa should have entered for tonight's meeting. There was nothing there, though. Simply the initial "C," a phone number and the appointment time. "Guess Larissa already had one foot out the door," Ginny murmured.

A thunderclap brought Ginny's head up.

Was it supposed to rain? Last time she checked, the sky had been clear.

There were no windows in her small, airless office, but when the lobby darkened considerably, she rose from her seat. The lights were still on, but the windows were almost black from the sudden storm. She came around the desk and stopped in the doorway, her heart flying into her throat when thunder rolled, immediately followed by a crack of lightning, briefly illuminating the empty lobby.

There. In the far end, near the visitation room.

Had she seen an outline of somebody or were her eyes playing tricks on her?

All she could hear in the muted stillness was the sound of her own breathing. In out in out. Something was missing. The gentle ticking of the grandfather clock. Had it stopped working? In the absence of enough light, she couldn't see the time indicated by the two hands. The sound of rain intruded, pelting the windows like Tic Tacs falling from the sky and thunder blustered again, followed by another blast of lightning.

A movement occurred in her periphery and she whipped her head in that direction. Nothing. Just the movement of shadow, surely.

The hair on the back of Ginny's neck stood up.

Slowly, she backed into the office and closed the door, twisting the lock. Roksana would be downstairs any minute. Of course Ginny was spooked. Her life had become a parade of the unusual. Things that never existed before were her new normal. Once a vampire makes an attempt on one's life, one may never feel truly safe again. Wasn't that a universal truth?

Someone knocked on the office door.

Once.

Pause.

Twice.

Pause.

A third time.

Roksana wouldn't knock.

Ginny reached back and gripped the desk, remaining as still as possible. Who was on the other side of the door? If it was a vampire that wanted to do her harm, there would be nothing she could do to stop them. Even if she had a big, nasty stake, she didn't have the skill or speed to drive it home.

Another, louder knock made her jump, her hand flying up to cover her mouth. "Ginny?"

Her hand dropped away. "Tucker?"

"What's good, sweetheart?"

She heaved a choppy laugh and unlocked the door, opening it to find Tucker in a rain slicker and Wellingtons. Gold chain. No shirt. "Crazy weather we're having."

"Yeah, it's not often I get outside before six o'clock in the fall. I feel like a kid again." Even as he made the joke, Ginny could see the concern lurking in the corners of his downturned mouth. "Where's Roks?"

"Bagging my dresses for tonight."

"I'm right here," the slayer said, striding into the room, wooden stake at her side. "What the hell is up with this storm?"

"You mind putting that thing away?" Tucker waited for her to tuck the weapon into her boot. "I don't know. It came on pretty fast."

"Too fast," Roksana muttered. "Where is the prince?"

"He's going to be late. That newbie he met with the other day is having an existential crisis. He'll meet us there." He hopped up onto the desk and tossed a wink at Ginny. "Until then, I'm putting the body back in bodyguard."

Fighting a smile, Ginny checked the time on her laptop. "My meeting is late. I'll just call him to make sure he's still coming."

She picked up the office phone and dialed, getting a series of beeps in her ear. "The number you dialed is no longer in service," she murmured, repeating after the robotic voice. "We'll give him five more minutes."

Her appointment never arrived.

A while later, as she, Roksana and Tucker carried her dresses out and loaded them into the waiting car, Ginny looked up at the sky and couldn't find the merest whisper of a cloud.

CHAPTER EIGHTEEN

I T WAS ONE thing to be the outcast of Embrace the Lace. It was quite another to have so many people witnessing the obvious shunning.

Ginny had been assigned to a display table in the mustiest, darkest corner of the church basement, complete with cobwebs and rattling radiator. The light panel overhead no longer worked, leaving her in the shadows. There was a clear division of her and everyone else, the other tables bathed in light and surrounded by friends and family, who'd come to see the hard work of their loved ones and place bids on the finished dresses.

Ginny had Roksana and Tucker.

They basically waltzed in, fell into the two metal folding chairs she'd been allotted and glowered at everyone who even considered a visit to the distant glacier that was her table.

With a final adjustment, Ginny stepped back from the mannequin to which she'd affixed her Christmas dress and removed the pin from her mouth. "Did I mention how glad I am that you're both here?"

The pair grunted and continued their hard scrutiny of every living soul in the basement.

"That being said, if you could try and appear just a *smidgen* less life threatening, that might help increase traffic to my table."

"This is just my face," Roksana drawled.

"This basement is a fire trap and the alley out back doesn't exit to a street. Coincidentally, if something happens to you, Jonas is going to set fire to my insides." Tucker held up his hands, palms out. "His words, not mine."

"How am I supposed to auction off my dresses if you're scaring everyone away?"

Roksana shrugged a shoulder. "*We* could bid."

Tucker batted his eyelashes. "Do you have anything in turquoise?"

Ginny slumped. She'd harbored no delusions that she would arrive tonight and suddenly be the belle of the ball. But she'd hoped, at the very least, her dresses would speak for themselves. That unlike the meetings, the expo would place the members on an even playing field. Not everyone in the room knew she was Death Girl, did they?

Determined to keep her optimism, Ginny took her next dress out of its garment bag and arranged it on the mannequin. As she was doing so, someone called her name from across the room and she turned to wave at Gordon. He stood with his mother at the cookies and coffee table in a suit and tie. And wasn't that nice of him to get dressed up for his mother's dress club, even if he looked distinctly uncomfortable fidgeting with his collar?

Yes, it *was* nice. A lot nicer than buying half of her funeral home without telling her first and then surrounding her in people repellent à la Tucker and Roksana.

Lord, that sounded mean-spirited of her. She was grateful for the protection of her friends, but Jonas being high handed and *princely* was only going to work if she had some input into the decisions that affected her.

A hot poker prodded Ginny in the sternum.

Anger?

Yes, that was anger.

In fact, she couldn't wait for Jonas to arrive so she could express it. As soon as he walked in, she was going to march right up to him and…and ask to speak to him privately! After all, she didn't want to make a *scene*. She just needed him to realize she wasn't going to live her life like a dog's favorite bone, constantly being buried for her own protection—and without her consent!

An elderly woman with a sweet smile approached the table. Ginny shot Roksana and Tucker a warning glance over her shoulder before welcoming the potential customer. A dress customer, not a funeral home customer, although her advanced age did technically qualify her for both. *Don't be dark. You're selling dresses tonight, not coffins.* "Hello," Ginny said brightly. "Are you having a nice time?"

"Yes, I am. Thank you." The woman re-shouldered her purse and leaned in to admire Ginny's Christmas dress. "This one caught my eye across the room. Look at the holly detail—I love it!"

"Less talk, more bidding," Roksana called, smacking her gum.

Ginny brandished a pin at the slayer and imbedded it in the table, in the V between her index and middle fingers.

Roksana looked impressed. "Just trying to help."

"I *would* like to bid, actually." The woman seemed wary about approaching the table. Could anyone blame her? She'd just managed to pick up the little, square bidding sheet when a voice split the air.

"I wouldn't bid on that one," Galina sing-songed. "It was manufactured in a funeral home. Who knows what kind of nasty diseases it carries. Honestly, there should be a rule against her selling them."

All movement ceased in the church basement. If Ginny had felt cold in the corner before, she was freezing now, inside and out, yet her face burned with heat. How she could listen to such comments her entire life and still have them land like daggers in her chest was beyond her. She *should* have been a seasoned pro. But in the wake of Galina's words, she reeled. Her hands shook. Every eye in the room was on her and it took all of her inner strength not to flee the room.

A chair scraped back.

"Can you please watch Ginny's back while I kill the dumb bitch?" Roksana asked in an oddly formal tone, receiving an immediate—and alarmingly bored—"*of course*" from Tucker, thus rousing Ginny from her stupor.

"No," she murmured to Roksana, though she even found it hard to look even her friend in the eye after her embarrassment. "I think...I can do this."

Until recently, she might have smiled and whispered some altruistic sentiment about killing people with kindness. Not now. Letting people step on her to elevate themselves had been fusing her to the ground for so long. And now that she knew what it felt like to be lifted up by friends, by purpose, she didn't want to stay down.

Roksana pursed her lips and sat back down.

"Galina." Ginny called, facing the room again. "Since you're so worried about the rules, they state that you must be a Coney Island resident to be admitted to the club and I'm almost positive you dwell in Gerritsen Beach."

Galina gasped and dropped the clutch purse she'd been holding onto her folding table with a dramatic *thwack*. Guests turned to look at her and she let out a high-pitched laugh. "Yes, but...very, *very* close to the border. And no matter where I live, my dresses aren't tainted, Death Girl."

Ginny's composure faltered when the woman set down her bidding form and scurried back to the bright side of the room. She could feel the crack running from forehead to belly, but she faced the basement and kept her chin up, ignoring the hot pressure building behind her eyes. She wouldn't cry. She wouldn't cry—

The air in the room changed.

Whipped up, lifting her hair as if on a breeze.

She wasn't the only one who felt the shift, either. Everyone in the vicinity looked around for the source of renewed energy, some people rubbing their arms, others whispering amongst each other. Even Gordon stopped yanking on the collar of his dress shirt and faced the entrance, just in time for Jonas to stride in.

Time slowed down and Ginny...she quite simply stopped breathing.

Remember you're mad at him.

How on earth was she supposed to do that when he walked purposefully in Ginny's direction, through a sea of dumbstruck guests, looking at her like she'd just completed work on the Sistine Chapel? Or perhaps turned water into wine. And really, the way he regarded her with such reverence would have been enough to tumble her tower of anger, but he looked...

Righteously sexy.

Careless, black hair. Eyes that held the weight of

dangerous knowledge. An air of total command—that was the part she was mad about. Or supposed to be mad about. What was happening to her? Was she melting?

Did he always look like this?

Yes. Yes, but...in a room full of regular, everyday humans, he was transcendent. He dropped the jaws of everyone he passed, one person dropping their Dixie cup of fruit punch, as well.

He wore jeans. Dark ones, much nicer than the pair he'd donned the night they met. Along with boots, a white shirt and an overcoat of soft, chocolate brown.

Flowers. There were flowers in his hand.

For her.

"Ginny," he breathed, stopping in front of her. "I'm sorry I'm late."

She nodded. Or shook her head. Hard to be sure.

He handed her the flowers, then cupped her face in his hands, brushing her cheekbones with adoring sweeps of his thumbs. Their lips met and they both shuddered, the cellophane crinkling beneath her grasping fingers. Ginny didn't have to look around the room to know they were the center of attention and she couldn't have cared less anyway. She only saw Jonas.

"Why are you over here in the dark, love?"

"Am I in the dark?" she whispered, his green eyes imbuing her with a sort of lovesick delirium. "It doesn't feel like I am anymore."

His expression softened. "I'll have you moved."

"No," she blurted, snapping out of her Jonas Hypnosis. "The proper way to phrase that question was, shall I have you moved? Or even better, shall *we* see if you can be moved?"

Cautiously, he took the bouquet out of her hands and set it down on the table. "I'm not following."

"You bought half of my funeral home, Jonas."

"Yes," he said slowly. "Owning property together is a way humans express commitment to each other, isn't it? I thought you would be pleased."

The fact that Jonas appeared perplexed by her anger dulled the edges of her irritation considerably. He genuinely thought she'd be thrilled by his actions. Still, she couldn't just let his highhandedness go so easily, could she? Not unless she wanted that kind of behavior to become the norm.

"I suppose I'm pleased that you *thought* of me—"

"I never stop thinking about you," he rasped, placing a hand on her hip and squeezing. "Ever, Ginny."

She lost more steam. "I never stop thinking of you, either."

His brow knit. "Then don't be cross with me."

"I don't want to be, but until very recently, you were planning to rob my memories against my will. I'm shuffled around among bodyguards and...and I have to find out by accident that you're going to kill yourself.

Then today, you buy the funeral home. You have to clue me in or I *will* feel like I'm standing in the dark." She brushed their fingers together and he immediately clung, bringing her hand to his mouth and mashing her knuckles to his lips. "More partnership, less prince and subject, Jonas. Please?"

Thoughts churned behind his eyes. "I'll do my best to discuss certain matters with you. If I feel it's possible to land on an acceptable compromise."

"You mean, land on a compromise you *like*."

His jaw ticked. "Every decision I make is with the intention of keeping you safe and close to me. I refuse to stop doing that."

"I'm not asking you to stop, I'm asking you to confide in me. I'm asking to be a part of those decisions."

"And if you disagree with my judgment?"

"Then we work on a new one together."

He huffed a mint-laced breath and started to respond with something she almost certainly wasn't going to like, but his shoulders stiffened.

A slight turn of Jonas's head and he was face to face with Gordon.

Well. Chin to face. Jonas was at least five inches taller than the collar-tugging ginger.

"H-hi, I'm Gordon," he said, backing away from Jonas's intensity.

The lights in the basement sputtered.

With a sense of impending doom, Ginny tried to insert herself between man and vampire, but Jonas surprised her by extending his hand toward Gordon. "Nice to meet you, Gordon. I understand you're a *friend* of Ginny's."

"Yes." He released a light laugh. "Well *kind of…*"

Jonas's eye twitched. "Kind of?"

Gordon straightened, as if gathering courage. Had he no his sense of self preservation? "We did go out on one date…and I was hoping maybe we would again—"

A popping noise sounded above their heads. Sparks rained down from the ceiling and the radiator behind Ginny's table started to whistle, shooting off steam in three directions. The emeralds in Jonas's eyes burst into flames and the ground started to shake.

Murmurs of alarm went up around the church basement.

"Ginny," Jonas said, sounding as if he was being strangled. "Can I speak with you privately?"

Distantly, Ginny thought she heard Tucker and Roksana laughing like hyenas, but she didn't dare look to confirm. No, she twined her fingers together with Jonas's and hustled him twenty yards to the back exit door into the alley, closing it firmly behind them.

Jonas walked straight to the wall opposite the church and ripped two handfuls of bricks out with his bare hands, smashing them to dust at his feet. "Ginny," he bit off. "Can we compromise on killing him?"

"*No.*"

"There you have it." He swiped out an arc of bricks, as easily as one might swat a fly, leaving them scattered in pieces on the ground. "Proof discussions don't work."

"I'm not having a discussion about whether or not you can kill someone simply for liking me. We went on one date, before I ever met you," Ginny said. "Besides, I'm not the first girl *you've* been with."

He turned to her with an incredulous expression. "You are my *feast*. Do not concern yourself with breadcrumbs."

"I don't. Because I can see it's pointless up against…"

Jonas stalked closer. "What?"

"What we have."

He kept coming until he'd backed her up against the wall. "What do we have? I need to hear you say it. Having you angry with me was torture enough, then this man thinks he can come within ten feet of *my mate*." He buried his face in her neck, inhaling deeply. Capturing her wrists and pinning them above her head. "You don't know, love. You don't understand what happens inside me when there is friction between us. It's like burning in hell."

"I don't like it, either." Spicy, little shivers raced all over her skin, pooling in the places where their bodies made contact. Chest, belly, thighs, lap. "But I'm happy you asked me to come outside instead of acting on what you wanted to do."

His laughter was devoid of humor. "Rip his throat out with my teeth, damn the rules?"

"Yes." She pulled his face from her neck and slid their lips together, side to side, eliciting a deep, male groan. "And what we have? It's forever. Nothing comes close to that, especially not one bad date."

Jonas's hips and chest surged closer, flattening her even tighter to the wall, almost to the point of not being able to breathe. His restlessness and aggression called to something inside of Ginny. Intuition pervaded her, raw and honest and *new*. Unique to the two of them. "You need to feed," she whispered.

Jonas made a broken sound and spun her around to face the wall, aligning his body tightly with hers. "Tell me again what we have," he growled, gathering her hair in a fist. "*Tell me*, love."

"Forever," she breathed. "And when we go inside, I'll tell him, too, if it makes you feel better."

He paused with his lips on her neck. "I like that. Not as much as I like the idea of killing him, but I like it."

"That's a compromise," she said, smiling back at him. "Was that so bad?"

For several seconds, he did nothing but stare at her, seeming almost mesmerized. "Nothing that makes you smile so beautifully could ever be bad." With a final, longing look at her pulse, he let go of her hair and stepped away. "Let's get you back inside. I won't have your reputation damaged because I can't control myself around you."

Turning back around, Ginny breathed a laugh. "I wouldn't mind a change to my reputation."

His brows drew together. "What does that mean?"

Was it so much to ask that this man who seemed to believe she was wonderful continued to believe it? "They have me in the dusty corner by the radiator because I'm Death Girl. I'm just the outsider." She lifted a shoulder and let it drop. "They think there's something wrong with me for wanting to work with the dead. I'm used to it. Or maybe...I thought I was."

Several more bricks popped out of the building across the alley. "Blind idiots," he said, his temple visibly throbbing. "Inside, love. You're about to to sell out."

"Oh no." She grabbed his arm before he could open the church basement door. "Jonas, you cannot compel people to bid on my dresses."

His hand curled into a fist on the door. "Compromise, compromise," he grumbled unhappily. "I will not compel anyone to bid, but I *am* going to...can *we* even the odds?"

The smile nearly leaped off her face. "Yes."

Regarding her closely, his lips parted on a prayer.

"People who are good and kind, inside and out, hold up mirrors to the malevolence around them. I've walked this earth for almost ninety years and I've never met anyone who exemplifies that truth more fully than you, Ginny. You are good in every sense of the word. And evil hates reminders of what they're incapable of being." He kissed her mouth softly. "Let them flail and sputter in their inferiority. You're a goddess among fruit flies."

He had to tug Ginny's hand to get her moving.

When she did, she had the urge to picture herself as one of her movie stars to boost her confidence. But after standing up to Galina earlier, and now with Jonas's words ringing in her head, she didn't need those illusions. Not tonight.

Maybe never again.

She walked hand in hand with Jonas through the sea of curious faces, stopping when they reached Ruth.

Jonas looked down at her and winked.

"Ruth," Ginny said, clearing her throat. "I'd like you to meet my boyfriend, Jonas." She looked Gordon in the eye. "He *is* my boyfriend. Sorry."

"She's not sorry," Jonas drawled, smiling at Ruth.

"No, I'm not," Ginny hurried to continue, feeling the crowd closing in on them to hear better. "And anyway, I'm wondering, if it's not too much trouble, if we could move my table into one of the more well-lit areas?"

Ruth didn't answer. She was too busy staring a hole in Jonas.

Ginny did a quick check to make sure he wasn't compelling her and relaxed when his eyes were their normal shade of seductive green.

"Mother," Gordon prompted, exasperated by his mother's shameless staring. "Seriously."

The dress club founder jolted. "Oh, I'm sorry…I…yes, yes of course." She fluttered a hand near her neckline, face turning a light shade of pink. "Gordon, would you help Ginny move the table—"

"That won't be necessary," Jonas cut in. "Thank you, Ruth. You're obviously a fair and reasonable leader."

Giggling, she fanned herself. "Well, I try my best."

Jonas put an arm around Ginny and led her away. They'd only made it about five feet when Galina called out from her table where she was surrounded by her dress club posse. "Ginny!" Her smile was almost feral. "Aren't you going to introduce us to your friend?"

"Boyfriend," Jonas corrected Galina, tucking a strand of hair behind Ginny's ear. "Of the eternal variety. If you'll excuse us." He guided her past the table, leaning down to mutter in her ear, "Fruit flies."

Five minutes later, with the help of Roksana, Tucker and of course, Jonas, her table was not only in the light, it was in the dead center of the room.

Ginny shifted on her feet. "Can't we scoot it toward

the wall a little—"

Jonas quieted her with a kiss. "This is where you belong." Next, he brushed his lips across her forehead, seeming fascinated by her widow's peak. "Do you want my help?"

"You've done more than enough." Her fingertips slid over his ribcage and he let out a low groan, stilling her hand in a tight grip. "I have to do the rest by myself."

He seemed reluctant to let go of her hand, but eventually did. Keeping Ginny in his sights, he went around the back of her table and fell into a metal folding chair the way royalty falls into a throne, one ankle crossed over the opposite knee.

Ginny took a deep breath and faced the room, which she had to admit, was a heck of a lot easier with the addition of Jonas at her back. Half of the guests were still gaping at him…and yet, he gaped at *her*. Before Jonas, she'd had tiny little seeds of resourcefulness inside of her that couldn't grow without sunlight. But they'd been there nonetheless. They were products of Ginny. Perhaps they just needed some encouragement to bloom.

She squared her shoulders and took a long breath, painfully aware of the people circling her table, scrutinizing her months of work and still not stopping.

Still not stopping.

Until someone did.

"Hi," whispered the young woman with a starburst

brooch, punch clutched between her fingerless gloves. "Everyone is talking about the Christmas dress and I love it. I do," she assured Ginny in a scratchy Brooklyn accent. "But…I have my eye on the white silk. That faux fur collar is to die for. Can I bid?"

"Yes," Ginny exhaled, stepping aside. "Please."

As the woman crouched down at the table and scribbled her number on the white square of paper, Ginny turned and met Jonas's eyes over her shoulder.

He winked and mouthed the words, "That's my girl."

She smiled, huger than she could ever remember doing. It reached all the way to her pounding heart—and she knew in that moment, she would never love anyone or anything more than Jonas Cantrell.

CHAPTER NINETEEN

J ONAS CARRIED A laughing Ginny into her bedroom over his shoulder. She was tempted to scold him for handling her like a sack of potatoes, but she was in too good a mood. The best mood of the century. The *millennium.*

"I can't believe it," she said, directly to his butt. "The highest bid of the night."

"I'm not surprised," he sniffed, ever the prince. "I know nothing about dresses, but I know I'd most like to see you in the ones you made."

Her face burned with pleasure. "That's how you judge, is it?"

"Yes."

"I guess the one downside to selling them all is you'll never see me in them."

"That *is* regrettable." Gently, he lifted Ginny off his shoulder and settled her on her feet, keeping steadying hands on her waist. She gasped when he used the belt to tug her up against his body, nipping at her mouth. "Speaking of dresses, love. *This* little fucking red one…"

Her knees turned to rubber. "What about it?"

"You know." Using his hold on the belt, he turned her in a slow circle, raking her with hot eyes all the while. "Yes, you knew when you put it on that I'd be obsessed with getting it off you."

"Obsessed?"

"Ginny, don't question my obsession with any and every part of you." Turning her to face him once more, he unfastened her belt and let it clank to the ground. "Just start assuming."

If only her lungs were working properly. "Are you going to spend the night?"

His fingers paused. "Would you like that?"

She nodded, never more sure of anything. Never wanting anything more than she wanted to forge that final connection with Jonas. "In my bed."

Jonas seemed to rein himself in with a deep, shuddering breath. "We'll go slow," he said, thickly. "God, I'm scared out of my mind I'll hurt you."

"That whole thing about the rules? Breaking one means breaking them all? That can't apply to us," Ginny said, pushing the jacket off his shoulders and running her palms up the cool cotton of his white, long-sleeved shirt, feeling his muscles strain and flex at her touch. "Nothing else seems to apply. I'm your second mate in a lifetime. I feel your pain. Until someone can explain any of that to me, I'm operating as if this is a-a…totally unique situation."

"We're nothing if not that," he agreed unevenly, watching her hands mold over his body. "You've done some thinking about this."

"A little," she admitted, in a vast understatement. "Have you?"

Jonas puffed a pained laugh. "Have I thought of getting you into bed?" He dropped his mouth to the valley of her breasts, kissing them both with a greedy, open mouth. "Almost as much as I've thought of getting you down the aisle."

Ginny's legs turned to mist. "What did you say?"

He straightened and looked her square in the eye, intensity radiating from every inch of his powerful frame. "You heard me."

Her mind stretched into an obstacle course and she had no idea where to begin conquering it. Was he serious? *Marriage?* Yet even as the holes in his plan presented themselves, she was filled with an effervescent hope that could have carried her up to the stars. "Jonas...our relationship is a secret," she said, common sense prevailing. For now. Holding back her happiness was like trying to plug a dam with a twig. "We're not even supposed to be together."

"You can be my secret wife just as easily as you can be my secret girlfriend," he said in a low, resolute voice, backing her step by step toward the bed. "All you have to do is say yes."

Before she could utter a word, he drew off his shirt and tossed it aside, leaving him in all his glowing, tousle-haired, muscular glory. Her blood had turned up the volume on every part of Jonas, down to his cloves and mint scent, the plush masculinity of his lips, the intensity with which he devoured the sight of her. All of him burned bright with hunger and beauty and possessive-ness. His fingertips brushed down the trail of dark hair beneath his belly button absently, drawing attention to the risen flesh below.

"Um…" she started, a ticklish feeling stirring in the deepest recesses of her stomach. This was all happening very quickly. She was still getting used to being a vampire's mate. Surely they could space out the surprises here and there? "I m-mean, we should probably live together for a while first. To see if we're…compatible? You do own half of this place now, remember? You could move in for a while and—"

"Compatible?" Appearing more than a little annoyed, Jonas sauntered closer, giving Ginny no choice but to fall back on the bed. He leaned over her, bracing his hands on either side of her head. "I live for you. I *crave* you without cease. Your beauty, your blood and your spirit sustain me. Yet you question our compatibility?"

"No," she whispered. "No, that was a stupid thing to say. I'm just trying to keep up with the rapid-fire changes. I need you. I crave you, too." She squeezed her eyes shut, feeling every word like a twist in her chest. "*Constantly.*"

When she opened her eyes, she saw the temper had ebbed from his face. His overt possessiveness remained, though it was tempered with adoration. "Compromise," he said to himself. "Moving in here could draw more unwanted attention to us. But hell if I'll be able to stay away. Or deny you anything you ask."

"We'll be careful."

"Ah, love. There's nothing careful about us." Jonas scrutinized her thoughtfully, hungrily. "Do you know exactly what it is you crave from me, Ginny?" He reached down and tugged up her dress, bunching it around her waist. "Is it time for me to show you?"

Her belly shuddered under his rapt regard. "*Yes.*"

He hit her with blistering eye contact while lowering his mouth to her stomach, licking a slow circle with the tip of his tongue. "Open your legs."

Ginny's feminine core clenched with such intensity, it hurt to follow his order, but she managed, her chest already heaving, trying to draw air. Simply from being on display in front of Jonas, her dress around her waist, thighs fallen open, her moon and star panties stretched over a place she'd never shown anyone.

"Such a beautiful offering," he groaned, ghosting his mouth over the waistband of her panties, then lower, nudging her mound with his lips. "Do you give yourself to me freely, Ginny Lynn?"

Her hands flew up and fisted the bedclothes. "*Yes.*"

The heat of his mouth warmed her, covering her in gooseflesh. Through the taut material, he pressed his tongue down on her sensitive nub of flesh and sparks danced in front of her eyes. *Lord Lord Lord*, it was already took much. The rasp of his shaking hands on her knees, the flex of his shoulders, the wicked portrait he made framed between her straining thighs.

Do you know exactly what it is you crave from me, Ginny?

Until he tugged her panties to one side, then ripped them off entirely, she hadn't understood. Not completely. The need to be claimed by him was already swamping her senses and plaguing her with a heavy, aching feeling right in the center of her belly. This was so much more than desire, though. She'd desired him from the moment he sat up on her table.

No, this ran deeper. Like she'd been waiting and pining and suffering without the weight of him on top of her. Without his mouth and flesh and breath.

She needed to the point of pain.

His tongue curled around her swelling button of flesh and she tore at the comforter. "*Jonas*," she moaned. "We're compatible. We're compatible."

A male laugh vibrated her nerve endings all the way

down to her toes. He rode his tongue up the split of her sex and made a guttural, satisfied sound, before batting her clitoris like a predator with its cornered prey. "Even sweeter than it looks," he muttered hoarsely, yanking her hips closer and laving her with the flat of his tongue, up and back until her head thrashed on the bed. "*Ginny*," he growled, squeezing her knees in his flexing hands. "Try and be calm. I'm getting too…excited."

The way he said *excited* made it obvious he was understating the truth by quite a lot, as did his eyes. They glowed so hot, the skin of her stomach and thighs was bathed in green. "It just feels so good," she gasped. "Please don't stop."

He groaned into his next lick, using his lips to draw on her nub gently, in between strokes from his tongue. She felt the pad of his middle finger at her entrance and held her breath, the promise of being filled making her realize how badly she ached for it to happen. And when it did, when Jonas's finger sank home, Ginny's hips bucked wildly and Jonas visibly lost the battle with his control.

His muscles bunched on a rasp of her name, his fangs slicing out.

"*Need.*"

Knowing exactly what he meant, she relinquished her right hand's grip on the bedclothes, sank it into his hair and instinctively drew him to her thigh. "Yours. It's yours. *I'm yours.*"

With an expression rife with possession and unholy thirst, Jonas pressed a second finger into her body and bit down hard on her inner thigh, groaning brokenly at the taste of her.

Ginny whipped headlong into an orgasm.

It was all the more brutal and beautiful for its unexpectedness.

Her being didn't know what to react to. His fingers sliding in and out of her wetness so expertly or the pleasure/pain of his fangs where they punctured her leg, drawing blood for Jonas to devour. One second the spot ached, the next it throbbed like an extension of her sex, sending pulsing ribbons of heat to the juncture of her thighs. And then only the pleasure remained, building and building like a funeral pyre until she screamed, bliss nearly crushing her in its intensity.

"*Jonas,*" she cried, her body arched in a near fit of pleasure. "*Jonas!*"

When his head lifted, she expected him to be sated, his hunger fulfilled. She never expected him to look as though he'd been teased. Slowly, he slipped his fingers from inside of Ginny, staring at them for a moment as if they'd been dipped in gold, before sucking them into his mouth.

Her hands moved on their own, trying desperately to get her dress off. She wasn't sure where the impulse came from, only that she needed to follow it. Needed to feel his chest on her breasts, his stomach on hers.

She needed him inside of her.

Now.

The emptiness was relentless. *Lord.* Was it supposed to be like this? Like she would die unless he took ownership of her body and soul and never let her go? She could see she already owned his soul, body. Yes, he was projecting that truth in no uncertain terms as he prowled higher, knocking aside her hands where they tried to remove her dress and ripping it clean down the middle, instead.

"Every thought in your beautiful head is translated by this sweet body, love. I asked you to be *calm*," he rasped, twisting the middle clasp of her bra until it snapped, then falling on her breasts like they were his last meal. "When you insist on rubbing your pussy against my mouth, you make it clear you'll be eager when I get you underneath me and I will have no choice but to be rough." He suckled her nipples in turn with a desperate mouth and by the time he finished, her legs were wrapped around his hips and she was begging for more, all of him, everything. "Please, Ginny, *stay calm.*"

"*I can't.*"

A violent shudder moved through him, his muscles looking as though they could burst free of his skin. "*Fuck.* I have to stop."

"No."

Panic turned his eyes to moss. "*I could kill you like this.*"

"You won't." Ginny forced herself to relax and space out her harried breaths. Ordered her thighs to stop squeezing his hips, her hips to stop shifting. Teasing the distended fly of his jeans and tempting him to take was not helping his state of mind. "Kiss me," she breathed at his lips. "We'll slow down."

His laughter was pained. "Kissing you won't inspire me to go slow."

"Look at me." She stroked the side of his face. "Look at me."

He pressed their foreheads together and sipped at her mouth cautiously. Their tongues met in a fleeting caress, just a touch, but he groaned like he'd been burned. Ginny slipped her fingers into his hair, scratching her nails along his scalp and let their mouths mate in a slow, rhythmic way that made her sex hot and needy. But she remained still, being seduced all over again by the restrained passion of his kiss, until she was finally rewarded by Jonas dropping his hips into the cradle of her thighs, the denim friction forcing her to trap a cry in her throat.

Jonas kept their mouths poised mid-kiss and reached down to unzip his pants, everything, everything balancing on a razor's edge. Their eyes locked and remained that way while he drew out his shaft in a fist, cursing as it brushed her damp femininity. "I want to know if you're hurting, love…" His jaw tightened to the point of near shatter. "But I also worry if you cry out in pain, my soul will leave my fucking body."

She shook her head. "This is inevitable, remember?"

"*Yes.*"

"Then trust it."

Affection, surrender, lust, moved in waves across his features. He fused their mouths together and trailed a hand down, down between their bodies, taking hold of himself and dragging the thick head side to side at her entrance. "Christ be with me, please. Hold me back," he gritted out, before surging his hips forward and planting every hard inch of himself inside her.

His animal growl almost deafened Ginny, but she was thankful for it, because it drowned out her shocked whimper.

Pain pricked holes in the euphoria his mouth had bestowed. But the buzz of cradling his sex within her body was a thrill that dulled the edges of her hurt. She let her neck muscles loosen, let her lids drift down and reveled in the knowledge of what he felt like inside of her, huge and uncompromising. Male.

"Mate," she whispered.

Jonas's lust-fogged eyes found Ginny's and she let him see her full comprehension of every facet of that word. Not only would she sustain his life, she would feed his soul—and he would do the same for her. Endlessly.

The wordless communication passed between them on the wings of velvet, sealing their fate in the history books and Jonas started to rock, his teeth bared, neck muscles straining. And the pain was no more, compared to her soaked welcome of this man's flesh. This man whom she loved.

"Mate," he croaked into her neck, his movements turning more and more frantic, his hips pumping and colliding with her eager ones. "My only. My only. Take me as deep as you can stand."

"Give it to me. I can stand it all."

"*Ginny*," he warned, then, brokenly. "Oh, fuck, *Ginny*."

The lamp on her bedside table popped and sizzled. In her periphery, she swore the lights on the Coney Island skyline dulled and brightened to a higher setting, but she could comprehend nothing more than that. Not with Jonas's mouth clamping down over hers in ownership, his hands scooping beneath her bottom and holding it securely in place as his pace kicked into a frenzy.

"So much *squirming*. Keep your tight pussy right where it is, love, or I'll think you're trying to take it away from me. We can't have that."

Oh Lord. Oh Lord.

Completion summoned her closer, brought on by Jonas's lack of control. She liked it. No, she loved it. The breakneck speed of him mating her, his grunts of her name, the good, honest sweat he built on her body.

She conformed the arch of her feet to his hips and listened to the resulting string of profanities in her hair. They were a glorious hymn and she wanted to memorize them and sing them out loud, all day, every day, proof she was this man's salvation and poison in equal measure.

"Look at you, moaning and trying to get your legs wider for me when you ought to be terrified. Beautiful, reckless girl."

Jonas changed angles, bearing down on her clitoris with rough grinds of his shaft and Ginny's romantic haze was blown apart by all-out lust. Her back arched on a moan and the green in Jonas's eyes whipped, holding her in thrall. She didn't think, she simply followed the urges of her body and reached down to claw his backside, urging him to go faster, chanting, "Don't stop, don't stop, don't stop..."

Everything happened so fast after that.

Fast and glorious.

"If your blood could not sustain me, Ginny," he growled, yanking her knees high and throwing them over his shoulders. "I swear this pussy would."

He stroked into her deep, the new angle allowed that slick, thick part of him unfettered access to *that spot—*

and she couldn't move her hips to meet him or grind up, she simply had to take it. There was a loud sound coming from a distant land and it took her several guesses before she realized it was the entire bed rebounding off the wall.

The wildness of it was her undoing.

Or maybe it was watching Jonas sink his fangs into the small of her wrist, followed by the further swelling and jerking of his flesh inside her. Knowing he was close to finding unimaginable pleasure after a lifetime of going without. His body stiffened at the same time as hers, his mouth released her wrist and fingers clutched at skin eagerly, pulling one another's bodies closer any way they could.

Molten heat poured inside of Ginny, mixing magically, addictively with her own release and she found herself flattened on the mattress, beneath a vampire in the throes—and it was a sight she would remember for the rest of her life. His blind eyes and exposed fangs, his thrown back head. His repeated groan of her name.

"*Ginny. Fuuuuck.*" He lunged for her mouth as if he was scared what might happen if he didn't kiss her. "You feel so good. It *feels so good.*"

When he collapsed a moment later, she'd never been more thankful for his beating heart because she could hear it rioting out of control, matching her tempo perfectly, and she loved him so much just then, tears clogged her throat.

He lifted his head, concern a living thing on his face. "Are you hurt?"

"No, Dreamboat," she managed between shallow breaths, allowing him to draw her protectively into his side. "No, I'm perfect."

"Truer words were never spoken," he said hoarsely into her neck, breathing her in like he was already starved for another course of her. "Are you satisfied, mate?"

"Yes. So very yes."

His relieved exhale stirred her hair. "While you sleep tonight, I'll try to come up with the adequate words to describe what we did, if those words exist." He wrapped her tightly in his embrace, tucking her head beneath his chin, his heart pounding wildly in her ear. "For now…suffice it to say, you are magic. My God, Ginny. You are…my magic."

CHAPTER TWENTY

G INNY HAD NEVER been afraid while inside the dream.

This time, however, she trembled while walking along the path on the outskirts of the fair. The funhouse sounds were distorted now and she could feel the sweat clinging to her palms, trickling down her rigid spine.

He was under the tree. The man in the newsboy cap and suspenders. More than ever, she desperately wanted to reach him. There was an urgency to be with him that had only been present in lighter shades before. Now, she picked up her skirt to run in his direction. Get to him by any means possible.

"Don't," he mouthed, stiffening and separating from the tree. "Please don't—"

The crimson hooded figure moved in her periphery and she broke into a sprint, desperate to reach the man beneath the tree. If she could just reach him, no harm would come to her. His protectiveness was somehow a given. It was understood, though they'd never even had a conversation. The closer she came to reaching him, the more the ominous presence dragged her back, making it impossible to run as fast as needed.

The wind whipped his hat off and for the first time, she saw the face of the man who waited for her night after night beneath the tree.

"Jonas," she whispered, extending her hand, knowing he'd take it if he could.

Somehow she'd already *known* it was him that waited, hadn't she?

Yes. Of course. She'd always known.

Everything went silent.

Silent and…vast.

Still dreaming, but she couldn't see.

Could only feel the breeze slithering around her bare legs, uneven ground beneath her feet. And Lord, she was cold. A shiver caught her in its grip and wouldn't let go, her teeth chattering. Her hands lifted to her face and found a blindfold there, across her eyes. Who had put it there?

Where was Jonas?

She whimpered his name as she drew off the blindfold, the air vacating her lungs in a terrified gasp. There was no time to prepare or find her balance. She teetered on the tiny outcropping protruding from the side of the cliff and slipped, falling down…down to the rocks below, her screams ripping in the wind behind her.

Ginny braced for impact that never came.

It never came, but she was blind again. Back on that unsteady ground, the air endless and noisy around her. *Noisy.* That was different. She couldn't be back on the cliff. Not wanting to startle herself into falling a second time, she slowly reached up and drew off the blindfold—and trapped a scream of horror in her throat.

Tears scalded her eyes, her knees shaking violently.

"*No, no, no, no,*" she sobbed, her lips numb from shock.

A body of water spread out in front of her, seemingly going on for miles, dotted intermittently by boats. And they were so small. Lord, they were so small, meaning she was extremely high up. Traffic rushed behind her. Wind thrashed and tangled her hair. Land to her right and left. Bridge. She was on a bridge.

On the ledge of a bridge.

Ginny stayed very still, afraid to even turn around and find a way off the ledge. The wind was so fierce that any shift of her equilibrium could knock her off balance and plunge her to the water below. Water that was nothing more than a horrible, mute blackness.

My heart is going to kill me.

It pumped with such force, her body moved along with the frantic beats.

"Jonas," she whispered, tears raining down her cheeks. "Jonas."

Something was wrong. Very wrong, or he would be

there. He never would have let her reach the bridge in the first place. She would have to save herself. Not only because she desperately wanted to live, but because Jonas might die without her and the mere possibility nearly ripped her down the middle.

She could die without telling him she loved him.

No.

No, she owed it to both of them not to lose hope. If he was in danger, she would damn well expect him to live. To make it back to her.

There was no way she could stand there for much longer without making a move. That was for certain. Already her legs were wobbling from maintaining total stillness on the tiny ledge—and yes, she knew without looking down that it was tiny, because her toes hung over the edge.

Panic welled in her throat and the condensation of her shuddering breaths wafted around her face. Anger broke through the soil of her fear like a little green sprout, growing larger and larger. Someone had put her here. Someone who wanted her harmed. Dead. Seymour might have been killed, but there was obviously *another* vampire who sought to do her harm. Had Seymour ever really been the threat to begin with? Whoever put her on this bridge was following the same pattern of not outright killing her, but flouting the rules by putting her in a position to do it herself. And this…just like her trip to the Belt Parkway, would look like a suicide, wouldn't it?

Whoever wanted her dead might get away with it.

No, she couldn't let that happen.

With a long, slow intake of breath, Ginny turned her head to the left, searching for a handhold. Anything she could inch toward and grasp, to keep herself from pitching forward into the icy black. There was nothing. Just a flat, light blue wall of painted-over steel. Light blue. *I must be on the Verrazano*, she thought dimly, trying not to succumb to the despair of finding no anchor.

Carefully, she placed her palms flat on the bumpy surface behind her, breathing in and out. In and out. She closed her eyes and tried to find her center, find anything that would help her maintain motionlessness.

She might have been able to stay that way long enough for Jonas to find her, if it weren't for the crash. In a weird way, she felt it coming. Perhaps because of the dream wherein she toppled off the cliff to the jagged rocks below.

This was unavoidable, wasn't it?

Tires screeched overhead and Ginny braced, her teeth drawing blood on her lower lip. Metal crunched and the bridge vibrated beneath her feet. All it took was the tiniest shake and she stumbled forward, her foot catching nothing but air. It didn't happen in slow motion, the fall. It was a downward drop at a hundred miles an hour with no control of her body, limbs pinwheeling, a shriek rupturing her vocal cords. Ginny squeezed her eyes shut and in those final seconds, thought of beautiful emerald eyes...

Weightlessness.

Her pulse rioted in her ears. A fog horn wailed in the distance.

No impact.

Nothing.

Another dream?

Had she been having another dream?

Cautiously, Ginny opened her eyes to find Jonas above her, mid-jump. *Jumping off the bridge*, his hands extended down toward her. As he drew closer, it became obvious that *she* wasn't moving. Was she hovering? A peek to the side told Ginny she'd stopped several feet above the ominous, black water.

"I've got you," he shouted, voice hoarse, commanding. "I've got you, Ginny."

He reached her then, wrapped both arms around her waist and twisted, flipping their positions so his back would hit the water first, and everything sped up. They landed with a splash, sinking down into the ink in a swath of bubbles, the freezing cold temperature flaying her skin. It seemed to take forever for them to surface, when in reality it was probably only seconds. Jonas took her face in his hands and scrutinized her closely, rasping indecipherable words to himself, appearing on the verge of total madness.

"*You fell. Christ, you fell. You fell. You fell.*"

Ginny sucked in a hysterical sound, her adrenaline taking a sharp nose-dive and she burst into tears, a ripple moving through her body before gripping her in violent shakes, stirring the water where they bobbed like buoys.

"Oh, Ginny. Love, no tears. Please, please." He kissed her mouth hard, followed by her cheeks, forehead and nose. Rough touches of his mouth that made her cry all the harder for some reason. "You just made my heart start beating again, baby, now you're tearing it out."

"H-h-how did I get there? I just...and then...I thought I was going to—"

He stopped her with another rough kiss, his unsteady hands stroking her wet hair. "I woke up with silver across my chest and you were halfway out the window. Fucking gone and I couldn't move. *I couldn't move.*"

"How did you get it off?"

"I don't know. I didn't know it was possible, but you were moving out of my reach and I just...I broke out. It had no hold over me."

Involuntarily, her hand touched his chest, as if to strip away the metal after the fact. She found a deep trench of red, angry branded skin, instead. "Jonas. Why isn't it healing faster?"

"You worry over a flesh wound when you just fell of a bridge?" he gritted out, squeezing her shoulders. "Jesus Christ, I have to get you out of here. I have to get you somewhere safe."

Ginny was too drained to protest when Jonas tossed her onto his back and started swimming. Her head lolled on his shoulder and she watched the water fly past at a rapid pace.

"Talk to me, love," he whispered morosely. "I keep seeing you fall."

Talk? She could barely keep her eyes open. Apparently her brain was handling the stress of falling to her death by calling it a day. "I dreamed of you," she murmured, dazed. "I was dreaming of you this whole time."

"Dreaming of me?"

She hummed, rubbing her face on his wet shoulder. "Outside the fair. You were waiting for me underneath the tree in your hat and suspenders." Absently, she noticed Jonas's back muscles bunching, the rhythm of his strokes faltering. "I tried to come to you, but the person in the red hood ruined everything."

"*Ginny*," he rasped, lifting her out of the water onto a dock and climbing out beside her. She started to lie down on the wooden planks, but he caught her in his arms, lifting her to his chest. "Stay awake." He shook her lightly. "Finish the rest."

"You told me to go back, but I didn't listen. I needed

you." She tucked her head under his chin and let the drowsiness close in. "We needed each other."

The last thing she remembered before sleep claimed her was Jonas staring down at her in shock. And oddly…recognition.

CHAPTER TWENTY-ONE

G INNY WOKE UP on soft, heavenly bed sheets to a
trio of angry male voices.

She cracked an eyelid open, expecting to find Jonas,
Tucker and Elias in the same room with her, but she was
greeted by nothing but darkness. Cautiously, she walked
her fingers across a fluffy pillow and found something
hard. A side table? She scooted over a few more inches,
levered up and switched on a lamp, finding herself
somewhere unfamiliar.

A hotel room?

Memories forged through her foggy mind. Her entire
body jerked when her fall from the Verrazano returned
to her in full force, putting her back in the center of her
freefall. She heaved a breath and sucked in more oxygen,
ironically wishing she had some water.

Jonas burst into the room through an adjoining door
wearing nothing but black sweatpants. His hair was still
wet, which meant he'd either taken a shower or it was
still damp from their impromptu swim. She hoped it was
the latter because it would mean she hadn't been out

long.

"You're awake," Jonas sat down on the side of the bed, his weight on the mattress causing her to roll toward him. Automatically, his finger threaded into her hair, his thumb massaging circles into her temple. "How are you feeling?"

She laid her head on his thigh. "I'm fine."

He watched her in silence, brows knit together.

"I'm glad the wound on your chest is fading. I didn't like thinking of how much it must have hurt."

"Hmmm."

Was it her imagination or was he acting odd? "What's wrong?"

"Nothing," he said quietly. "Everything."

"Oh is that all?"

Not a hint of a smile from Jonas.

"What were you arguing about?"

"Now, we weren't arguing," Tucker said, clomping into the room with a pinched grin on his face. "Your mommies and daddy were just having a discussion."

Ginny sat up all the way with her back against the headboard, realizing too late she was wearing an unbelted white hotel robe. Thankfully, Jonas yanked the sides shut and secured the belt around her waist before she could flash Tucker. She glanced at the adjoining door, waiting for Elias to join them in the room, but the entrance remained empty. "How long was I asleep?"

"Two hours," Jonas answered. "We're at a Hilton in Staten Island. It was the closest place I could find."

Tucker cracked a laugh. "Listen to the disgust in his voice over the three-star rating."

Jonas was still staring at her strangely. "It'll do for the night, but you should always expect better."

"What's going on with you?" she whispered, reaching up to scratch his chin. "You're looking at me like I grew a unicorn horn." Her eyes widened in mock concern. "Oh my God. Did I?"

"No." His smile was lopsided, eyes intense. "You're as perfect as ever."

She must have left her shame floating in New York Harbor, because even with Tucker in the room, her nipples turned to sensitive peaks inside her robe and she contemplated pulling Jonas down on top of her in the bed. Just to remind herself of the delicious press of his weight. Oh wow. *How she missed his weight.*

"My God. That racing pulse of yours…" His gaze fell to her mouth and sparked. "Stay calm for me, love." Ginny reined in her galloping libido with two hands. Or tried to, anyway. Jonas ruined her progress by leaning down and speaking right on top of her ear. "Do you remember what you told me before you fell asleep?"

Ginny clawed through her memory, but couldn't remember a thing after climbing onto Jonas's back in the water. "No."

313

"Mmmm."

"What does mmmm mean?"

"Eli*as*," Tucker called to the other room. "They're ignoring me."

Cheeks heating, Ginny shied back from Jonas. "Sorry." It was hard to concentrate when Jonas refused to stop regarding her like some kind of riddle he was attempting to decipher. "Um. What are we arguing about?"

"*You're* not arguing about anything," Jonas stressed. "You're resting."

Elias strode into the room, hoodie up, once again shielding his face from view. "She has the right to know you're leaving," he said, voice casual.

Jonas closed his eyes. "Fuck you, Elias."

"I've heard that plenty." The room's newcomer sprawled out on a couch in an unlit corner of the room. "Doesn't change the facts."

Ginny felt as though she were standing back up on the ledge of the Verrazano. Winded, unbalanced and preparing to tumble end over end. "What does he mean you're leaving?" Her mouth was dry as dust. "Where are you going?"

"I was going to tell you once you'd slept a while more." A line flexed in his cheek. "I'm going to approach the High Order. About you. About us."

Her blood chilled. "No. *Why?*"

Silence ticked by. "How long have you been having the dreams, Ginny?"

It came back to her then. Clinging to Jonas's back while he sliced through the water and telling him about the man under the tree. Him. "Since I met you."

"Met me." His laughter was flat. "You've known me a lot longer than you think." There was so much weight in his eyes as he studied her, she could only exist in their line of fire. "Or maybe not. We didn't speak the first time. Not really."

"What are you talking about, prince?" Tucker asked slowly.

"That's what I'd like to know," Elias added.

His voice scratched when he spoke. "My mate. She vanished without a trace and I could never find her again. I saw her the first time outside a school dance. She was only eighteen—and human. I stayed away. I *tried* to stay away, just watching over her, until the night at the fair."

Ginny's heart rapped against her eardrums. She could taste the roasted nuts in the air, smell the spun sugar, hear the tinkling notes of the rides. Most of all, she could sense Jonas beneath the tree. The atmospheric click of being right where she was supposed to be, with him, the hand of fate sweeping her closer.

"I swear she knew me," Jonas rasped now. "I swear...*you* knew me."

"I did. I'd been waiting."

Emotion swarmed his face. "I didn't have two mates. I simply found you again." His voice shook as he caressed her cheek. "Where did you go?"

Icy wind from the past cooled her skin. "Off a cliff," she whispered, numbly.

Heavy moments passed while they stared at one another.

Slowly, Jonas rose from the bed, fists pressed to his temples. He walked in one direction, switched and stopped, doubling over and letting out a deafening roar. Ginny rushed to cover her ears with both hands, ducking toward the comforter as sparks flew from every light source and outlet in the hotel room, singeing the carpet with little hisses.

"Is it my sire who does this?" He pulled at his hair. "Would my sire try and take you from me twice?"

"Of course he would," muttered Elias. "He's a ruthless bastard,"

"I don't understand," Ginny said, transferring a look between the men.

Jonas paused, staring into space. "He's the common denominator. When I found you the first time, I was freshly Silenced. No one else knew about me. I'd assumed no responsibilities yet under his command, so no one would have struck out at me to spite him. And it's the same pattern. Putting you in danger with just enough room to fail on your own." He raked a hand down his face. "A cliff. A bridge. My God, he's behind this, isn't he?"

"He's sure as shit powerful enough," Tucker said.

Ginny blinked. "He wants me dead so you won't break the rules and have a relationship with a human?"

"He controls everyone around him, like puppets on strings. Finding my mate would bring my devotion elsewhere." Jonas cursed. "But why come after you again *now* when I've made it clear I'll have nothing to do with him, anyway? And how did he find you the second time before we'd even met?"

"You can't just march in there and demand answers to your questions," she said, her voice thick. "Right? It's too dangerous."

Please don't go.

As if she'd spoken out loud, his eyes plead for her understanding. "He wants the oath of fealty I refused to give to him. Giving this oath would mean I could never challenge his seat, something only I can do. I'm going to offer the oath now in exchange for leniency. And above all, your safety."

Ginny reached for her closing throat. "What if he says no?"

"I can't live forever in fear of you being taken from me. If he seeks to get me back in line by hurting you, I can't ignore the problem. I have to face this head on.

Please understand."

"He could put you to death for breaking the rules," she said brokenly, standing and pulling him close by the front of his shirt. "Don't. Please don't."

"Ginny…" he said miserably against her forehead.

A realization occurred and she clung to it like a life preserver. "How are you going to survive? If you go, you have to take me with you."

"*Never*." Never was a firmer word spoken. His glittering eyes accompanied it in a plume of green sparks. "You will stay here with Elias and Tucker. I will do *everything* in my power to come back to you." He paused, looking away. "And if I can't, your life will be much safer. Trust me on that, love."

"So much for compromise," she gasped, fleeing to the bathroom and locking the door behind her. Nothing was within her control.

Nothing.

After experiencing the sensation of free falling that night, she desperately needed the opposite. Firm ground. A clear plan. Waiting and hoping things worked out might be the way she'd operated in the past, but not now. This was her future on the line and she didn't want to wait and be guided down a predetermined path by the hand of fate, she wanted to carve the damn path herself. The fragile human had to remain behind and…

Fragile human.

She'd just sat down on the lip of the bathtub when someone rapped on the bathroom door three times. Her mind was still spinning with possibilities—was she really considering this?—so she ignored the knocking and continued to think.

The metal doorknob lock popped open and Jonas took a brisk step inside, closing the door behind him. "I can't leave with you angry at me."

She swiped a tear away before it could fall. "Maybe I'll stay angry forever so you have to stay."

"Ah, Ginny. Don't break my heart."

"Don't break mine," she whispered. "I'm in love with you. And you could go tonight and never come back. Because of me."

Clearly ignoring every word out of her mouth, he came toward her as she spoke and knelt at her feet, gathering her resistant body and drawing her close, despite her protests. "Don't you dare tell me you love me and push me away."

"You can't compromise only when it's convenient, Jonas." She twisted in his arms and he purposely lost balance. Ginny ending up on the floor in his lap, his arms around her like steel bands. "That's not how it works."

"I'm in love with you, too," he said gruffly into her hair. "And now I know why it overwhelms me at every turn, this love I have for you. It's been fucking doubled.

I've been struck down twice by the same beautiful soul."

"Is it my soul you love most?"

He took her chin, lifting it so they made eye contact. "It's *all* of you," he answered, almost angrily. "Your soul, your heart, your body. I said everything."

"Will those things change if I become like you?"

Jonas reared back like he'd been struck. "What did you say?"

She said nothing for a moment, simply letting him see she was serious. It took an effort to struggle free of his arms, but she managed it and gained her feet. "My lifetime is going to pass in the blink of an eye for you. And every single second of it, we'll be worrying about it being cut short too soon."

"Ginny, stop this," he breathed, standing. "Turn around and look at the mirror."

With a heavy swallow, she glanced back over her shoulder, finding herself alone in the bathroom, even though she knew she wasn't. Could never mistake being alone with standing beside the magnetic life force that was Jonas. "If your argument is I won't be able to look at myself in the mirror, you're going to have to do better."

He seized her shoulders. "I will worship you no matter what form you're in, but you could hate yourself like I did. I won't be responsible for extinguishing your humanity. For making you dependent on blood. I won't."

"You will. Because I won't live without you. And changing me will protect you against the High Order. Don't leave me behind with the knowledge that I'm the reason you were put to death."

"If the choice is between me dying and you dying, *there is no choice*."

"You think I'll be better off, don't you?" Ginny said slowly. "You're still chained in that room, sentencing yourself to death so I won't have to spend my life keeping you alive." His flexing jaw told her she was at least partially correct. "Dammit, Jonas. I made that decision myself and you're not respecting it. You're not respecting *me*."

Appearing agonized, he turned Ginny and pressed her against the door, planting a fist hard above her head. "I *revere* you," he said, mouth against her ear. "But I will not do it. Not when there's a chance I could save us with my vow of fealty and leave you human."

His firmness told Ginny she'd been defeated. And that defeat allowed the imminent fear of losing him to penetrate. It shook the ground beneath her feet and made her ache. If this was the last time she saw Jonas, she wouldn't waste a single second. Lifting her chin a notch, she reached between them and untied her robe, shifting her shoulders until it fell from her body and pooled on the ground. "If that's your decision, then make love to me like it's the last time. It might be."

Jonas stiffened against her, his hands dropping to her hips, hesitating before cradling them. "Is it your intention to shatter me?"

"No, it's my intention to make us feel whole," she managed, her bones already liquefying from one simple touch. "Give me something to remember you by."

"*Ginny.*"

Before he could say more, she pulled his face toward hers for a kiss. His lips were stiff at first, but she made an entreating sound in her throat and he shuddered in response, flattening her body between him and the door, his mouth slanting over hers with a jagged groan. His surrender paired with Ginny's desperation was a match being thrown on a powder keg. They exploded into movement, his fingers twisting in the sides of her panties, yanking and shoving them down. They slipped down her ankles and she kicked them off, never breaking the kiss.

She couldn't.

He was consuming, and he consumed. Stealing her breath and storing it inside his body greedily, keeping her alive with strokes of his tongue and massaging hands that seemed to land everywhere. Her hips, her waist, her bare breasts.

When his thumbs smoothed over her erect nipples, she broke away with a whimper, only given a split second to suck down oxygen before he was kissing her furiously again. "This is not calm," he growled, pressing their foreheads together. "I am not calm."

"If I was like you," she whispered against his mouth, "you could take me as hard as you wanted—"

Eyes flaring like burnished jewels, he cut her off with his mouth, sweeping his tongue inside her mouth as if memorizing every corner. Flames kissed every sensitive spot on her body, nerve endings sizzling. Even with her eyes closed, she could sense the lights in the bathroom dimming and brightening and the proof of Jonas being affected heightened her need. Made it wild.

Craving even more proof, of the physical variety, she trailed a hand down his naked chest, encountering his hard shaft where it swelled free of his sweatpants waistband, straining against his stomach. Through the soft material, she molded him in her hand. His hips thrust in response, throwing her hard against the door and knocking the wind out of her. And for the first time, she took seriously the threat of his physical strength having the ability to injure her.

"Christ," he said thickly, releasing her mouth, but still undulating his lower body toward her touch, as if compelled. "Did I hurt you?"

"No." She shook her head while pushing the sweatpants down his hips, her body in pain without him as close as possible. *As close as possible.* "No, but we should probably slow down," she said in a gasping rush of tangled words.

"You're saying one thing and encouraging another," he muttered, boosting her up against the door, leaving her feet several inches above the ground. He dropped his mouth to her breasts, licking a path between her nipples before sucking on each one deeply, his cheeks hollowing in a way that turned her instantly wet. Ready. Needy.

Her thighs wrapped around his hips automatically, her toes digging into his taut backside. No choice but to cling, squeeze him between her legs. Her core was so sensitive, so exposed. "Jonas, Jonas, Jonas."

"You don't want to make love, Ginny." His teeth raked over her nipple, tonguing the sting while he made blistering eye contact. "You want to fuck, don't you?"

That word coming from his perfect lips blew lusty sparks at her already overwhelming hunger. "I think so. Yes?"

"You're a little furious at me, is that why?" He worked his hard sex against the damp juncture of her thighs, his jaw slackening over the friction. She knew, because she felt the incredible slide and grind of it, too. "You want to send me off knowing you're angry, so I'll try harder to come back and make up."

Moisture rushed to her eyes. "Maybe."

His nod was resigned, but his eyes remained molten. "I'm incapable of denying you anything. Anything." He reached down and fisted his thickness, notching the smooth head inside of her—and ramming himself home to the tune of Ginny's strangled cry. For a moment, Jonas said nothing, his mouth open against her ear. Then, "You're even tighter when you're pissed."

A tickle roared downward in her belly, her thighs jerking violently as the orgasm whipping through her. "Oh my God." She squirmed, desperate for an anchor, a branch to grab onto while being shot down the raging rapids. "*Oh my God.*"

"Tell me you love my mouth," he said through his teeth, moving his hips in a slow circle beneath her. "The filth I say to you. Tell me you love my cock. Your body is already confessing."

"I love it!" She screamed in her throat, alarmed, delighted, overcome by how long she was being pitched uncontrollably in the throes of pleasure. "It feels too good. I can't. I can't."

"Do you know the effort it's taking to leash the monster inside me, Ginny? If the leash snaps, I'll fuck you clear through this door, so help me God."

So help *her* God, she almost encouraged him. Told him to do it. To give her his worst. Because she hated any part of Jonas being held hostage, kept away from her. She wanted every single piece, every facet of this man she loved. But he would never forgive himself if she was hurt and that—surprisingly not self-preservation—had Ginny kissing him softly. "Calm, Jonas." She stroked the side of his face. "Calm."

"Goddammit. Too late," he rasped, shaking his head and starting to drive himself inside of her, sliding her up and down the door at a jarring pace. "Too late."

Ginny tried to speak and couldn't. Not with her back teeth clacking together and the pressure of his size filling her over and over again, her ankles shaking from the impact where they dangled helplessly on either side of his hips. His hands were bruising on her bottom, holding her in place for his powerful pumps. Behind her, the door protested the continual abuse of its hinges, the handle rattling loudly.

"I don't mean to make it hurt, love. I don't mean it. I don't mean it."

She was pulled back from the precipice of alarm when her body started to respond to the wicked pace and intensity of Jonas inside her, chasing his release in a frenzy. Her own monster woke up where it had been dormant inside of her and she closed her eyes, listening to the repetitive *slapslapslap* of their sexes meeting. She thrilled to the grip of his hands, the possessiveness of his fingers digging into her flesh. Exhilaration danced down her spine at the hungry grunts he made into her neck, the sound of his fangs slicing out.

"I hold my entire world in these hands," he said hoarsely, licking the pulse at the base of her neck. "I drink from you with gratitude and worship every beat of your heart."

And when he sank his fangs into her neck, growling brokenly, the culmination of her derived pleasures collided and she was overcome. For long, rapturous moments, she couldn't move. Could only listen to him feed from her neck and derive strength, his body pulsing with renewed life right in front of her eyes. Her erogenous zones tightened and shivered and sparked, his feasting mouth weaving an emotional sense of completion inside of her, especially when he eased his fangs free, healed her with a lick and regarded her like some kind of angel.

She wasn't one. Not now.

Her fingernails of one hand scored his shoulders, the other tearing at his hair and she started to ride, as much as she could with limited movement, his body pressing her so tightly to the door, the rolls of her hips were almost futile, but they were something. They were something and she needed to move. To get over the edge of the cliff looming closer, closer.

"Come with me," she urged, whimpering when his rough drives resumed, their bodies moving like a sensual machine. "I love you, I love you, stay with me. Don't take yourself from me."

He slammed his mouth down on top of hers, kissing her with the passionate brutality she was starving for, the door rebounding hard off the frame behind her. *Bambambambambam.* "I'm sorry, my love," he said hoarsely. "My fucking *life*."

Ginny pitched over the edge so fast and so hard, her climax was almost painful. Her thighs shook around Jonas's hips, her body arching off the door, her scream echoing off the bathroom walls. He pressed his forehead to hers, looking her in the eye as he followed her off the cliff, hips jerking wildly, *Ginny* on his lips. Behind him, the bathroom bulbs shot sparks and went out, leaving them in the barest light where it crept in from beneath the door.

"Send me with your love, not your anger," he said once the most tremendous wave of passion had passed, his fingers brushing back her hair. "Tell me you'll marry me when and if I return to you. Give my heart a reason to keep beating. *Please*."

"Make me like you and I'll marry you now," she said in a pleading voice, willing to beg with everything she had to keep him alive. "Now. Today."

Agony bled from his every pore, but his words were threaded with steel. "I won't do it."

The need to throw her arms around Jonas was fierce. To tell him she loved him and would forgive him even the worst transgressions. But the fear in the dead center of her chest wouldn't let her lie. And anyway, he would have known by her pulse if she wasn't truthful. Her voice trembled as she answered. "I send you with both my love and my anger."

Jonas's eyes burned into her, rife with misery, but she held firm.

After what felt like an eternity, he stooped down and collected her robe, wrapping and belting her inside of it, along with the weighted silence. Once his pants were back in place, he stared hard at nothing, seeing what? She didn't know. Words remaining unspoken created a terrible pressure in her throat, but she didn't say them out loud. Her anger prevented her. How dare he reject the only solution that would keep them together? How dare he make decisions for her?

Tears burned her eyes as she stepped away from the bathroom door and opened it, allowing him to pass through. The prospect of his permanent absence turned her legs to jelly and she dropped to the floor, clutching the robe around her, tears scalding her cheeks. She listened to him open the hotel room door and leave with her heart occupying so much of her throat, she could barely breathe.

"Wait," she whispered. "Wait."

Once again the door opened and she scrambled to her feet, intending to take back all of her anger. To send him with love. What had she been thinking? He was going to face the firing squad and she'd have him secure in how she felt, not devastated over their fight. But when she rushed into the room, it was Elias that greeted her from the shadows, not Jonas.

"We can save him, you know," said Elias.

Hope surged, alleviating some of the awful weight in her stomach. "We can?"

"He'll hate me for it. But I can't let him play the sacrifice."

"I don't want that, either."

"Good." Elias took one step in her direction, and another, raising goosebumps on her arms, for the first time revealing the angry scar that bisected his mouth. "Then we give them you instead."

CHAPTER TWENTY-TWO
Jonas

EVERY INCH JONAS drove in the opposite direction of Ginny was a new nail being driven into his chest. Hands strangling the steering wheel of the car he'd borrowed from Tucker, he took deep breaths, limiting how often he swallowed so he wouldn't lose the taste of her too soon and go mad.

She had every right to hate him.

He'd turned her into a servant. Couldn't even make love to her without piercing her perfect fucking skin and sucking out the substance keeping her alive. And what they'd done in the hotel bathroom tonight hadn't been making love. He'd been too rough. God, what if she was sore? What if she needed him?

It took every ounce of his self-control not to whip the car into a U-turn on the two-lane highway, but somehow he stayed the course, already breaking his own rule and swallowing greedily. He would never make it back to Staten Island before sunrise, anyway. His only option was to keep the gas pedal to the floorboard and reach New Hampshire before dawn broke the horizon.

Though wouldn't it solve everything if he just lay down in a field somewhere and let himself burn? If he ceased to exist on this earth, Ginny wouldn't be forced to act as his perpetual meal. She'd walk down the street without fear of violence from monsters he'd brought into her life, simply by being her mate.

Her mate in two lifetimes.

He could hardly fathom it, but on another level, he couldn't believe it took him so long to realize she was his first love reincarnated. When he'd sat up on the embalming table and spied her across the room, he'd felt the deep sense of recognition. But that call from the past had quickly been drowned out by the present. His overpowering infatuation with Ginny—and trying like hell not to act on it—had required his full concentration. That initial recognition had fallen by the wayside, even though he'd continued to experience it at every turn without fully acknowledging it.

Jonas's heart thunked fast and heavy in his chest. The off-pace tempo of the newly awakened organ hammered out its distress in Morse code. *Go back, I miss her, go back, I need her. Why why why?* Why were they speeding away from their reason for living? From the woman whose extraordinary essence had woven from one century to another and fallen right into his lap again? If that wasn't a decree from fate that they had a connection that could not be severed by place or time or circumstance, nothing was.

And *because* he loved Ginny, he would put himself between her and harm.

He'd been too green the first time to save her from falling off a cliff, but he wouldn't fail her this time. She would be left safe, if it was his final act on this earth. There was no doubt her face would be the last image imprinted on his brain and he was glad of it. His heart would still be clamoring, begging to return to her side, but his mind would be at rest, knowing he'd removed the threat of harm from her life.

Currently, his mind was far from peaceful, however. It continued to replay a grainy horror film in which Ginny fell from the Verazzano Bridge while screaming his name and he was still back at the on-ramp, a quarter of a mile from the center of the bridge where she dropped. That fear of not being able to reach her in time would never go away, never fade, just like his love for her.

The image changed and now she toppled from a cliff, while he was none the wiser, wondering where she'd gone. Giving up his exhaustive search and mourning her while serving at the right hand of the man who had potentially killed her.

He wouldn't be blind this time.

Not with Ginny.

Jonas forced his grip to lessen on the steering wheel, lest he rip it off.

I love you. Please forgive me for leaving.

There was a chance she *wouldn't* forgive him and he'd factored that into his decision. It seemed like the only option. Do anything to keep her breathing. But now, as he approached the exit that would bring him to the High Order dwelling, a yawning pit opened in his stomach. All the progress they'd made on compromise, wiped out in one swipe of his hand across the board. Would every second of their relationship forever be soured in her memory by his highhandedness?

The exit he took was narrow and closed for repair, as it had been for decades, and he wove the vehicle through traffic cones and roadblocks, before turning left onto a road densely wooded on either side. He drove for ten minutes, muscle memory making him slow the car at the thirteenth bend and pull over. He crossed the road to pull a series of tree branches to the side, revealing an overgrown path, just large enough for a car to fit. After driving through the opening, he got back out and replaced the branches before continuing on his way. Several bumpy minutes later, he arrived at an abbreviated turnoff leading to nothing but a shoddy hut.

Jonas remained in the car staring at the decaying shack, memories rushing back of the first time he entered through its rusted door. A young man steeped in grief and confusion over the disappearance of his mate. Needing an anchor, anything to keep him from being peeled off the earth into the atmosphere.

Back then, he'd trusted his sire, the vampire within—and he wouldn't make that mistake again.

His instinct urged him to rip down the surrounding trees, bring them down on the hut and smash it to pieces. To go below and wreak havoc on everyone who resided with the High Order. As far as he was concerned, they were all complicit in trying to hurt his love. His life.

Go back.

Go back and apologize and compromise.

If you survive this, you've lost her.

Jonas's hand flew to his chest where his heart remained half-beating in protest at being apart from Ginny. He slammed a fist there to start it pumping correctly again, his body slumping in relief when it sputtered and functioned once more, if dully.

He closed his eyes and thought of her before climbing out of the car. Of the excitement on her beautiful face when someone bid on her white, silk dress. Her bravery climbing onto his lap and offering her neck while he rattled the silver chains like a beast. Her peacefulness when she slept, her voice reciting words from a movie along with Maureen O'Hara. The way her palms felt on his face, in his hair, on his shoulders.

With a miserable sound, he propelled himself from

the car and approached the hut, staring up at the overhead, pinhole-sized camera until he heard the click. He opened the door and crossed to another, passing through and traveling down a set of stairs that led to steel elevator doors.

Floor after floor ticked by while he worked to keep his burning ire under control. Oddly, he felt no apprehension over seeing his sire again after so long, like he'd always imagined he would. He was no longer a misguided youth. He'd been out in the world cleaning up the havoc wreaked by malevolent leadership and every ounce of hero worship he'd once had for the king was now extinguished. All that remained was a demand for answers and the urgent motivation to keep Ginny safe.

The elevator doors separated, revealing a suited vampire, hands folded at his waist. His eyes might as well have been made of glass for all they gave away. He simply inclined his head at Jonas, turned on a wing tip and strode away through the high-ceilinged foyer. Jonas followed, unintimidated by the lack of greeting. After all, he knew the process well. Anyone requiring an audience with the king was first made to understand they were insignificant, no matter how old or young. A lot like he treated his public.

The sound of their footsteps was muffled by the royal blue carpeting. Lights flickered on the wall and cast shadows that shifted as they walked. Stone staircases crisscrossed overhead, leading to drawing rooms and sleeping quarters. Somewhere a single violin played a haunting melody and Jonas rolled his eyes because it was all so goddamn dramatic.

One of his less important reasons for leaving the High Order was their refusal to update their antiquated existence. The members of the union and their groupies haunted this place like specters, their robes dragging behind them while they drank blood from gold chalices and the like. Frankly the gold chalices were the most embarrassing part. Show him the rule that said vampires weren't allowed to shop at Bed Bath & Beyond.

For all their showboating, however, the High Order was dangerous. Each and every one of them possessed superhuman strength and knowledge that was only earned by centuries of living. He might find them and their frippery somewhat ridiculous, but he wouldn't let down his guard or underestimate them.

Only a fool would do so.

The suited man led Jonas down the far right corridor and down a set of stairs that expanded toward the bottom, emptying into the Great Hall.

And there they were, right where he'd left them, four of earth's oldest vampires sitting in high-back, velvet inlaid thrones lining the far back wall. Jonas was surprised to find the chair beside the king—*his* chair— still remained empty, but he showed no outward reaction.

They'd been anticipating his arrival, that much was obvious.

The High Order didn't assemble in the Great Hall unless there was an important matter at hand, but here they were, watching Jonas with an air of expectancy.

Jonas's sire was tight-lipped and impassive, his salt and pepper hair in waves around his shoulders, though his eyes were sharp with humor. As always. Watching, measuring, deciding how best to amuse himself. If there was a fleeting flicker of affection in his sire's eyes, he either imagined it or didn't care.

The other three chairs were occupied by faces he recognized. Faces that hadn't aged a day over the course of a century or longer, in some cases. There was Griselda, a German female who'd been Silenced during the Second World War. David, a Scotsman whose wife had been so distraught when he took ill, she'd hunted down and bargained with a vampire to Silence him, so he'd live on forever. Unfortunately, that same vampire had failed to successfully Silence her, too. Lastly, there was Devon, a steely-eyed black man from Chicago who'd once been a roadie for blues singer Robert Johnson.

Finally, his sire leaned forward, just the barest inch. "Perhaps with your fancy new heartbeat, you've started behaving as an entitled human, daring to address this council in sweatpants?"

"I've had a busy night," Jonas returned, without a second's hesitation. "As I suspect you well know."

Clarence slowly tilted his head. "Why, whatever could you mean?"

The gut-crushing memory of his Ginny pitching forward off the bridge shot him through with white-hot rage. While he did his best to control his outrage, because losing his composure would serve no one, he would *not* play the fucking game. Not after three attempts on Ginny's life. "You know damn well what I'm talking about. You've been waiting for me to figure it out."

Silence ticked by, followed by a low laugh from the king. "How does it feel to be a hypocrite, son? Such an idealist and a rule follower, aren't you? Traveling the country, turning my constituents against me with your bleeding heart." He drummed his fingers on the armrest, the movement very precise, a glimpse at the irritation he tried so hard to conceal. "Until a pretty face—a *human*—comes along and the rules become inconvenient. Not so noble now, are we?"

"*A pretty face?*" Jonas took an involuntary step toward the foursome. "You speak of my *mate.* My devotion to her is not a whim. I could no more stay away from her than I could turn myself human again."

Silence fell. "She is still alive then?"

They had no idea, did they? They had no idea he

could never be standing there and forming words if she was dead. He'd be nothing more than dust motes carrying on the breeze. Furthermore, they had no idea he'd saved her. Or how. And he'd hold on to any potential advantage. "Yes. She is alive," Jonas answered, voice clear.

The king's eye twitched. "A rule has been broken. You've most boldly entered into a relationship with a human. Would you have us ignore your insubordination?"

"Who will make the ruling on what *you* have done?" Jonas shouted. "Leaving her in a position to die is the same as killing her. So is sending another vampire to put her in harm's way."

"Ah yes, Seymour. He agreed to the mission in exchange for his mate's freedom. When he didn't report back with his progress, I assumed he'd failed and executed her for the crime of feeding from a human." He tapped his lips. "Though I can't imagine what happened to Seymour. Care to fill me in?"

Jonas stared back unflinchingly, intuition telling him to leave the question unanswered. The longer he could keep his new abilities to himself, the better off he would be if he needed to fight. "Don't distract from the issue. You've tried to kill my mate, too. *Twice.*"

The smallest dash of regret bloomed in Clarence's eyes, but it was masked immediately. "I wondered if you'd figure it out. Well done."

"Why?" Jonas worked to steady his voice. How easily his sire admitted to subjecting him to unimaginable pain. "Why kill her and not me?"

"Is it so outlandish that I desire to have *my only son* reign at my side?" shouted the king. "That you would covet the accolade so many would kill for?"

Jonas hid his shock over Clarence's vehemence. "If that is so, if you are being truthful and you care anything for me, please accept my vow of fealty in exchange for…a life with her. A life out of this Order's reach."

The king's eyes widened just slightly, enough to let Jonas know he'd surprised him. "First you choose your precious conscience over the life I offered you. Now you choose a human girl over the honor of sitting on the High Order? How many times do you think I'll allow you to humiliate me?"

"I do not seek to humiliate."

"It matters not. Perhaps I'll give you what you want, my son. Perhaps I'll sentence you to death. Once you're gone, I'll no longer *have* a reason to fear a challenge." He cast a look just beyond Jonas's shoulder. "Isn't that right, Larissa?"

Jonas reeled from the shock of Ginny's stepmother waltzing past him in a crimson robe, her movements so smooth, she didn't seem to touch the ground at all. She curtseyed to the High Order and folded her hands at her waist. She'd just opened her mouth to speak when the suited vampire who'd greeted Jonas at the elevator reentered the room. "King, we have visitors."

The king's mouth turned down at the corners. He beckoned the suited servant forward, gesturing for him to come closer. The vampire whispered in Clarence's ear and he started to laugh, quietly at first, then louder and louder.

Fear prickled Jonas's skin for the first time. He watched the staircase with the anxiety writhing in his bones. It couldn't be Ginny. It couldn't be. But he didn't like the way his sire watched and waited for his reaction, almost gleeful in his anticipation.

God no. What was this?

The pure scent of Ginny reached him and a bellowed denial ripped out of his throat with such force, he tasted blood. And when she came into view, he could barely register what his eyes were telling him, the scene was such an abomination to his senses. Elias dragged—*dragged*—his Ginny into the gigantic hall by her hair.

"Oh my God. *What is this?*" she screamed, twisting in Elias's grip. "Why are you doing this? Please let me go, let me go, let me go. I just want to go home."

Jonas's vision tripled and swarmed back together, his equilibrium diminished almost entirely. Somehow he remained standing under the weight of denial. Ginny in this place. His mate surrounded by beings that could break her neck with the snap of a finger. Vulnerable. Scared. Brought here by a man he'd considered his best friend. No. No.

Was she hurt? *Jesus Christ*. This betrayal couldn't be happening.

He'd been prepared to exchange his life for her safety and now she was in the midst of wolves. Exposed. No. Please God no.

"*Elias*," Jonas shouted, sounding and feeling like a wounded animal. "What have you done?" Elias threw Ginny down to the ground and she looked up at Jonas...

...as if she didn't know him. Had never met him in her life. Her gaze went right through him like a sword cutting into water, her pulse erratic and wild, like it had been when she fell from the bridge. "Ginny?" With a shaking hand extended, he went toward her, intending to pick her up, cradle her, find the injuries and try to heal them. *Now now now*. It was his duty and he craved them, even in the midst of his utter terror. "Come to me, love. I'll make it all right. I won't let them hurt you."

"How do you know my name?" Ginny breathed, crawling backwards, away from him. Away. From. Him? "I don't understand why I'm here! What is happening?"

Jonas ran into an invisible barrier, ice forming a frigid layer on his skin. His voice emerged sounding like a wheeze. "What do you mean, how do I know your name?"

Elias's dark laughter rang out. "I did what *you* were too weak to do. She remembers nothing of Jonas Cantrell." With a hateful smirk in Jonas's direction, he turned to face the High Order and executed a sweeping bow. "For years, I've urged him to resume his duties and he refuses. He does not deserve the honor—an honor I covet above all else." He flicked a wrist in Ginny's direction. "Take this as my show of good faith. Consider me for his council seat instead. I will spend my every waking breath undoing the damage he's done to your reputation—in a way only I can. I know every place he's been, every vampire he's met with, every safe haven he's established."

Torment seared Jonas's insides.

He'd been dropped into hell to be roasted among sinners.

A violent ringing started in his ears and vibrated down his spine and if he had a functioning stomach, he would have emptied it on the ground at that moment.

No.

No.

No.

Yes, the betrayal was equivalent to a spike being driven into his stomach, but he could focus on nothing but Ginny. His love looked right through him as if she'd never met him. Never spent hours speaking to him, never kissed him or enraptured him with her laugh.

Every magical minute since he'd woken up on her table…gone? How could that be? How could such valuable, perfect hours cease to exist? His mate didn't know his touch. She didn't know he would keep her safe. Didn't know him at all. These realizations hit fast and hard, leaving him bereft, stumbling sideways in front of the Order and nearly dropping.

"Look at him," marveled the king. "A shell. Over an inconsequential human."

"I'm going to kill you, Elias," Jonas choked out, doubling over, bracing his hands on his knees. "How could you do this?"

Not only to him. But to Ginny.

How many times had she begged him to leave her mind intact? Once upon a time, had he actually considered erasing himself from her memories? The pain of occupying no place in her mind—and therefore her heart—was unfathomable. His bones were turning to dust where he stood.

"I am entertained," cooed the king, steepling his fingers beneath his chin. "Anyone else?"

The High Order murmured their agreement.

Clarence got more comfortable in his throne. "You want to know why I put Miss Lynn in such perilous situations?" He waved at someone or something, Jonas couldn't be sure, couldn't feel or deduce anything. "Larissa, please come closer."

Jonas watched Ginny's eyes widen, just a fraction, her attention training on Larissa. Her skin turned the barest shade lighter, as though some blood had left her face. Recognition? Shock? It all happened in the split second before she went back to looking confused and fearful.

That was odd.

"The poor thing is so confused," murmured the king.

"Does she not remember me?" Larissa asked, peeling the red hood back from her face. "Jesus. H-how far back did he erase her memories?"

"Far. Years," Elias supplied quickly.

Too quickly?

What are you looking for? Hope in a void?

Stop.

Elias had betrayed him.

His only mission in this life was to get Ginny out of this place unharmed. He would be put to death and thus, she would no longer be a conduit for his hunger pains. There were no other options. None. He couldn't sustain himself on her blood when she didn't even fucking know him. It would be against her will and he would die first. He *would* die first.

"Larissa is a seer. An immortal, such as we," said the king. "She came to me around the time I sired you, bargaining protection from us in exchange for a vision she'd had. Always scouting for her next payday, my darling seer." He regarded Larissa fondly, but his expression quickly soured. "She told me you would challenge me one day for the throne—and win." He unfurled his index finger and pointed it at Ginny. "But it would only happen if and when you found your mate."

"Mate?" Ginny echoed, regarding him with renewed terror. "What are you talking about? Who *are* you people?"

Her words were a blow to Jonas's chest and he closed his eyes to absorb the jolt, attempting to soak in what Clarence had revealed at the same time. "That's why you tried to kill Ginny before I even met her. You didn't want us to find each other." He turned his focus on Larissa. "All this time, the threat was right down the hall."

Larissa seemed to be having a hard time taking her eyes off Ginny. "I was hired to keep tabs on the girl. Killing her didn't strike me as necessary until you arrived in Coney Island." Her chin went up a notch. "After that, I didn't have a choice but to alert the king. The prophecy was in motion."

"But prophecies can be changed," stressed Clarence, eyeballing the seer. "Now that I've sentenced Jonas to death, you foresee me as king indefinitely."

After the barest hesitation, Larissa inclined her head and the king looked satisfied. "I'd have found the poor creature in her next life, too, thanks to Larissa, and did what needed to be done," said the king. "Oftentimes, rules must be bent slightly to preserve the integrity of the Order."

Ginny's stepmother had been watching Ginny with an uncomfortable expression, but started at the mention of her name. "Yes," she said, voice raspy. "It took quite a while, this time around. But if she came back in yet another form, the patterns left behind by her soul would be easier to follow."

"Please, no," Jonas rasped, bowing his head in contrition. "Please take me now and let her go live her life. If I'm gone and unable to take your throne, you'll have no need to harm her. The prophecy will be void."

"Unbelievable," murmured the king. "You came here prepared to willingly sacrifice yourself to save her humanity. Is separation from her so favorable to Silencing her?"

Jonas thought he knew the answer to that. If someone had asked him yesterday, he would have given an unequivocal yes. *Nothing* was worth stopping her exquisite heart from beating. But now he could hear her pleading with him to Silence her. Could hear the bravery in her voice and he wasn't so sure he'd done the right thing denying her. A future together. An endless future with his love. Had he honestly rejected one without even considering Ginny's wishes?

The words scraped his throat raw. "I...refused to

take from her what I gave up without knowing the hell that followed."

Again, Clarence seemed to blanch before retreating into his shell of hatred. "Well." His face arranged itself in a sneer. "I find myself in a magnanimous mood. Jonas, since you're so enamored with humanity, why not mimic one of their most ridiculous practices, shall we?" He met the eyes of each member of the Order. "It's only fair Jonas be allowed a last meal."

Clarence's smile was sinister as he gestured to the suited servant.

"Bring him his mate."

"*No,*" Jonas roared, even as his fangs descended, his appetite gathering like hurricane clouds. He watched in horror as the servant seized Ginny beneath her arms and began carrying her toward Jonas. Eyes wide with fright, she fought—and he couldn't move. His mouth salivated with hunger, already tasting the pure, perfect flavor of her. The flavor he *required.* The animal inside him wailed to life, demanding satisfaction. *Mine. Mine. Mine.* He could already feel her softness giving way in deference to his bite and the rush of life on his tongue. *Ginny. My mate.*

This lifetime's worth of yearning took place in a split second and then all he could see was her pain. Another vampire daring to place a finger on his love? The lights in the great hall dimmed and flickered. *Hold it in check.*

Hold it.

Jonas caught Ginny before her sudden lack of balance made her hit the floor. He gathered her close, moaning at the feel of her in his arms. She struggled against him and his brain demanded he let her go, *let her go right now*, but he couldn't.

Oh God, he couldn't.

The High Order laughed at his weakness, but he ignored the grating sound and focused on the precious beating of her heart. Just one second more. One second more and he'd let her go. Jonas's mouth moved in her hair, inhaling her scent like a greedy miser, his hands tracing every inch of her back. "You don't know this, love, but I would kill, steal and die for you. There is nothing to fear."

Ginny pulled back just enough to make eye contact and what he saw in their beautiful depths turned his world back to color. Furthermore, her pulse beat true once more. Trusting and steady.

She…knew him.

She knew him and loved him.

Her memories were intact.

"I know," she whispered. "I have no fear, Dreamboat."

Then in the subtlest of movements, the reason for his existence tipped her head to the left, exposing her neck.

CHAPTER TWENTY-THREE

T HEY REALLY, REALLY didn't have time for a reunion.
Ginny wished the opposite were true. That she
had endless hours to bask in the return of Jonas, because
he'd gone missing the moment she pretended not to
know him, lost to grief, the light extinguishing in his
eyes. She would have nightmares about the last ten
minutes forever, they'd been so painfully horrific, but
she'd followed Elias's plan to a T. If Jonas would stop
staring at her like she'd come back from the dead, it
might work.

No, it *would* work.

"I love you," she mouthed, still trying to free herself
from his grip and thankfully, being unsuccessful. "Now
compromise."

A ghost of a sound puffed out of him, such love
shining down at her, she would have buckled under the
weight of it if he wasn't holding her up. Very slowly, his
attention moved to her neck and he swallowed, fear
tightening his features—and she remembered what he'd
told her about Silencing.

There's a venom inside of us that only releases when a victim is close to…dying. It's involuntary, a product of our true nature as predators and it's the only thing that can transform a human…

These circumstances were far from ideal with near-death on the agenda, but what choice did they have?

Ginny bucked and twisted in his arms, drawing more laughter from the High Order. Elias came forward, as if to get a better view of Ginny and Jonas, but he was pulled away by three guards. Past Larissa.

Larissa.

It didn't seem possible that her flighty stepmother had been the figure in the crimson robe that appeared in her dreams and was now working for the High Order. That her prediction had nearly been the catalyst for Ginny's *murder.*

Twice.

It made sense now, why Larissa never seemed to age. Although…why had she tried so hard to convince Ginny to leave Coney Island with her? To keep her away from Jonas, and thus the wrath the High Order? Had Larissa been truthful about loving Peter Lynn? Ginny hoped so. Badly. The wool being pulled over her own eyes was one thing, but Larissa duping her sweet father was unacceptable. Ginny couldn't think of that now, though. There was too much on the line. Her future with Jonas. His life. Hers. And she could only keep up the pretense of struggle for so long before the High

Order realized she'd been acting.

"Look at him. Suddenly back to being so noble." The king's disgust was palpable. "Thank goodness the prophecy has amended itself. This council would never have survived under his weak leadership."

"You are stronger than anyone I've ever known," Ginny whispered, pushing up to speak right against Jonas's ear. "*Jonas.* Now or never."

They locked eyes briefly and she tried her best to communicate her total confidence in him. How rock solid it was. How much she loved him. He must have translated her look correctly, because he took a shuddering breath and closed his eyes, as if soaking in her words in as deeply as he could.

When he opened them again, they shone like emeralds.

Whereas minutes ago, he'd been ashen, barely able to stay on his feet, he resembled a determined warrior now. Fierce. Unbeatable.

He tilted Ginny's head to one side and leaned down, pausing with his fangs an inch from her neck. "Please forgive me for the pain. Stay with me through it all. *Stay with me.*"

"Eternally."

His fangs slid into the thick vein of Ginny's neck and her limbs turned limp. She gasped at the ceiling, recognizing the difference instantly in the way Jonas took her blood. It was fast and ferocious and purposeful. He'd been afraid of killing her before, but now...in a way, killing her was the point.

Dizziness assailed Ginny, her eyelids growing heavy. Jonas's hand twisted in the material of the hotel maid uniform Elias had stolen for her to wear, pulling her ever closer, his gruff sounds of satisfaction turning into desperate growls. This was it. The change he'd told her would come over him—his true nature as a predator. She wouldn't be around for much more of it, because her vision was already growing dim and she couldn't feel her feet, her hands, her lips.

Her head lolled backward and she caught sight of Larissa creeping backward into the shadows, pulling the hood back over her head. Maybe Ginny's lack of blood had her imagining things, but she swore the seer gave her a quiet nod.

"Enough," said the king, but of course, Jonas didn't listen. At being ignored, Clarence's fist rapped off the throne and made Ginny's head pound. "*Enough.*"

Whispers rose like a funnel cloud in the hall.

He's turning her.

He's turning her to circumvent the rule.

A searing pain ripped into her neck and Ginny bit down on a whimper, but it wouldn't be contained and it turned into a full-fledged scream. Jonas almost broke away then, but she somehow found the strength to reach up and hold him fast. With a choppy sound of alarm, laced with definite hunger, he pulled deeply of her blood, taking her all the way down to the floor and quite simply preying on her, his full weight pinning her to the carpet.

The pain in her neck dulled.

Everything dulled.

A light appeared in front of her eyes and helplessly, Ginny followed it—

Jonas's weight left her suddenly and in the hazy distance, she heard a loud crash. Someone picked her up and wind licked at her skin, before she was set down once more. When she managed to crack open an eyelid, she found herself at the bottom of the wide staircase she'd come down…hours ago? Minutes?

The numbness inside her dropped out and the pain lashed back in, holding her organs hostage in a clenched fist. Her mouth opened on a silent scream and she started to shake. Was this it? Was it happening?

"Jonas," she whimpered pitifully. "Jonas."

Ginny clawed at her chest, ready to rip it open to reach the agony in her heart and it seemed to go on forever, cracking like a whip to the rest of her insides, inflicting damage—and she experienced every brutal second of it. No way out, *there was no way out* and the human inside of her searched for help on instinct, turning onto her side and attempting to call out.

No one heard her. Not with the battle taking place.

The High Order no longer sat in their thrones. They surrounded Jonas in a circle, their robes in tatters. And Jonas...she'd never seen him as he was. Like a God. He fended off the attacks they hurled in his direction, capturing their energy and sending it back twice as powerful. Felling them one by one.

But they continued to rise, regroup, attack again. Unfazed.

"You shouldn't be able to last a minute against us," said Clarence, awestruck. "Where did you gain such power?"

Elias appeared at Jonas's side, his gaze rife with meaning and emotion. "Threaten a vampire's mate once, he grows stronger to protect her. Take her life? Threaten it again and again? You've created your own worst nightmare."

"We don't have nightmares anymore," droned Jonas's sire. "We don't sleep."

Not acknowledging Clarence's comment, Elias instead nodded at Jonas. "It's time. You've got this. I have your back."

"How touching," Jonas's sire sneered, sailing a bolt of opaque air in Elias's direction. Elias rolled to the side, but not before he was winged by the moving force field. With gritted teeth, he got to his feet and started to rejoin Jonas in the middle of the circle, but something caught his attention and made him smile. It didn't take Ginny long to realize what it was. Tucker.

Tucker…and an army. Hundreds of men and women.

They thundered down the stairs around her with a deafening war cry, running head first into the fray with Tucker at the lead. The army moved at such a high speed, there was no mistaking them as vampires. One man in particular fought balanced on a prosthetic leg, a baseball cap pulled low on his forehead. Several of them were knocked to the ground before they could reach the High Order—who were now unmistakably the enemy—but it was impossible to stop them all.

Despite the miserable state of her body, Ginny couldn't help but watch in breathless triumph as the High Order were captured, one by one, held down and subdued by the makeshift army. This was it. The rightful beginning of Jonas's rule. It all started here and she was proud of him. So proud.

Jonas stood over Clarence, his shoulders rippling with ferocity. "You die now in her name," he rasped, raising his right hand, fisting it until his sire started to choke, scratching at the invisible hands around his throat.

"Don't you see she is dying?" The king gasped a laugh. "*She is dying.*"

Jonas's fist dropped to his side. He stiffened and twisted around, his gaze landing on her immediately.

"No," he whispered, reaching her side in an instant. "You…" He frantically ran hands over her body, brows drawn together in confusion. "You're not supposed to be conscious. *Ginny.*"

She tried to speak. Nothing came out.

"*Elias*," Jonas roared, his eyes wild. "*What the fuck is happening?*"

The light she'd been trying to walk toward loomed brighter, swallowing her, but she only made it halfway through, darkness crushing in on one side, searing heat on the other. She was being rent in two.

"Did your venom release?" Elias shouted.

"*Yes.*"

"All of it?"

Their voices faded little by little as Ginny started to move away from her body, like fog rolling off a bay. Jonas's anguished below made her fight. She clawed her way back to full wakefulness, even though that was where the pain resided. Better to be in agony than separated from Jonas at the end.

"I don't understand," Jonas rasped, tipping her face up. "Her heartbeat is strong, but her skin cools so quickly."

Ginny tried to communicate with her eyes that nothing was his fault. That she would find him again in the next life and the one after that…but a movement just beyond his shoulder caught her eye. Jonas was drowning too deeply in his misery to notice Clarence had broken loose of the vampires holding him down. The king disengaged their hold, spun around long enough to grasp a stake and fly in Jonas's direction, weapon raised. Vaguely, Ginny wondered if the king's movements would normally appear as a blur to her and nothing more, but now? She could pinpoint every step, could see the revenge flame in his eyes, hear the carpet fibers move under his feet.

And with Jonas in jeopardy, her body took over.

Power ripped through the cobwebs of pain and spiked in her stomach, shooting out to her fingertips, legs, hair follicles. Denial followed. The weight of responsibility. Without a formal command from her brain, Ginny lunged to her feet and threw herself in between the king and Jonas.

"*Ginny!*" Jonas boomed. "*No.*"

Yes.

Surprise was on her side or she would have been toast.

Her fist knocked the stake free from the king's hand and it clattered to the ground, at her feet. The king stared at Ginny in shock for a millisecond, before springing forward—propelling himself right into the stake she'd picked up at an unfathomable pace and now held in her fist. Air left his open mouth like a deflating ball, his eyes ticking to Jonas, holding, and he became nothing but embers, then ash.

The remaining members of the High Order screamed, the sound echoing off the hall's high ceiling. Ginny fell like a stone, her final reserve of energy expended.

No more.

She couldn't stay another second. Numbness stole through her and she collapsed onto her back in a fit of trembling.

Jonas's frenzied expression filled the space above her. "*Elias, give me your knife.*"

"What are you going to do?"

Distantly, Ginny sensed the exchange taking place. "What my gut tells me," Jonas said raggedly. "I have no choice. I refuse to walk this earth without her."

She cracked a single eye in time to watch Elias blade slash diagonally across Jonas's wrist, blood welling in the cut—and something inside her swelled eagerly. He held the wound above her mouth, letting several droplets fall before bringing it flush to her lips. A drop slid down her throat and Ginny's back arched off the floor. A moment ago, her hands were devoid of strength, but they clung to Jonas's wrist now, holding his hand immobile while more and more blood dripped into her mouth.

Her heart scrambled, pumping harder and...*louder* than she could ever remember, as if she was listening to an ultrasound at full volume.

The taste was paradise.

It was partially her own blood, yes, but it carried Jonas, too. Somehow her taste buds could pick out the individual molecules that held his essence and she savored them most of all, moaning as they slid down her throat.

"That's it. Come back to me, love." Tears clogged his tone. "Ginny, *please*."

Her eyelids fluttered down and she dropped into the scene from her recurring dream, but the perspective changed. She was now Jonas standing beneath the tree, watching herself approach. A different version of herself, but herself nonetheless. The bone-deep yearning, the hunger, the obsession was Jonas's. All for her. She shook in the face of it.

Next she saw herself in the embalming room, dressed in her green plaid dress and white coat. Thirst wrapped around her throat and squeezed, inner willpower wrestling back the urge to pounce, to subdue and conquer. Claim. Had he really been fighting such ferocious urges in her presence? How had he managed it all this time?

Relentless had been his ache. Not touching her had been nearly unbearable for him. Leaving her before sunrise had left him bereft, over and over again, to the point of despair. That despair infiltrated her now and she understood it.

Now she was living his reality, her human love colliding with something elemental, something animal and irreversible. *Exploding.*

She let go of Jonas's wrist, turning boneless on the floor, hands flopped out at her sides, but she had to reassure him. Craved his easement so much that she smiled. "Oh, thank God," he said, falling forward to writhe his forehead on her belly. "I almost lost you. I almost fucking lost you."

You didn't, she wanted to whisper, but couldn't locate her vocal abilities.

"Listen to her heart. It never fully stopped." Jonas lifted his head, sounding awed. "That means...I'm...her mate, too. The bond was already in place. Even when she was still human?"

"That must be why she felt your pain."

"We can sustain each other," Jonas whispered.

"She won't have to be woken by her mate," Elias said, crouching down beside his friend. "Her heart never slept."

Jonas leaned down and kissed her mouth softly. "I'll never let it go silent."

Ginny looked up into the eyes of the man he loved, noticing four separate shades of green for the first time. His breaths caressed her eardrums. She could feel the bow of his muscles through two sets of clothes, hear the friction of clothing on his skin—and she had to spear her fingers into the carpet to keep from pulling Jonas down on top of her, craving the press of his body, his mouth on hers.

Jonas's mouth curved against hers. "Still going to have a problem being calm, are we?"

Oh Lord, the sound of his voice. It unwrapped her like a present. "I was led to believe we wouldn't need to be…calm anymore."

The tips of their tongues met on the barest stroke. "I'm really looking forward to that."

"Me too." A throb landed in her throat. "I'm sorry…about Clarence. He was your father, in a way—"

He cut her off with an incredulous sound, his eyes whipping with intensity. "I have need of you and no one else." Jonas's hands shook as he cupped her face. "Some things a man doesn't get over so easy," he said, quoting *The Quiet Man* and making her heart soar. "Loving you is one of them. I will do it *eternally*, Ginny. But if you *ever* put yourself in danger again—"

"Without consulting you first?"

"Yes…"

"Sounds familiar, doesn't it?"

Emotion swept his features. "Who knew I could be so grateful knowing I'll be having the same argument about compromise for thousands of years?"

Jonas picked up Ginny and cradled her against his chest. He didn't take his attention off her once as he crossed the hall and settled into the throne where Clarence had sat. Then he looked out over the gathering of vampires he'd helped in their time of need, his face impassive as they each took a knee and pressed a fist to their chests.

Their voices rang in unison. "To the king."

Jonas drew Ginny closer. "And his queen," he said.

EPILOGUE

Three months later

G INNY LOOKED DOWN at the bouquet of roses clasped tightly in her hands. In a word, they were pink, to match her wedding gown. But they were so much more. Tiny dew drops clung to the buds. The green leaves were shot through with tiny, intricate veins of varying sizes. If she listened carefully, she could hear the moisture being carried through them to hydrate the roses.

Wonder curved her lips and she hugged the bouquet to her chest.

Her feet were planted on the roof of the funeral home, but she could have been levitating, for all the hope and optimism in her heart.

Today she married her love.

Her mate, her best friend, the king to her queen.

Ginny stood behind a veil of flowers, waiting to walk down the aisle, and even though she was aching from being separated from Jonas—even by mere yards—she needed to savor the moment. To acknowledge the journey toward reaching such…completion.

There was a quiet hum of conversation coming from the guests on the roof and she could pick out each individual voice. Elias and Tucker sat in the front row, beneath a waterfall of fairy lights and roses, Tucker no doubt exceedingly uncomfortable in his suit. The rest of the voices were newer to Ginny, but growing more and more familiar. They belonged to the Silenced Jonas had counseled over the years, now members of his royal court. Jonas ran his kingdom the way he did everything else. With heart, fairness and wisdom and the vampires who served him were loyal, not only to Jonas, but to Ginny.

When Jonas took the throne, he'd immediately begun making changes to the High Order's policies and was in the process of sending ambassadors to all major cities to guide vampires through their transition from human to immortal. Feeding from humans was still illegal. And now Silencing humans at will and thus, leaving them without guidance was no longer allowed, either. But at Ginny's urging, Jonas had compromised and decided to make rulings over Silencing matters on a case-by-case basis.

After all, weren't they proof a vampire and human could fall in love and choose to spend eternity together?

Compromising with her fiancé was a beautiful thing…if sometimes a bit of a challenge.

For instance, Jonas had been adamant that Ginny remain with him at the High Order's underground palace, which they were in the process of giving a much needed makeover. But she'd reminded him of the importance of her father's legacy. Not only that, while her preferred location was by her future husband's side, she wasn't the kind to sit back and let everyone else do the work.

P. Lynn Funeral Home was a funeral home no longer.

They'd sealed off the windows, turned the morgue into a series of bedrooms and it was now a halfway house for freshly Silenced vampires.

At first, Ginny worried that she would miss being a mortician terribly. Being entrusted with the important job of sending the deceased off with care and respect. But, in a weird way, she was still doing relatively the same thing, wasn't she? Vampires came to her and Jonas, confused and alone. Through counseling and giving of resources, they were able to send the undead off to a new life, armed with the support they needed. Her new undertaking even fulfilled her with a sense of family that had been missing in her prior line of work. Now she had friends *and* a purpose.

For Ginny's part, she'd required little guidance transitioning to the vampire lifestyle. She and Jonas had spent a lot of time speculating *why*, usually in between bouts of passionate lovemaking that often resulted in broken furniture.

Jonas had a theory that went like this. Fate had selected them as mates, vampire or otherwise. And thus, Ginny's body had been prepared, even in its humanity, to step into the role, no matter what it took. That was why she'd experienced his pain. Why her spirit had traveled through time and found him again. Fate had deemed it so—and the consummation of that destiny would change the course of the vampire world forever.

Ginny looked out over the lights of Coney Island, her attention lingering on the Shore Theater where Tucker and Elias still stayed on occasion, when they weren't at the palace. They'd been given the job of searching for Larissa—and they had. Far and wide with no luck. In the beginning, Ginny had felt betrayed by her stepmother. Like she'd spent years having her privacy invaded. But now...

The more she replayed the night Jonas seized the throne, the more she remembered. When Clarence asked Larissa if the prophecy had shifted, she said yes. When it clearly had not. If Larissa hadn't lied on their behalf, the night could have ended quite differently. In an odd way, Ginny now felt indebted to the seer. And if her father was still alive—and Lord, she wished he was there to witness her wedding tonight—he would want Ginny to forgive Larissa and so she had. Forgiveness was pretty easy with love occupying every inch of her heart and soul.

A lone violin started to play and Ginny's fingers tightened around the rose stems, her body going through the motions of taking a deep breath, though it was hardly required. Jonas was waiting for her and she could already pick out his pulse among dozens, true and heavy, anticipatory. Her fangs almost dropped in response, but she pressed her tongue hard to incisors, placating herself with the promise of *later*.

Later Jonas would crowd her into to a quiet corner and take rough hold of her backside, lifting her so she could reach his neck—and when she broke his skin and *took*, his moans would shake the rafters.

"Easy there, tiger," came a voice lightly accented with Russian. "You'll give new meaning to the term 'blushing bride.'"

"Roksana?" Ginny breathed, whirling around. And there was her friend, who'd been missing in action for over three months, standing in the moonlight. In a persimmon gown. "You're wearing the dress I made you."

"I am." She picked up the skirt and lifted it, revealing a series of stakes strapped to her thighs. "Very convenient for hiding weapons."

"Are you going to complain if I hug you?"

Roksana sniffed. "I'll endure it on your wedding day.

Even though you're a bloodsucker now."

Ginny threw her arms around Roksana's neck, surprised when the slayer returned the embrace. "I guess this means you'll have to slaughter me now," Ginny whispered.

"Yes. Tomorrow."

Emotion weighed Ginny's chest down as she stepped back. "Walk me down the aisle?"

Roksana scoffed, but her eyes turned suspiciously damp. "You want a slayer to walk you down the aisle at a vampire wedding?"

"Yes. Please?"

Her friend started to answer, but grew tense when Elias joined them behind the veil of flowers, filling the air with electricity. "The king grows impatient for his bride…" He trailed off when he saw Roksana, his gaze slowly raking her top to bottom. "You're here. In a dress." His scar turned a stark white, anger igniting his deep brown eyes. "Where the hell have you been?"

"Wherever I want to be."

"You…" A muscle slithered in his cheek. "You left my credit card behind on purpose so I couldn't track you."

Roksana's voice was breathless. "Get used to it. I'm leaving as soon as I walk Ginny down the aisle."

He stepped into Roksana's space. "*Where are you going?*"

Was that fear in the slayer's eyes? "Russia. I've been called back and rightly so."

Elias choked a sound.

"Yes. It's...been real." The slayer forced a smile and skirted around a stiff Elias, hooking her elbow with Ginny's. "Shall we?"

Ginny wanted to question her friend—and she would. Whatever was in Russia was not good. Not good at all. She would find out what it was and use her new power as queen of the High Order to help, by any means possible. Roksana had protected her when she needed it most and she would return the favor.

At that moment, though, Jonas came into view in between the two standing sections of wedding guests and everything else ceased to exist.

If she'd had breath in her lungs, the sight of her fiancé in a tuxedo would have knocked it clean out of her. Ginny's heart picked up the slack, hammering wildly in her throat. *Mate. My mate.* Lord help her, she almost picked up the hem of her dress and ran down the flower-strewn aisle to meet him.

Jonas appeared to be contemplating the same—a run up the aisle to acquire her in his arms. His expression shifted between impatience and awe, the green of his eyes lit up like twin flames. "My love," he mouthed, grasping at his heart. "Come to me."

Beside her, Roksana laughed and slid her arm free of

Ginny's. "Go ahead."

With a sound between a whimper and a sob, Ginny tossed her friend the bouquet. Then she picked up the hem of her wedding dress and ran toward a waiting Jonas.

Into the arms of eternal happiness two lifetimes in the making.

THE END

Acknowledgments

Thank you so much for reading Reborn Yesterday.

Anyone interested in Elias and Roksana's book? Stay tuned.

This book was inspired by so many things, mainly timing. Time itself has become such a large presence in my life lately. The passage of time, the swift nature of it, the lack of it. The unfairness of it, on occasion.

My father, to whom this book is dedicated, passed away two weeks before I started writing this book, at age sixty-two. It's a very personal thing, losing a parent. Something you really can't put into words. So I wrote a book where death and timing and loss are themes, which I normally wouldn't do, but in the moment felt right and inevitable. Somewhere in between the words and chapters (and humor) I tried to weave some healing and rewrite sadness into a happy ending—and that's what's magical about this genre. Optimism. Hope. I'm so grateful for both.

I love you, dad. Thank you for being so proud of me, even when I refused to give you credit. You deserved a lot of it. Maybe even all of it. I don't think I'd be here without the confidence you instilled in me. I'll see you someday.

Thank you to Eagle at Aquila Editing for being with me on this project from inception to finish.

Thank you to my cover designer, Hang Le Designs. You cooked up a breathtaking masterpiece and I'm still in disbelief that I get to call it mine.

Thank you to the readers for taking a chance on me when this isn't my usual type of story. Readers make my world go around and I take not a single one of you for granted.

Off to plot Elias and Roksana's story…

Subscribe to Tessa's newsletter and never miss a new release!

tessabailey.com/contact

Follow Tessa on Instagram:

instagram.com/tessabaileyisanauthor

Available Now from Tessa Bailey

This unlikely getaway driver never expected to help the mayor escape...

After a six-year absence, Addison Potts is back in Charleston to stir things up. And what better place to make her villainous return than her estranged cousin's wedding? Only, the nuptials hit a snag when the bride doesn't show, leaving Addison to play getaway driver for the jilted groom. A groom whose heartbreaking smile and deep, southern drawl she should not be noticing...

Elijah Montgomery Du Pont is the future mayor of Charleston. From his military career to city hall, every detail of his life has been meticulously planned. Until now. His only respite from life's sudden upheaval is Addison, his new, improbable best friend. She makes him happy. Grounds him. And public disapproval be damned, he's not willing to give her up. But with an election on the line and public pressure rising, Addison—and the cruel hand of fate—might not give him a choice.

Get it here:
goodreads.com/en/book/show/38324363-getaway-girl

CPSIA information can be obtained
at www.ICGtesting.com
Printed in the USA
FSHW022032100520
70116FS